BUILD
UNIVERSES

Sue Slipman

Tales from the Alpujarra

To
Louise,
So good to be working
with you.
Sue Slipman

europebooks

ISBN 979-12-201-0353-4
First edition: November 2020

Tales from the Alpujarra

ACKNOWLEDGEMENTS

This book is dedicated to Gideon, my son, and to my sisters Jacqueline and Tandy.

I would like to acknowledge the support of friends throughout writing who also acted as my readers and critics.

Firstly, thanks to my brilliant friend Sue Larner who nagged me into writing and has been my inspiration over the course of many years.

To Patricia Prett, who was my researcher and reader in chief and who together with Anne Dickson has given me constant encouragement in progressing these stories. We met at the school gates delivering our children into their reception year and made friends, as women do. Both have supported me through more than the odd life crisis.

To Russell Prett for his thoughtful critique of my stories in this book and beyond.

To Yvonne Peters who is at the centre and to the many awe-inspiring women who over the years have shared their life stories with me.

I would also like to thank my editors at Europa Books, Ginevra Picani, Elisa Giuliani and Sirna Bonucci, who have taken such an interest in this work.

Under the Mountain
Seen from above
The foam in the curving bay is a goose-quill
That feathers... unfeathers... itself.
Seen from above
The field is a flap and the haycocks buttons
To keep it flush with the earth.
Seen from above
The house is a silent gadget whose purpose
Was long since obsolete.
But when you get down
The breakers are cold scum and the wrack
Sizzles with stinking life.
When you get down
The field is a failed or a worth-while crop, the source
Of back-ache if not heartache.
And when you get down
The house is a maelstrom of loves and hates where you –
Having got down – belong.

–Louis Macneice (1907-1963)

AN INTRODUCTION TO JOANNA

In her, by now, broad experience, Joanna had been often surprised by the things that the people who stayed chose to tell her. Sometimes these had been the most intimate details of lives you might not entrust to those nearest to you, because the revelation might cause you shame, or hurt them, or break open a fragile family truce where everyone would have their own clear memory of an event and none of these would tally. Sometimes you might only entrust your truth to a sympathetic stranger in whose house you had found a temporary respite that was way outside of your own time and space. Sometimes you might feel that the secret which had to remain locked there was here, in this space, free to be shared or even urgent to be told.

Respite was a word Joanna liked to associate with her guest house: a place of rest and recuperation where people brought their stories and where sometimes those stories unfolded in the cool of the evening, when alcohol could loosen tongues and the mountains had done their magic work of applying balm to the soul. Mind you, none of that would have been possible if anyone other than Joanna had been in charge. There was empathy to Jo, that could not have been manufactured. She had an openness and enthusiasm for life and other people that was immediately obvious and compellingly infectious.

She was blunt, but not brutal. She would ask you outright what you wanted and expect an honest reply. She was impatient with the polite niceties which are the masks behind which the English hide in their fear of being known. In fact, there were times when people doubted she was English as a result.

Above all, Jo wanted to know. She wanted to exercise her keen intelligence; to remain curious and open, and from time to time this appeared almost childlike, and would probably have given rise to cynicism in the wary, but to other and basically warm people it was endearing.

At her *posada*, guests could relax on the roof terrace, around the small pool where Thomas, her husband, would offer them an occasional cold beer, whilst they luxuriated in the sunshine and soaked in the peace and the smells of country and soft pure air, and as they watched the ever changing play of light on the mountains across the valley. The light was especially beautiful in this part of the Alpujarra. In the morning the light was sharp, clear and precise, pinpointing every shrub and tree on the hillside. At noon it was often harsh and glinting, perhaps turning hazy in late afternoon when moisture from the sea breezes blew in before, later still, turning the hills a gentle pink, as if preparing the stage for the spectacular sunset that would come yet later, before the gentle inky blackness of night framed a million stars. At night, the warm softness gave relief from what in summer could be the brutal heat of the day. It was a softness that would envelop and relax the soul as eyes focused on the growing clarity of the emerging stars. At this end of the village there was very little ambient light and as the night wore on, the stars could overwhelm the blackness, until it seemed as if they were descending en masse. It was that point of the balmy evening when the stars begin to swell their numbers, after supper with an abundance of the surprisingly smooth local wine inside them, that a guest might choose to open up to Joanna.

A Yorkshire woman by birth, Joanna had been a successful teacher of languages at a school in Leeds. She had loved being a teacher. She thought of it as a dynamic process of engagement and inspiring growth. Although a spark might only have been lit in a single child, it gave her huge satisfaction when the light of knowing went on behind the eyes. She had enormous energy and enthusiasm: enough to get her through the endless annual repetition of *je m'appelles* and *ich bins* of the year one pupils. She particularly enjoyed teaching the older ones who had mastered enough of the language to open up to a different politics and culture and literature with curiosity and sense of adventure. Whilst in general the British remained resolutely of the view that others should learn their language, there remained the few who hankered after a broader understanding of the world beyond their narrow little island. Although she realised towards the end as the world tilted on its axis and new powers arose that, although French might still stand them in good stead, she should probably retrain to teach mandarin Chinese.

After twenty odd years in the frontline she had loved, she became head of the Department and this she found she hated. Teaching was becoming endless form filling and outcome focused, with exam results being the only measure of success as kids started climbing the increasingly greasy pole of academic and professional success. Curiously, she noted that middle class jobs were receding from their grasp, even as more and more pupils were being fed into the machine seeking successfully to churn them out. Education for the sake of learning and growing was a curiously outmoded idea. It might happen in the margins of a curriculum, but more by accident than design. It had been a living ideal for her generation: education as the basis of a culture and a spur to intellectual – nay, perhaps even spiritual and moral growth. It seemed to her increasingly that everywhere she turned it was becoming only about the money. She increasingly thought of her school as a factory with children as fodder for the classroom machines. It seemed to be what parents wanted for their children, regardless of what their children might have wanted for themselves. Her job as Department Head was to keep the mechanics running smoothly and to ensure her team achieved the exam results that would give the school its status in the league tables. After some years of this she felt defeated; her seemingly eternal enthusiasm waned and she began to hate the job and to want out.

It wasn't that Joanna was a raving leftie. She approved of people getting on in the world if they could, just as she had. She approved of aspiration and discipline and hard work. She just wished there could be more joy in the way they did it and perhaps more kindness and payback to support those who were still struggling. Increasingly she disliked the lack of solidarity between generations and classes and the emergence of it being okay to denigrate the poor in what seemed like an inexorable move to a pride in displaying wealth and ignorance.

Joanna had been a working class kid in a family that had little respect for education. Her father thought education was, if of dubious value for a boy, totally wasted on a girl. He had left school at fourteen but had done an apprenticeship in the print industry. He was a strong union man and a stickler for rules. Her mother would never stand up to the father; just didn't have the strength and, in the end, it broke her will. He had been a cruel and controlling man and his will had prevailed in the family. Her mother would later describe the day he died as probably the happiest of her life. From that point she would re-discover a life free from the tedium of his power.

Joanna was the oldest girl in the family. She was at loggerheads with her father from the get-go and remembered the beatings this had brought her as he tried to bend her considerable presence to his will. She had become increasingly determined to continue her education so at sixteen, when he insisted she leave school and get a job, she had left home instead and gone to live with her maternal grandmother, who hated Jo's father almost as much as she did. She worked evenings to pay her way and continued at school, qualifying top of her class and going to University in the town. When she graduated only her grandmother and the next youngest sister, to whom she remained close, had attended to applaud her. Her mother had sent her a note saying she had wanted to come and was proud of her, but in the end she dared not.

Jo had become a teacher with a sense of service and because she'd wanted to repay those who had inspired her as a working class girl from the rougher side of town to start on the intellectual journey that had changed her life and prospects. Teachers had been respected. Now they were more often reviled. She wanted out more every day.

She was in her fifties. She and Thomas had been married for twelve years. For both it was a second marriage. Her husband had left her when their children were not yet teenagers. She was a victim of the early, pre-Facebook, social media creation of Friends Reunited. It was a website that offered the opportunity – school by school, year by year and class by class – for old school friends to get back in touch and renew old friendships. More appositely and as a by-product rather than as a design feature, it offered the opportunity for old romances to be re-kindled. She had used it first searching for her one time best friend Isabel, with whom she had lost contact when she, Joanna, went off to Leeds University and Isabel off to a poncy, posh girls' teacher education college somewhere down south. They had found each other and then discovered they had very little left in common and after a few, half-hearted drinking sessions, had let the relationship fade away. Unfortunately, at the height of her enthusiasm for the possibilities of the site she suggested to Eric her erstwhile husband that he might like to try to contact his old best friend Simon.

She and Eric had met at Leeds University and married before the end of their course when Joanna was already pregnant with their first child, a girl they had called Erica at Eric's insistence when Joanna, full of hormones and weepy with love for her new daughter, had not had the inner strength to resist, but for which she had never really forgiven him. Eric did not find Simon, but he did find Ruth, his first love. Joanna supposed later that Friends Reunited had been responsible for many divorces through renewed old liaisons. It was certainly the myth spread about it, but in her case it was accurate. She had never really liked Eric's weak chin, which was now forever nestled in the ample bosom of Ruth, leaving her free to feel relief and loathing in equal measure.

In her youth Jo had been a biker: motor bike that is. Even now when tamer gangs of bikers were out on the mountain roads on a Sunday she could still identify makes, models and horsepower at a distance. She was like a human dynamo machine. When Eric left her, Jo had started riding with a small gang of female friends as a biker pack, that is, whenever she could get a babysitter. She said she had loved being dressed in her leathers giving the powerful bike some free throttle and zooming down the highway Easy Rider style. She had particularly loved stopping with her gang at a café or pub and striding from her bike, taking off her helmet in front of groups of the slightly paunchy, often over tattooed male bikers gathered outside to reveal her long auburn hair as it slithered half way down her back. She said it made her feel powerful and sexy and totally out of their league. She also said she thought she liked it so much because when she was cruising with her favourite gang like that, it was a kind of revenge on Eric and even if he never saw her she could still envisage him under her wheels.

Thomas was the widower who lived down the road. He had a son who was the same age as her child. They started to share lone parenthood duties as Eric was useless with and neglectful of their children. Thomas became useful in her life. They shared shoulders to weep on, a school run, and later the occasional drink and meal and later still the occasional bed which proved to be far more rewardingly tantric than either had expected – but first they had been friends. It was a very welcome surprise that the sex was so spectacular, but it seemed significant that first they had been friends. Joanna had discovered that a weak chin had not been Eric's only failing attribute and when over the shock and initial pain of the unsought separation, she came to feel grateful to Friends Reunited and one day wickedly gave it a five star rating on the feedback form for freeing her from that man.

Thomas had long had a dream of moving from the cold northern city. He longed for sunshine and freedom. He designed industrial pipes for firms across Europe. They didn't care where he worked. Anywhere a computer could be plugged in and Wi-Fi provided, would do. Their children, though still young, had more or less grown and moved away. Joanna had had her fill of boredom and bureaucracy. After a mad night of too much red wine and sex, they decided to do it. The where and what came later. By a process of elimination they decided on Southern Spain. They were clear that they didn't want to be in the expat fifty mile nightmare strip of coastline around Malaga. They looked on the map and stuck a pin at random in far enough into the hinterland to be away from people they had no doubt they did not want to meet, but close enough to the coastline to have days out. They found the Alpujarra, that stretch of mountain that precedes the grander Sierra Nevada range north of Granada. Thomas had been there once as a boy with his parents.

"It's beautiful," he said, "but as I remember it, it felt a bit remote."

They agreed that both these things met their essential criteria. They were both keen walkers and Joanna fancied giving pursuits like bird watching a whirl. From their research, these two seemed to be the most common reasons people went to the Alpujarra – rather than the cheap booze and dubious company of the by now Russian dominated costa.

The issue was how they would make a living. They planned on Thomas having his job and doing it remotely, but Joanna needed something to do that definitely was not teaching but that would bring in some money. In her head the idea of a bed and breakfast place had already started to form. Neither spoke Spanish but Joanna was confident it would not take her long to pick it up, and besides her ideal market for attracting guests would probably still be in the *UK*.

They booked a two weeks holiday and the flight to Almeria airport, hired a car and drove nearly two hours to a place called Ugijar, which had seemed like a good base to begin their search. They had sectioned the map and each day they drove off in a different direction to explore and make contact with estate agents where these existed. On day five of week one they were exploring the eastern Alpujarra. They drove through a sleepy little village which seemed to have one shop and a restaurant. Peculiarly it also had an estate agents office. They wandered in and found Anna, an eccentric English woman who, like most of the few English people they found living around the area, had fetched up there completely by accident. She was escaping a heart that had been broken in Majorca.

Anna was an extremely bad painter of weird gigantic goddess figures without arms, that resembled nothing so much as the Martians in popular American comic books. Anna had been living in Majorca with her female lover, who had left her for a more virile looking Spanish fisherman. She had come to the mountains to nurse her broken heart and paint her lover with a mixture of longing and acrimony, as far away from the sea she felt had betrayed her as she could get. She had bought an enormous house for the ample studio she felt she needed, and built herself a small flat within the large dimensions of the house, leaving a number of rooms and an attached larger flat unoccupied.

Believing that the housing market was saturated nearer the coast and people would start having to buy property further into the countryside – at which point she would make a killing – she had set up as an estate agent. Anna had a short attention span and after a few years she got bored by her obvious lack of talent as an artist and the fact that the property revolution just had not happened. She also noticed, increasingly, that when the light was clear enough she could see the ocean. Even though her heart had recovered sufficiently from her disappointment in love, this irritated her and she knew the time had come to move on again.

It turned out that Anna already had the perfect property to sell them. It was large and rambling on the edge of town in Barrio Alto. It had two flats and six additional bedrooms. It had an open roof terrace that had turned out to have those unwelcome (to her at least) clear views of the sea when the light had that crystal clear quality it sometimes got in winter. In short, it was her house.

Joanna and Thomas were enchanted with the house. It was built with its back into the hillside rock, so no one could build behind them and it had everything that Anna had promised. They bought it from her and she disappeared almost overnight never to be heard from again but, they discovered later, leaving them an unusual present of the six hundred euro unpaid electricity bill that she had, either absent minded or just conveniently, for her at least, overlooked.

This was how Joanna had come to be the doyenne of a guest house in paradise, where ten years down the road she was standing as she surveyed her domain. The sun terrace was also graced with a small pool that somehow looked much bigger in the pictures on the website than it proved to be in the life.

Joanna consistently got five star ratings or just below in guest reviews. Others around her believed that although the accommodation was fine and the setting breath-taking, the high ratings came because of Joanna herself. She was a big, confident, handsome woman, with a long angular face and large teeth almost always showing as she smiled constantly. She had long, now greying, once truly dark brown hair – now helped a little by hair dye – that framed a vitally alive face with eyes that often sparkled with amusement. She was as gregarious as her husband was shy and reserved. She needed company and was one of those people who was genuinely interested in everyone's story and prepared to listen patiently while they told it. People felt her empathy from a hundred paces. This was why people who were otherwise complete strangers would immediately trust her. After a few days of snatched conversations they would ache to tell her their secrets, and most often they were safe with her. She would sometimes tell her other more permanent friends to illustrate a point or elaborate a theory, but only ever with respect. She did not ridicule others. She would find the lives of her guests amusing or sad, inspiring or depressing, but hardly ever boring and she always longed for more stories. After a few years as well as a few five star ratings, she got repeat business so often over the ten years, she had watched the children of families who came to stay as they grew in annual instalments. She had seen marriages falter and new romances prosper.

She was a fund of stories and people loved her and gravitated towards her. They recognised her as a story collector and gave her the gift of their own. In return she gave them space, nourishing breakfasts, information on the mountains, maps for walking, advice on what birds they could expect to see, and useful tips depending on the time of year, like in March where to find wild orchids and how to avoid the toxic pine processionary caterpillar, that marches in long joined lines across the mountain paths when they hatch from huge spider web like tree nests each year.

As time went on, Jo found herself wanting to do more than listen. Often she wanted to give advice. Sometimes she did. She was perhaps a little less successful as an adviser than she had been as a listener. This was probably because her essential Yorkshire would out, at times. As a therapist she veered towards the "pull yourself up by your bootstraps" variety. This was not always welcome to those who were still wallowing in their misery and looking for some company in the swamp, rather than wanting to crawl out of it. But Jo had been there, done that, and knew you could get stuck in victimhood if you blinked for too long. By all means, she thought, experience your feelings, but then, for God's sake, deal with them. She knew a lot depended on how damaged the cruelties of life had left you, but she also knew people who had suffered the worst kind of abuses who had survived and those who had bailed at the first hurdle. She knew the difference between coming to terms with pain by exploration and being perpetually trapped in the whinging groove. Increasingly she found her patience with those in the latter category diminishing as her respect for those in the former grew. Her growing discernment between those who with a bit of tender concern would pull through and those who could not find the guts to move on did mean she was not universally liked. She found she had to be careful with what she actually said, with the rating of her business on Booking and Facebook and AirB&B to think about and keep high. It was Thomas who got an earful late at night about her frustration with the whingers of the world and as Joanna often said to him: "You just can't please all of the people, all of the time."

And he would reply: "But in this business you surely have to try."

HOW REBECCA FOUND
AND THEN LOST LUCINDA

There were two relationships in Rebecca's life that collided in the village one Easter in a less than a helpful, nay, better said cataclysmic way. It took over fifteen years or maybe longer for the threads to develop, then intertwine and tighten around her neck until, one perfect Easter Sunday evening, they strangled her.

Rebecca had met David when they were both students. They had met at a student conference, stayed in touch, became friends and then lovers.

The complication in their relationship was that he had married young, had two young children in what he claimed was an open marriage, and had had previous dalliances. Though she was shocked when she discovered he was married, the arrangement suited her. She was happy to have access to a man part-time. It meant she could get on with her studies and have a life involved in feminist politics and later a career and keep a part share in a relationship.

She had no ill will towards David's wife nor would she have dreamt of depriving their children of their father. They saw each other fortnightly for a weekend or a few days and then willingly she gave him back. The arrangement seemed to suit everyone, and it was remarkable how fresh and inviting it kept the sex.

By the time Rebecca met Lucinda, she had had ten years of creating a thread with David. The sex was no longer quite so fresh, and whilst Rebecca had moved way beyond the occasional heavy drinking bouts of their student days, David had not. For him spending a lot of time in pubs and drinking a lot of alcohol had become a daily ritual. In Rebecca's opinion he was not yet an alcoholic, but he was probably not far off. She had already started falling into the habits of what would become co-dependency: speaking for him in social situations when he got to the word slurring stage of an evening out, and hoping that friends had not noticed either this itself or her growing embarrassment at his condition. But at this stage he could still hold his liquor and slurring did not occur with the frequency that would later become inveterate.

Lucinda was posh. She lived in Hampstead and had been to a highly trendy girls' school in Camden. She had a bohemian mother who had not been married to Lucinda's Italianate sounding father. Lucinda herself had a daughter, Chloe, who went to an even posher private girls' school, which, it turned out, was paid for by the daughter's father to whom Lucinda had never been married, but with whom she had lived briefly until she met the love of her life, Brendan, with whom she had gone off with little baby Chloe in a Moses basket.

Lucinda was interesting. She had had a career in publishing, which she'd left when Brendan, a scientist by trade, suggested the rat race should not be for them and proposed they buy a boat and sail it round the Med and see what happened. So, they took the three year old Chloe, who had outgrown the Moses basket, and set off round the Med, coming to berth mainly in Majorca.

Their sea adventures continued for five years, until the then eight year old Chloe told them she wanted an English education and asked them to take her home. This they did. They had little money, so ended up living in the spacious rent controlled flat of Lucinda's mother, Gwen.

They decided they still didn't want conventional careers, so Brendan became a jobbing gardener and Lucinda got a job as a secretary to the director of a small national charity. Two years later Rebecca got the job of director of the charity, creating the second thread in our story.

In her first day in the job, three remarkable things happened to Rebecca.

Firstly she'd struggled up the narrow stairway to their first floor offices, having noted through olfactory evidence that they had the kind of doorway where down-and-outs would take a piss of an evening, to be greeted by a poster asking her if she thought she might be a lesbian. Now, Rebecca had nothing against lesbians. Indeed, some of her best friends were and she was not without some experimental tangling with other women – but she didn't understand why she was being asked this question in a professional environment. Indeed she thought it was offensive that the women who struggled up these ridiculously narrow, steep stairs to get help, with all their belongings in hand and two hapless kids in tow, should be asked anything about their sexual preferences.

Not appropriate, she said to herself briskly as she tore the poster down.

The second remarkable event was that the union shop stewards, of whom there were three for thirty members of staff, came to see her to request paid leave to take the organisation's banner on a 'support the miners' demonstration. She found the fact that their small national charity had a banner hard to understand. She asked to see it and told them she would keep hold of it for the time being and that, by the way, if they wanted to support the miners they should do so in their own time, as she doubted whether their funders would be much amused to discover that their money was going to fund staff to go on demonstrations. At this stage of her career Rebecca had been a trades union official for a number of years, representing low paid manual workers – mostly women – and led more strikes and disputes than the three ridiculously leftist over privileged representatives of the middle-class sitting in front of her could easily contemplate. *So, even more not appropriate*, she said to herself as she thanked them for their visit. She'd met plenty like this through university: lefties who were just as desperate to lose the appropriate use of the 'h' in speech as Rebecca had been in her youth to acquire it.

As the door closed behind them she was thinking: *what the hell have I walked into here?*

She'd been delighted to get this job, though she'd understood from afar that there would be difficulties to overcome. The previous Director had left in a hurry, as had the one before her. Also, she had refused Rebecca's request to meet to give her any kind of briefing or hand over. So there was clearly a story to be told and Rebecca felt as if she was beginning to get a handle on its plot.

After only a few minutes the door opened again and in walked Lucinda.

"Well, hello to you," she said in an even more cut-glass accent than the three who had just disappeared. Rebecca knew immediately that this was not someone who would ever drop an aitch even in jest.

Lucinda was pretty. She had mid-length brown hair that was secured by a black velvet Alice-band. She had a round face in which sat a pert, slightly upturned nose. As she moved, her hair bounced around the confines of its Alice-band, giving her a jaunty air. There was something stagey about her voice, but it might just have been the dusky undertone of the seasoned smoker. She was dressed in a white shirt with a Peter Pan collar with a small single pearly necklace, just showing in the gap between the collar. She had a navy cotton cardigan and a loose, flowing needle cord skirt with small, neat white flowers on a navy background. It was a very neat, very Sloane Ranger outfit, finished off with a pair of flat, patent loafers with a snaffle bar trim.

Lucinda was as perky as she was pert and prone to laughing, which Rebecca felt was unlikely to be a bad thing. She also blushed frequently, which gave her the air of an upper class head girl visiting the school head. It was oddly attractive.

They completed their introductions and had a cup of coffee together, while Lucinda took her through the office routines and briefed her on the monthly round of meetings. Then, together, they toured the building to say hello to the other twenty six staff members Rebecca had yet to meet.

The third remarkable thing happened at lunchtime; although, had it not happened, Lucinda's entry in itself might have been enough to count. However, Lucinda invited her to lunch. They went to a local pub and sat outside. It was early autumn, and one of those last days of Indian summers where the days start off cool but by lunchtime have the kind of languorous warmth that you don't want to miss, because by evening the incipient chill of winter insinuates itself in your consciousness reminding you of the shorter, darker days that are just around the corner.

As they sat in the sun with their sandwiches and fruit juices, Lucinda looked at her and said: "Look, I don't know you, but I have decided I must trust you to sort out the mess that is this organisation."

"Well, it's what I think I'm here to do. How bad is it?"

"I am going to tell you only because I saw the poster was missing, and guessed it must have been you, and I heard about you taking the banner away. So, well done you! When I've told you, you'll go away thinking I am completely barking mad and have made this up – but I swear to you I haven't".

She stopped to take breath and Rebecca thought: *how bad can it be? Maybe it's worse even than I thought.*

"Ok. Here goes. The previous two directors had nervous

breakdowns. I don't know about the first one, because I only started work here two years ago, when the second director came into post. I quite liked Deirdre. She was a legal expert with quite an academic approach – not a bad stick, but she was weak and didn't like confrontation. Mostly the staff here ran rings around her, and she hid in her office. But then things really got crazy when the Head Finance person, who is an evil woman, seduced her and then blackmailed her into letting the trades union run the organisation."

"Sorry?" said Rebecca.

"I know it sounds mad but, believe me, it happened," said Lucinda nodding vigorously. "I don't understand why it would matter if she had a lesbian affair – except of course in the workplace, with an employee, could be dodgy. Look, I'm not sure I've got the whole story," continued Lucinda. "There was something about the custody of Deirdre's child being fought out in court with a former partner and Jenny offering to give evidence that Deirdre was not a fit person to get custody. I assume she'd have claimed that the Director seduced her, but I don't know that level of detail."

"Well, that's quite a story." At this stage Rebecca was staring at her with a more than slightly open mouth.

Lucinda, wearing a serious face, said: "Deirdre was under a lot of strain. She'd been stringing the management committee and the Chair along about how well things were going, when in reality it was like the Wild West with no sheriff round here. Anyway, she had a nervous breakdown and had to leave and now I think there are a lot of financial problems as well. The Head of Finance took sabbatical leave shortly afterwards and won't be back for a year."

Of all the remarkable things that happened on her first morning, this turned out to be the most remarkable. If Rebecca had had a 'flabber', it would have been truly 'ghasted'.

She told Lucinda she was grateful to be entrusted with the story but that, clearly, she needed to think about all its implications.

When she got back to the office, she asked Lucinda to send the Deputy Finance Officer in to see her. Hence she spent the afternoon discovering just how big was the hole in their finances and learnt that, thankfully, she had a second ally in the Deputy who hated her recently, if temporarily, departed boss with a passion, though she managed to disguise it just enough in what Rebecca thought was a reasonably professional manner.

This was how the start of a four year journey of turning the organisation around, and in which Rebecca and Lucinda were firm allies and then, or so Rebecca always thought, firm friends. It was a successful partnership. The organisation went from strength to greater strength as a key champion for parents bringing up children on their own with little or no support from erstwhile lovers and husbands and often nowhere to live.

From time to time Lucinda came across David, if he came to pick Rebecca up after work or they went out for a drink before heading home. Occasionally Rebecca came across Brendan and Chloe in similar circumstances, but they didn't see a great deal of each other outside of work and though they shared family news their lives were not intertwined.

During this period Rebecca learnt two significant things about Lucinda: she was a woman of enthusiasms – for people, for books for music and for knowing things. There was a large streak of nativity and innocence in her enthusiasms and she could be unforgiving if any of the objects of her passions disappointed her. The second thing was that she wanted everything to be, in her words, 'proper'. Rebecca, who was up for kindness, politeness and a whole load of other possible modes of behaviour that might come within the scope of being considered proper, could go along with this to a certain extent – but when it tipped over into obeying convention for its own sake she departed company. At some stage she realised that Lucinda's urge to propriety had its root in her shame that her parents had never been married, whereas Rebecca had never given a flying fuck that neither had hers – well, at least not until she was six years old, which she supposed might have made a difference to her social acceptability in a less enlightened time. For Lucinda, however, it was serious. It was as if she felt this fact alone caused her to be socially marginalised, somewhat spoiled goods, and never fully belonging as the genuine and impeccable middle-class article she aspired to be. The blame for this slight chip on her shoulder was laid firmly at the door of her hapless mother. Rebecca accepted this personality quirk, because hey ho and after all, no one is perfect.

The one thing that did surprise Rebecca was Lucinda's unexpected quest for religious faith. She thought it was perhaps an enthusiasm that would wain, but surprisingly Lucinda embraced it thoroughly. She sought instruction from a priest. It made sense that she would seek solace in the Church of England but go for high church variation. It had the pomp and circumstance.

Rebecca had a generally poor view of religion. She didn't mind a little light C of E, albeit highly diluted in the general culture in order to keep people law abiding and rioting and looting off the streets, but she just didn't understand faith and didn't have any. Also, religious bigotry and the piety of the Pharisee really disturbed her. Nevertheless, she didn't believe in trashing other people's beliefs providing they were not actively hurting others. On the whole, she believed that whatever got you through this vale of tears was probably ok. She supported Lucinda's quest on this basis and even went to her confirmation ceremony in St. Paul's Cathedral, which she had to admit was grand and proper in every sense of the term.

In these first few years of her growing friendship with Lucinda, her relationship with David increasingly came under strain. He was drinking more and more. He had come to live in London for a year to take a social worker course and it made sense for him to stay with her. She was busy and often had evening meetings and at the weekends he went back to see his wife and children, which was fine by her. It took her some time to notice that he was more often at the word slurring stage after drinking than was usual.

At first she thought that maybe it would go away as a problem, because she could see no reason for his drinking to excess. She found herself increasingly having to cover for him in any social situation they shared with friends. He was never aggressive, though sometimes belligerent about a point that seemed to him to be about principle but that he couldn't entirely articulate, as his brain was clogged by too much alcohol and he had gone way beyond the loquacious stage, through the insistently garrulous, to the downright tediously verbose, and, finally, into the unrestrained repetitive.

Eventually for Rebecca this became a descent into hell and the feelings to which it gave rise were those of panic and dread and eventually anger. He seemed to have lost any art of conversation and the knack of blending in to a social occasion, and Rebecca increasingly found herself becoming a shield for the protection of the others they were with, constantly trying to save him from himself and herself from the embarrassment of being with him.

She learnt a truth over a painful period of time, that drunks are really boring as well as very sick, and that you cannot believe a word they say.

She believed she had tried hard to help him. At first she believed the drunken promises to stop drinking and pull his life back on track – but learnt that there would no memory of this conversation the following day. Moreover, she came to know that this pattern of promise and failure was just a well-known downward path to drunken perdition.

She was very relieved when his year of staying at her place came to end and he went home. They had been together for nearly fifteen years and though she no longer respected him, she still felt fondness for what they had once shared, and she felt responsible for him and not a little guilty for no longer desiring him.

Inevitably, she started seeing another man: an old friend she never expected to be a lover. She was occasionally overwhelmed by guilt and then, when she discovered she was pregnant, overwhelmed by confusion and not just about which of her two lovers might be its father.

For a long period she later recognised was caused by shock, she was unable to be clear about what she felt and for whom. The only thing that she was clear about was that her priority would have to be this child, to which she would dedicate herself whatever the circumstances of its birth.

David begged her to let him be the child's father. He claimed it would be his salvation and give him a purpose for living he had not felt for years. Stupidly, she allowed her feelings of guilt to win his case for him. She felt that she owed him for all the time they had spent together and besides, though it was deeply unlikely, he might just have been the father. To her shame, she was not seeing things too clearly, and the small contribution that one or other had made to the creation of this child did not seem overwhelmingly significant. Later she would put this conviction, that had taken precedence over any consideration of the future rights of her, as of her yet unborn child, to know its real father, down to the hormones coursing through her system. But she was explaining – not excusing – her behaviour.

For a while David was reasonable. He seemed to love Daniel. He gave up drinking – or so she thought. He visited in the same pattern as previously, and his wife and children knew about the new baby. They had even travelled up to Scotland to meet his mother and sister, who had been really welcoming.

Then, when Daniel was about eighteen months, Rebecca went one Sunday afternoon to a reunion of her old school. She was only gone for a few hours and had left David in charge. When she got back, Daniel was wandering around unsupervised with a stinking, overflowing crappy nappy and David had passed out on the floor of the flat. There were two empty bottles of red wine on the table.

With the heaviest of hearts, Rebecca realised this was a failure from which David would not recover and, even if he did, she wouldn't. She had heard all the promises he had made over the last few years and they all suddenly stuck in her gorge. She almost choked on her rancour. For her he had been in the last chance saloon where she had just discovered him drinking. It was too much. She knew she could never again trust him with her child and in that split second realised the meaning of co-dependency. She couldn't help him to slow or reverse his descent and she recognised that continuing to try was too much agony to take. She let him sleep it off and next day she threw him out and told him not to come back unless he sobered up for good.

The next time she saw him was a further year on, when he asked to see Daniel and she allowed him a visit which she supervised. He smelt of booze. She sat open mouthed as he told the two year old Daniel that he was going away to Spain to stay in the mountains with his new partner, a wild Spanish woman who had a child about Daniel's age, and wouldn't that be nice?

"David," she asked, "have you completely lost your marbles?"

During all this time Rebecca was truly grateful for Lucinda's support for her. Daniel had been conceived and born in year five of them working together. He had been a severe baby asthmatic, that carried on into his childhood, capable of collapsing and needing hospitalisation at any moment. Whenever they travelled Rebecca took a portable nebuliser with them and had learnt to manage his condition, but there were frequent hospital stays and huge amounts of steroids, and Lucinda unfailingly sorted out workplace issues so that Rebecca could take off whenever she was needed and drop anything in her haste to get to whatever local hospital to which Daniel's childminder had taken him. There were a couple of occasions that had proved life threatening and Rebecca had needed considerable periods off work to get him over the crisis. Her gratitude was a huge bond between them.

Increasingly Lucinda had been talking about what they – her and Brendan – might do when Chloe went off to University. One plan might be to resurrect their sailing life, but that was a short lived dream, judged impractical and too physically demanding. Eventually, after a few years, one did arise and took shape and then it took roots and grew branches.

They would go to live in southern Spain. It would be as far away as possible from her mother whilst still being in Europe. Her relationship with mother had never been easy, and by the time she and Brendan left they would have had to share her flat for nearly ten years. Their new home would be, by preference, somewhere mountainous and remote. It would be in a village, not a town, and she would learn the English as a Foreign Language teaching method and qualify so she might be able to earn a living. It started as a dream but over a couple of years became a plan.

The year after David had set off for his Spanish jaunt, Lucinda and Brenden spent their summer holiday in the region they had chosen as their future home. They travelled round the villages day by day just asking people in their exceedingly poor Spanish if they knew of any house for sale and eventually they found one.

It was a house that had belonged to a Juan Molino, then quite long dead. They told the story with glee of how the whole family gathered and sat around an oblong table along with the notaria while Brendan divided the money into equal piles of cash before each of them and when the piles had reached the requisite height a nod of acceptance was given and the deed was done. They had toasted the sale with glasses of *Manzanilla* and plates of unspeakable parts of a pig that had been recently slaughtered.

Eighteen months later, in fact the same day that Chloe went off to University, Lucinda and Brendan went off to their new village life. At first, they kept in touch through letters. Rebecca felt bereft for a while, but life carried on in pretty much the same track. Meanwhile Lucinda was having a major adventure in a Spain that had only emerged from dictatorship some fifteen years before. It was still economically backward. The main form of transport in their village was the mule. People still kept animals in the basements of their houses and kept pigs for pets until they grew enough to be turned into sausages and blood puddings, then, with some ceremony but little sentiment, that's what they became. There was subsistence farming all around; little in the way of technology and a bureaucratic grip that reached into every facet of commerce and public life.

The exchange of letters went on for a couple of years. During this time Rebecca went on seeing Chloe in her university holidays when she came back to stay with her grandma in London and they became close. Then, the following summer, Rebecca and Daniel were staying with some friends in a small village a short drive from the sea in Almeria Province for three weeks. She asked if she could pay a visit and was asked to come for a weekend and bring Daniel and his friend. This she did.

The drive was a hairy one on single track roads where there were roads, and dirt tracks where there weren't. She'd never driven mountain roads before, so was unused to sheer drops with no barriers. She remembered this journey later as a bit of a white knuckle, buttock clenching ride and it didn't help that Daniel's friend was sick round many a bend. At one stage she took a wrong turn and she recognised the name of the village to which David had escaped and where he had lived with his tempestuous Spanish lover for nearly a year until she had had enough of him and turfed him out. It was overwhelmingly beautiful and majestic. It reminded her that she had not heard from him and that she felt nothing but relief.

The weekend had gone well. Both Lucinda and Brendan had been very pleased to see her and were tolerant of the boys. She remembered that Brendan, ever the scientists, had found rocks with them and showed them how to distil the mercury from them. The only sour note had come when Rebecca offered a financial contribution and got as a fierce response from Lucinda that she was insulted that a guest should think of paying. Rebecca remembered feeling embarrassed that she had got the etiquette so wrong, but she knew they had as little money as she had herself at that stage. The issue of money, and the misunderstandings around it, and the unspoken resentments to which it would lead, would later prove to be a significant factor in the explosion to come, but at this stage it was still a few years off. She took them out to supper in the only half way decent restaurant around to thank them, and the rest of the weekend was great fun. In fact, it all went so well that they invited her to come out for a week the following Easter, and she was delighted to accept.

So started what became an annual visit each Easter.

Rebecca and Daniel would travel with Chloe and hire a car to take them all to the village. They would spend their days on long walks through the mountains. As well as bringing Chloe, Rebecca would ask what they needed and load up with the things desired, along with lots of books for they were all avid readers. In the evening she'd sit in the kitchen while Lucinda cooked, unwilling to have any help or more likely what she saw as interference. They would catch up on village gossip and Lucinda's adventures whilst putting away glasses of the local wine that Brendan – a teetotaller – called 'electric juice' – getting quite merry. After supper there would be games of Trivial Pursuit and long talks about books they were reading.

They were good times with many jokes.

Wary of the money topic, Rebecca would offer to pay on shopping trips, and occasionally Lucinda would let her.

Over these years, Lucinda would make a new best friends who would be initially praised nonpareil. There was something quite touching but deeply naïve in her attachment to them. They could do no wrong for a period of time, then, suddenly, they could do no right and Lucinda would be full of complaint as to the many ways in which they had betrayed her trust. Rebecca had met two of them: a Dutch nurse and a Spanish teacher at the local school. Both seemed ok as human beings go, but she could not see what was exceptional in either to deserve either the exaggerated initial love or the vilification in which it ended. Rebecca didn't get to have many independent conversations with people in the village and she knew little Spanish, but whenever she did people would say to her that Lucinda was a *'una poca nerviosa – pero buena'* which she cottoned on meant 'highly strung – but good'.

Rebecca didn't take these things to be warning signs. She had known Lucinda for too long by now, and their relationship had been forged through a strong bond of trust and mutual support. She never believed she would go the way of some of these newer friends.

There had been a lot of changes in Rebecca's working life. She'd had a few jobs since their charity days and had recently been head hunted by a company who paid her a lot more money than she had ever earnt before. Later she realised that this was the moment she should have offered again to make a financial contribution when they came to stay, but then she remembered Lucinda's initial ferocity on the topic and clammed up. But from that moment on the relationship began to feel slightly strained and Lucinda more edgy than she had ever been.

One year during the Easter visit Lucinda showed her a house in the village she had heard was for sale. She encouraged Rebecca to think about buying it as she now had more money and it was very cheap. It needed a lot of remedial work doing to make it habitable, but Lucinda promised help with the legal transfer of the deeds, as by this stage she was a fluent Spanish speaker and keen to show off her skills. She also promised help finding the builders and painters and decorators that would transform this shell. She thought about it overnight and decided that she would buy it, despite a little warning voice that told her this would be a challenge for her relationship with Lucinda. After all, there were few English people in the village at this stage – though many more came in later years.

Lucinda had been a kind of doyen in the village. She had cornered the market in teaching English to the village children. She had started a conservation society that challenged those who broke the building regulations by putting extra floors on their houses, which violated height restrictions. This society fought cases through the hugely corrupt Spanish legal system, which they inevitably lost when the other side bribed the judge. She had started a small book exchange for the few English speakers in the area. She went to local council meetings and followed events closely. Above all she had been the access point to the village for Rebecca and Rebecca knew her friend would not easily reconcile to her now having direct access on her own terms. Nevertheless, Lucinda was as good as her word.

She accompanied Rebecca to the vendors' house, a couple called Gonzalez, where Rebecca, with her non-existent Spanish, had been unable to follow the guttural exchange whilst offers were made and accepted, as she sat mesmerised in the seldom used sitting room where a red neon pulsating heart of either Mary or Jesus flashed on and off.

They had just been given a tour of the Gonzalez house, which was huge and built on the side of the village below the main road. Outside of the immediate living accommodation were seven bedrooms: one each for their six children and one for themselves. Each of the six bedrooms had the requisite numbers of beds for each of the children and for the children they had produced. Though each door was quickly closed Rebecca had lost count at thirty beds. All the children had moved away to find work, but their rooms were constantly ready for their return, even if this was just for the summer months when everyone returns to the *pueblo* to visit the *abuelos*. It was this adherence to family that was as alien to northern European culture as was the neon beating heart of Jesus.

After the house tour was completed, they were once more led back to the throbbing neon, given a cold drink and serious conversation was resumed. At one stage Lucinda said in English: "I'm about to tell you what they want, and you mustn't laugh out loud because it is quite funny," and then proceeded to tell her that they wanted her to pay three hundred euros more and they would throw in the farm equipment in the basement and the table in the kitchen of the house that had lost one of its four legs. Rebecca did her best to be solemn and then the deal was done and hands were shaken with an agreement to meet at the *notaria* the following day to sort out the legal process.

They managed to get round the corner before the laughter bubbled up and they realised they needed a glass of wine to celebrate at the village's only café before staggering up the steep hill past the church and Rebecca's new house before arriving at the top *barrio* where Lucinda lived.

David had turned up again in Rebecca's life a few years previously. He had met and married a delightful woman who worked in hostels for women and children who had suffered domestic abuse. They were living together in the Scottish Highlands, near Balmoral. For some reason they were in London and David asked her to meet them both because he wanted to prove to her that he was turning his life around. He was no longer drinking. Rebecca liked his new wife. They offered to take Daniel for a few weeks in the summer and Rebecca agreed to let this happen because Daniel was keen to go and as she was working very full time at this stage, the long holiday was otherwise boring for him and David had a nephew the same age who was also going. She also thought it would be good for Daniel to become a little more independent and if she had doubts about David's ability to look after him, she had no doubt about the adequacy of his wife, and the visit was a success.

The following year, during the Easter visit when Daniel was around twelve, there were things to celebrate. Chloe, a few years out of university, was working as a teacher in a private school. She announced that she had just got a promotion to the Head of Classics and that, by the way, she and the friend who had become a boyfriend were thinking of getting married. It would not happen for a year or more, but she had wanted everyone to know. However, he wanted to do things the proper way so in the summer he would come out with Chloe to ask Brendan for Chloe's hand in marriage. Rebecca already knew and rather liked him as they'd come together for lunch a couple of times over the course of the previous year at her new house in London.

That Easter Rebecca and Daniel had stayed in their new house in the village. They had had enough work done to make it habitable, but it was not yet comfortable and major works where scheduled to start later in the year, when Rebecca had gotten that year's bonus payment from work and would be able to afford them.

In Autumn both Lucinda and David suffered different blows that sent them reeling.

Lucinda's mother came to live with her in the village. She was in her mid-seventies and her consistently vague, wandering mind had finally being diagnosed as Alzheimer's disease. She had continued to live in the London flat as Chloe was still living there, but Chloe could not be expected to look after her grandmother as she deteriorated further. She had a responsible job and a career to think about and was within a year to be married. Something had to happen for before too long Gwen would need full time care and there wasn't the money anywhere in the family to pay for it. The crunch came when Gwen forgot the pan was on the stove and set fire to the flat. The decision was made that Lucinda would care for her but only if they brought her to the Alpujarra to live with them.

All her life Lucinda had been angry with her mother for failing to give her the respectable family life she craved and for being too much of a free thinker with bohemian tendencies. Yet here she was, approaching her fifties, having to devote herself to her mother's care at a point where increasingly her mother was less sure every day of her own and her daughter's identity.

Gwen had always been physically robust, although a lifelong smoker with a persistent cough to prove it. As she lost her grip on the world, she lost weight and became quite suddenly physically frail. This was the worst thing that could have happened to Lucinda, who had never been a patient soul. She had escaped the responsibilities of home and moved as far away from her mother as possible. Being her mother's full time carer was a prison sentence and she would have to serve her time. She was resentful that life had dealt her this hand, but grimly determined she would play it as best she could. The outlook was decidedly bleak.

Whilst this was happening to Lucinda, an equally traumatic blow, though rather more self-inflicted, was being delivered to David. His second marriage had fallen apart. He had fallen off the wagon and his wife couldn't cope with the awfulness of living with an alcoholic. She had left. Rebecca had every sympathy for her, but was far from delighted that she would re-inherit David, which she did, albeit mostly on the phone. Over the following month he climbed back on the wagon and he stayed there for several months. He cleaned up his act and partially mended his relationship though it was clear that his wife would not agree to live with him again.

During their phone call at Christmas David asked Rebecca a favour. He wanted to re-visit the Alpujarra and see again the village where he had spent nearly a year living with his Spanish gypsy lover. Rebecca felt the accustomed sense of dread descend on her while he was talking. She said they would have to see and only if remained sober. This theme became a constant of their phone conversations. She discussed it with Daniel and he'd thought it would be ok, so with great reluctance, feeling churlish and manipulated by guilt she agreed. The sobriety condition still applied but she made another: David would have to come out with them at Easter on the same flight and he would stay the week with them and return on the same flight. He agreed.

As the Easter trip got closer Rebecca felt the knot in her stomach harden. It became a tight lump the day that he told her he had decided not to take the flight with her and Daniel and the other two friends who were coming out for a short holiday. He wanted to drive alone through France, into Spain. He would leave a day or two before their flight and arrive around the same time. It would, he said, be a test of his sobriety and his independence and he felt up to it.

Would she support him, he asked? What could she do?

Well, she agreed she would, but told him that if he did not stay sober during this test, he should not bother to come to the village because he would not be welcome.

Rebecca, Daniel and her two friends arrived at the house. It was still far from luxurious but there were no longer mushrooms growing on the walls, which had to be an improvement.

On their first night in the house she got a phone call from David, who was on the French side of the Pyrenees. He told her he was looking up at the stars over the Pyrenees. It was when he told her three times that he was looking up at the stars, she noticed the slight slur. By this time she knew all the signs of his descents, but when she asked him outright if he was pissed he denied it. So, she told him again that if he was lying he needn't bother to cross the Pyrenees and could just turn round and go home.

During that week the weather was perfect. Every day they went for long walks breathing deep the crystal air, enchanted by birdsong. Daniel sometimes accompanied them, but he was a teenager much given to sleeping late and prowling at night with the friends he'd had in the village since he was five years old. He was also accompanied by the guitar they kept at the house, which he played astoundingly well. All week there was no sign of David and no more phone calls and bit by bit the stomach knot had unclenched as Rebecca chose to believe he had taken her advice.

She had been round to see Lucinda early in the week taking the usual supply of books and aspirins, brought from the UK as they were so expensive in Spain. Lucinda had looked strained and a little haggard and had said sorry but that she had no time to see her as her mother was taking up all her time.

On the last day of their stay Rebecca's little party minus Daniel had stopped for lunch before their walk, in a restaurant about eight kilometres from the village, where she bumped into Lucinda with Gwen and Chloe. Rebecca had smiled at Lucinda and seen a look of fierce aggression on her face. To cover her confusion, she asked if they were there about arrangements for Chloe's wedding, which was to take place that August and to which she was looking forward. Lucinda just ignored her and pushed past to take Gwen to the loo. Rebecca felt a little shaken by the encounter but figured that Lucinda was having a very hard time and required the cutting of some slack.

Their walk was long and they got back to the house in late afternoon.

As she was walking up the stairs, Daniel lent his head out of his bedroom where he was practising guitar and said that David had arrived, and was asleep on a mattress he had put out for him upstairs in the living room, and that, by the way, he stank of alcohol. All the dread that Rebecca had been holding back flooded her system. He had driven through Spain drunk. She had last heard from him six days before so, who the hell knew where he had been or even if he had killed anyone on the roads?

Reluctantly she went up to see him, but couldn't get him to wake up. He was clutching a half empty bottle of red wine and he'd pissed himself. He stank. She yelled at him that he could sleep it off but that they were leaving at six the following morning to get their flight and she would throw him out of the house as she had to lock it up and was not prepared to leave him there. He had opened his eyes but they had not really focused.

They had cleaned up the house that morning so that all that remained was to clear out the fridge as they eat leftovers for supper and give the kitchen floor a quick wash the following morning before they left as well now as washing David's sheet. As she usually did, she took whatever they hadn't eaten during their week round to Lucinda. She remembered there had been some uncooked lamb they had frozen – so if Lucinda and Brendan didn't want it, it could feed their dog.

Lucinda came to the door and obviously didn't want to let her in. She agreed they would take the bags of goodies that Rebecca had brought her, but then said: "In this house we are deeply offended."

"What? Why? Have I done something to offend you?" Rebecca asked.

"Don't pretend you don't know. You gave that drunken fool David permission to break and enter our house. I found him passed out on my living room couch when we got in. It was disgusting. I had to clean up his vomit."

Rebecca felt the braid that had taken so long to inter-twine through so many years and accidents of fate tighten round her neck.

"I'm sorry," she mumbled, "but I would never have let him think that would be ok." She was prepared to go on to explain more, but a look at Lucinda's face silenced her. Lucinda did not want to know: so Rebecca in her shock walked away.

On her way back to her house, Rebecca saw David's car parked haphazardly in the narrow streets. She looked inside and saw several empty bottles. When she got back to her house feeling a little shaky and more closely questioned

Daniel, it turned out what he had omitted from his account of David's arrival was that he had stumbled in, having been dragged down the street by an explosive Lucinda. Daniel's teenage myopia had allowed his mother to walk unprepared and unshielded into a war zone she had not known existed. Later they discovered the whole story.

David, who did not know where to find Rebecca's house, had drunkenly wandered up to a Spanish neighbour in Lucinda's *barrio* and in slurry Spanish asked for directions to the house belonging to the English woman. The neighbour had naturally assumed he meant Lucinda and had helpfully taken him to her house. There was no one in but no one locked their doors in those days, so he assumed it was Rebecca's house, wandered in and like Goldilocks had found the most comfortable place to collapse. She never discovered if he had pissed himself as well as vomited in Lucinda's house, or if he had saved that particular pleasure for her alone.

David had not appeared at supper time, nor by the time they decided to get some sleep in before the early start for the airport. The following morning she woke him at five a.m. with coffee. He was bleary eyed. She told him he could have a shower but then he had to leave and at six o'clock he left as she packed up the hire car, locked up the house and prepared for departure.

Rebecca felt like she was carrying the weight of the world on her shoulders. She knew this Armageddon had cost her a cherished friendship; that it had been the taper that lit Lucinda's fuse, justified her growing anger with her erstwhile friend, and allowed her the outlet to pile her murderous rage with her mother entirely on to Rebecca. She did not know if the damage could ever be repaired.

It took some time for Rebecca to recover. It was painful and she felt depressed for a while. She was never exactly disinvited to the wedding but it was clear that nor was she expected to be there. She got news of David again many months later from his sister who phoned her to say that David had driven back and was arrested in Folkestone driving out of the ferry terminal. When released he had returned to Scotland by train. Some days after his return he had had a major stroke and for a couple of days lain on the floor of his little cottage on the River Dee, immediately east of the Cairngorm Mountains. He had eventually been discovered and was in a coma for six weeks and at that point in time was wheelchair bound with the use of some fingers on each hand, living in a home further up in the highlands waiting for some therapeutic rehabilitation on the NHS. This tragedy compounded the grotesque farce that had led to it and did nothing to alleviate Rebecca's guilt.

Mutual friends, when they heard the story of his drunken intrusion into Lucinda's house, thought that one day Lucinda would laugh about it – but instinctively Rebecca knew different. All those years before Lucinda had decided to put her trust in Rebecca to sort out the mess and she had. This time it was way beyond anything Rebecca could control and she realised that for Lucinda it was she who had brought one more mess into Lucinda's already highly pressurised life.

Lucinda was a powder keg; her dynamite of resentment was not getting the financial support she wanted and was too fiercely proud to ask for; it was Rebecca usurping her position as the only Englishwoman in the village; it was having to look after the mother who was her animus and vexation, but who at some level she loved and who was dying mentally and by degrees physically; it was the strain of having to organise her daughter's wedding and finally, it was her tendency to destroy the heroes she had created for herself. David's unexpected visit had lit the blue touch paper and the explosion duly occurred and not all of her supposed church going Christian commitment could tip the balance towards forgiveness – not then and, as it turned out in the longer run, not ever.

HOW REBECCA MET JOANNA

Her friend Elena, an accomplished sculptor who believed everyone had their sphere of creativity, had been with her for a week before Aunt Betsy had arrived.

She was always urging Rebecca to do something creative; normally it was to let her teach Rebecca life drawing. Rebecca always resisted, fearing her lack of hand eye coordination that made her such a spectator sport at tennis would also let her down as potential artist material. If truth be told, she was terrified of failure before her so competent friend, whose work she really admired. One evening, in their after supper chats, Elena had said: "I've got it. You should write. I bet you've got a novel in you." Over Rebecca's protests, she added, "Well at least you could write about your life. Why not try?"

Rebecca didn't believe she had a work of fiction inside her. She knew it was said that everyone has a book in there somewhere. Some people secretly believe that if only they sat down and gave it enough time, a perfect story, full to the brim of human wisdom, would emerge from the inner recesses of their soul and brain and translate to paper to enhance, nay, grow, the experience of what it is to be human. Not her. She not only didn't believe it, the mere thought of the potential humiliation at the public exposure of such empty vanity was enough to give her an anticipatory cringe. She knew she would be scared to provoke the contempt that she felt an attempt at high art on her part would occasion.

This does not mean she had no stories inside her or that

her life was not worthy of its own expression and would offer no reward to the putative reader. On the contrary – she had so far lived a full and, even if she would say so herself, unusually eventful life. So, after her chat with Elena, she had decided that yes, this might be the year that she would spend the summer in the village writing her life's story.

Her fine intention went into cold storage with Betsy's arrival, for it turned out that her life did not get off to a promising start. Her mother had not wanted to carry her to term. Her Aunt Betsy had let it slip on her first night and clearly many years after the event itself, that her mother had had an abortion in her thirtieth year. This her mother had confessed to Betsy in a whispered conversation, late one night after a glass, possibly too many, of red wine in the caravan park near Sheerness, where the sisters had holidayed with their husbands from time to time in the latter years of her life.

Rebecca had been born when her mum was thirty one. Rebecca's slightly addled brain worked out this meant that either her mother had tried without success to abort her in the early months of her pregnancy or that she had an abortion and then poor hapless thing had got pregnant for a second time with Rebecca and decided not to tempt fate twice.

Betsy bigmouth was unable to keep the secret for life – although to be fair to her she had hung on to it for several years, only revealing it to her niece now, some ten years after the mother's death when the daughter could neither challenge nor verify its veracity. This revelation had been made sitting on Rebecca's Spanish roof terrace on what started as a balmy night in August.

Rebecca had invited her recently widowed aunt to give her a break from her determined, grim faced mourning. After supper she and Betsy were sitting on the roof terrace, enclosed in a soft and subtle night, watching the stars and the bats emerge.

Rebecca's son and his friend who had come with him had taken off for a stroll into the village, but Betsy had had a little too much of the local delicious but highly potent dark rose wine and Rebecca had stayed with her out of politeness and affection. Perhaps Betsy told her the tale because sitting under the same intense but balmy sky had reminded her of that intimacy with Rebecca's mother. They had been close in the periods when they were not locked into determined rivalry. Rebecca loved having Betsy around. In her company she got a faint whiff of the mother she had adored.

Betsy was meandering her way around a number of topics as she always did. She had a habit of starting in the middle of a story with the assumption that you knew all the characters involved and the interconnections between them and could segue between several different stories in the one telling. It was hard to keep up with her. Sometimes you would think you were making sense of a particular thread, only to realise she had changed horses in mid-stream and was trotting off in a completely different and seemingly unrelated direction. Sometimes, when it became too difficult, like then in that balmy night, Rebecca zoned out allowing her discourse to become a background hum requiring minimal response to permit its flow.

She later remembered she had been lying in the hammock they'd bought in the travelling market earlier that day and strung up on the roof terrace. She was comfortably, if idly, gazing into the myriad star clusters in the inky blackness above them. She always got a thrill when she caught sight of a shooting star and there were many to be seen in the August night sky. The Perseids meteor shower which delivered dynamic meteor fall was a highlight of her summer night sky watching in the village.

She loved the allusion to Perseus, but had been disappointed to discover that they were really space debris from the comet Swift-Tuttle, but in light of this information, if the sky failed to deliver a dying star, she would pick out a satellite, of which there were many and watch its slow progress across the sky, always feeling some surprise at how long it took to travel across her horizon.

Betsy had been talking about the people she had met in the market when they had bought the hammock – a couple from Yorkshire who ran a B&B in the next *barrio*; this had led her round to how privileged Rebecca was to have a holiday house in this fabulous place and how such a luxury could not have been dreamt of when she and Eva had been growing up in the 1930s and 40s.

"Yes, your mother had a very different life then."

Rebecca expected her to start to reminisce about the hand me down clothing from better off relatives and the one pair of shoes that had to last a year or more, or the living conditions of shared loos in the tenement building in Whitechapel where they had lived. All this she had heard before.

These stories were part of the weave and warp of her childhood and indeed she had visited her grandmother often in the two up two down terrace she'd lived in when Rebecca was a child, from which you could spit at the just still standing tenements. It was the life and the journey of each immigrant wave into and through London's east end.

By now Betty was beginning to slur slightly, but pouring herself another small measure for the road downstairs and to bed, she warmed to the theme of their childhood poverty and they were back in the tenement and the newspaper cut into squares and skewered together and strung on the door of the communal outside loo.

Rebecca was just surfacing from her childhood memories of the sheer foreignness of the old men with their side curls, sitting outside their houses, drinking the sweetened black lemon tea, playing chess and babbling in Yiddish, when she tuned in to the gist of Betsy's comments.

Betsy had gone off on a completely different track to a different time.

"It was just as hard when she got married – first to Jack and then later to your father. There was a time they were so poor and your dad was out of work – quite a long time after the war, she must have been about thirty – she fell pregnant and went for an abortion. They were hard days."

Rebecca had stopped pushing her foot against the floor to maintain the gentle sway of the hammock and was struggling to sit upright and astride the beast. This did not seem physically possible. Eventually she swung her legs over the side and sat tentatively on the edge, feeling a little sick. Yes, it was the shock of recognition that her mother had given birth to her in her thirty first year.

Betsy was oblivious to the consternation she had just caused. She had barely realised what she had said and didn't seem to register that it had any special significance for Rebecca, who, meanwhile, sat in stunned silence. Later she didn't know why she had not immediately challenged her aunt – but at the time she let her burble on until she had finished her wine and her anecdotes.

Betsy announced she was ready for bed and took herself a little unsteadily, clinging on to the bannister, down the narrow stairs to the bedroom below.

Rebecca stayed on upstairs, clearing the last remnants of the meal up, putting glasses and stoppered wine bottle on the tray to take downstairs to the kitchen. But, instead she took the stopper out of the bottle and poured herself a small glass. If she hadn't given up smoking many years before, and had not now hated the smell of tobacco, she might have rootled around for one in the packet that one of her son's friend had hidden behind the new purpose built brick barbecue earlier, in a futile attempt to hide from her the fact that they had started smoking. She sat down at the empty, still messy table with a sharp out letting of breath.

What had Betsy been telling her exactly: had her mother tried to abort her but failed – or had that other scenario played out? Of course, abortion was only backstreet then and she may have figured that chancing her life once had been enough, and providence or biology had seemed to decree she would have another child whether she wanted it or not.

She didn't know what to think or feel.

She looked up into that infinite space and saw the moon just rising over the mountains to her distant right. It was so bright and almost full, but as she watched its ascent some small dark clouds moved across it, diffusing its brightness. A wind began to pick up and as the clouds thickened and began to swirl, the moon was encircled in plumes of silvery black like a messy imitation of the rings of Jupiter.

It was a witchy sky. She loved these nights of summer where the tension having built for days demanded the release of a storm. She particularly loved them when the night was still balmy but the wind was picking up and the rain would fall during the night, leaving the following morning clear and fresh until the powerful southern Spanish sun built up its inescapable heat. On nights like these, had she possessed a serviceable broomstick, instead of the rather over-used and now broken and unserviceable, one that leaned against the newly build brick barbecue, she would gladly have taken off from her roof terrace to swoop into the growing wildness of the night to howl at stars.

Well, here was a surprise. When she was calm enough to examine her feelings, she realised that the most significant thing she felt was relief, as if some ancient tension held deep inside her had suddenly relaxed. Betsy had unconsciously given her the key to unlock the mystery of her relationship with her mother and to understand some of the deep well springs for her own mental and emotional structure, her perceived shortcomings and her not always consistent behaviours. It was a significant step along what was proving to be that haphazard journey to hopefully better self-understanding we call living.

She had loved her mother deeply all her life, and from early childhood believed with all her being that it was her job to keep her alive. She had been five when he mother first got the cancer that would nearly twenty years later be the reason for her death. It was not that her mother did not love Rebecca; in her way she did – it was just that for a while she had preferred Rebecca's sister, the first born, favoured child.

Unlike her solidly built sporty sister, Rebecca had been a sickly child: unlucky enough to get measles as a baby in the days before vaccination. She was certainly luckier than some. Her sight was unimpaired and she did not lose her hearing, but it was affected and she had problems throughout her childhood and was a frequent visitor to the ear, nose and throat department at the local children's hospital.

She remembered the agony of constant earache during the winter months and the thick green pus that, from time to time, would pour out of her ears. She remembered the intramuscular penicillin injections in her backside when she lay, tense and tight and flat as a board, over one or other of her parent's laps watching in terror as what seemed like an a needle big enough to floor an elephant advanced towards her arse, carried by the starched nurse lying to her that 'it would not hurt a bit'.

When she was three she went into hospital for an operation on her ears. It was never explained to her what would happen, or even that she was to be left there. It felt like a terrible betrayal when her parents did leave her. She screamed for an age. Eventually, she screamed herself to sleep and had no memory of being prepared for an operation. When she came round, she had a huge bandage round her head, that flopped over one eye as her head was very small and it had not been done up tightly enough.

She had been allowed to sit up and was presented with food which she resolutely refused to eat.

Her parents turned up at some stage and sat anxiously round her bedside, but she would not talk to them. She remembered that she had felt that the enormity of their betrayal had made them strangers to her. She no longer knew how to talk to them and felt timid and shy and unable to meet their eyes.

She thought they had rejected her and had no expectation that they would soon take her home and away from that place. She felt they had abandoned her but did not have the words to say it, as is the way of children who have powerful emotions they do not know how to match with clarity of expression. She had neither the linguistic facility nor the requisite boldness to try to express what she was feeling, but the intensity of this experience was to remain with her. She held that image of the clarity of her feelings in stark contrast to her childish incapacity to express it. What she felt most was that it must somehow have been her fault, and she felt guilt in her gut that was to become her chief driver in life and might well have been ethnically induced.

Jewish guilt. It is a thing. It is different in kind to other forms of religious and ethnic guilt, which she was prepared to admit did exist. Jewish guilt is closely connected to humour, because if you bear the moral weight of the universe on your shoulders you may as well laugh or you will cry, and maybe you will do both.

Unlike catholic guilt, you couldn't cleanse it away every week at mass. It was a permanent condition barely touched by having only one day of atonement in the year. This guilt may have started in the religion, but her family was not religious; they didn't even keep high days and holy days and

Rebecca's only real brush with Judaism was that she went to a Jewish kinder garden. In Rebecca's case guilt had turned her into a righter of wrongs, and in her way a fighter for what she perceived to be social justice.

It seemed that Aunt Betsy's news about her mother's attempted or actual abortion had crystallised that experience for her. This piece of information merely focused intensely the underlying sense of rejection she had always felt from her mother.

Her mother had grown to love her, but Rebecca now knew that initially her mother had not wanted another child. Oddly, it did not seem personal. Her mother had not wanted any child. It wasn't specifically Rebecca she hadn't wanted. Indeed, whatever the truth of the story, she had gone on to give birth to her – so in an odd way had chosen her.

From that night Rebecca began to feel relieved. She now understood that her deep love and dedication to her mother had been a way of proving to her mum that she had not come to love Rebecca in vain. *Well*, she thought, *I may have been needy and sickly as a kid but if I survived an attempted abortion there could have been a reason for that. At least I now understand just how tenacious I must have been.*

Even as a child Rebecca had possessed a lively wit and was almost naturally very naughty. She had an impish nature and was always keen to find something to laugh about. She used humour as many weedy children do, as a method of self-preservation.

Also, she could never walk away from a dare or a challenge. She was not stupid and would never have done anything to put herself in real jeopardy. Even though she was scared of her own shadow, a dare was a badge of honour that had to be worn, like it or not. Scared or not, she just had to do it.

This, she thought was her other motivational driver.

In later life she believed this compulsion to do what felt

like it had to be done had served her well.

Also, she was brought up in a household that was very conventional in some ways and completely unconventional in others. As a result, she had never been able to accept the boundaries set by convention. She fully accepted then – and still did – the need for boundaries around behaviour in a civilised society, but either wanted to set her own rules, after considerable thought and moral grappling, or to negotiate them closely with others. She would not have other people's rules arbitrarily imposed upon her.

As a young child at school, when the lesson was boring or totally obvious, she did not disrupt the class. Simply, she would quietly leave the classroom and head off to the library where she would read a good novel until what would otherwise have been torture for her came to a natural conclusion. She rarely got caught.

That night as she sat there on her Spanish roof terrace awaiting the gathering storm, she reflected that we are, all of us, strange mixtures and amalgams of personality traits. Some embedded in us as if part of our DNA – some learned through our experience.

Identity is built through the close wrapping around of both our inheritance and our environment. It is in neither one nor the other that the explanation of ourselves is to be found.

So, what about hers? As was her habit Rebecca would go on pondering this, occasionally talking to friends as if it were a hypothetical examination of the generality of lives, but in reality feeding this constant inner dialogue of hers.

She didn't remember feeling insecure as a child, or ever entirely unloved.

It was true that children were left to roam back then. For a good few years her parents had run a pie and mash shop. It was odd for this most traditional cockney fare to be produced by a Jewish family, particularly one that had done a

58

deal with the local kosher butcher in Brixton to supply the meat. But many things about her parents were odd.

Rebecca remembered, and perhaps it was her earliest memory, even before her hospital visits, needing to go to the toilet in the very early light of a winter morning when it had been snowing.

Their toilet was outside the house and as she opened the back door the snow in the yard was gently heaving up and down like a living being. This memory was a surreal dream. She ran back inside without the pee she desperately needed and into her parents' bedroom babbling something about the yard being alive. Her father, never at his best this early in the day, went to investigate and discovered that the crated eels that would shortly be cut up, cooked and jellied had somehow escaped from their crates and were gently undulating under the subsequent layer of snow that had fallen.

Weird things happened on a daily basis in her family, largely because of her father.

He was a man of many colours. She thought of him as a cross between a not quite realised super hero and a failed gangster. He was crazy as a loon; an anarchic force who appeared not to give a toss for society's mores and its rules.

He told her once that when he had just turned thirteen he had been in a convalescence home after an operation for appendicitis. They had served bacon for breakfast. He thought about God before he ate it and waited for the Lord to strike him dead and when nothing happened decided that after all God did not exist and then refused his bar mitzvah because, after all, who makes a covenant with a non-existent God? This was much to the chagrin of his parents and the shame of his community. His Jewishness never left him, but it was never again to be expressed in religious belief or practice – not even when he got older, when many people facing death return to their roots.

At one stage it was expressed in politics, when he had briefly been a political activist and as a young man had helped drive Moseley and his fascist troop out of the east end of London in the Battle of Cable Street. For a period he had been a thief – unfortunately a bad one – been captured and sent to prison in, prosaically, Brixton and, more exotically, Mexico and San Francisco, although he would never tell her what the latter two stints had been for and she never knew if he was really a bit of a Walter Mitty fantasist who just made it up.

Then he met and fell in love with her mother and, like the swan, he mated for life.

Rebecca had learnt a lot from her dad, and one particularly significant lesson in life.

Her Bubba Anya had died when she was about eleven and she remembered being driven over to the East End by her dad as the relatives gathered. They were squabbling over Anya's old bits of furniture. It wasn't as if she had much. One distant aunt had hold of a three-legged wooden stool from which one leg had become detached. Anya had used it when for the Shabbos soup she plucked and gutted one of the chickens that had roamed her yard until she'd rung its neck, roundly cursing her neighbours in Yiddish while she did so. Anya had lived in London for over thirty five years before her death, but had poor English. She was diminutive and terrifyingly fierce, got madder as she grew older and ended up convinced her German neighbours were running gas pipes under the floorboards into her house to gas her.

Rebecca's Dad had looked at the unseemly scramble for what he called 'bits of toot' and asked her to promise him she would never stoop to behave like these family members of his for whom her felt nothing but shame. He took a photo of his parents with him and his brother – the two youngest boys – and told her that in reality he didn't even need that because they were in his heart and his soul. She remembered feeling very proud of him at that moment and knew that she had just learnt something profound about what matters in life and what does not.

The photo that her father took still had pride of place in Rebecca's living room and when she looked at it she saw the hypersensitive young man that had been her father and she remembered her promise to him.

Her father could be scary. He had a vicious temper, which her older sister had inherited but she had not.

He had taken her out for the day of her eighth birthday. They were on route to see the film *Robin and the Seven Hoods*, which only he could think appropriate for an eight year old, and which she had loved. Beforehand they were having lunch in Lyons corner House in Charing Cross. As they were heading downstairs, two men had pushed past of their way up saying: "Get out of our way, Jew Boy".

Her dad had pushed her to one side out of the fray, making sure she would be safe and then one after another he had picked up these men and hurled them headlong down the stairs. Both had run away and Rebecca and her Dad had just resumed their day.

Sometimes, particularly when her mother's ill health started to dominate their lives and he felt vulnerable and exposed, he could turn the anger against his children and genuinely scare them, and it could take several days for him to calm down. Though she had hated the violence of his temper tantrums, Rebecca felt later that her exposure to them from a young age had given her the ability to tackle difficult men, which was a daily occurrence in her professional life and for this she also thanked him though perhaps not quite so fulsomely.

The other and perhaps most salient feature of her father was his gift as a story teller. He was genuinely, side split-tingly funny. He didn't tell jokes: he told stories about things that had happened in his every day.

As a teenager creeping in rather later at night, and she was officially allowed, she would often find her serially insomniac father sitting in their kitchen having a fag and a cup of tea. She would be longing to sleep or day dream about the latest fancy in her life and her dad would beg her to keep him company for a while. Then he started to tell her stories. Sometimes she would still be there at five a.m. holding her ribs that ached with laughter, wiping the tears from her eyes and begging him to let her go to sleep.

He had died, like her mother, far too young – the same age that she had just attained – from a massive coronary from all the fags and the bacon sandwiches he had learnt to consume when he rejected God and his religion.

Her parents had been a genuine love story and Rebecca had grown up around this utterly intense love affair that had ruined her capacity to settle for normal and compromise in any future relationship that would be on offer.

Families, thought Rebecca, *what strange amalgams they are of loves and loathing, of unmet needs and frustrated expectations and many guilty secrets. Turns out they are maybe the best worst option for getting human beings into and through this world. Thank God for friends.*

With these thoughts still swirling round her brain, she noticed that the clouds had gathered thickly; the sky was overcast. There was a rumble of thunder followed by the first lightening streaking across the sky. These, along with the first drops of rain broke through her self-absorption and knowing she would get soaked if she remained on the roof terrace any longer, she gathered up the tray and went inside, firmly shutting the door in a feeble attempt to keep the geckos from venturing in out of the storm. Before long, as she prepared for bed, she could hear the hailstorm begin. Soon there would be ice the size of golf balls falling on the roof. She was relieved to hear the front door open and to know that Daniel had arrived back with his friend, Will.

After their late night conversation, Rebecca had been relieved to put Aunt Betsy on the plane a few days later at the end of her week's stay. Whilst she remained very fond of Betsy, she was hard work. Rebecca had been tempted to return to the topic of that conversation and to probe it like a tongue unable to resist exploring the sore part of a cavity in an aching tooth: but she had resisted. She'd driven Betsy the nearly two hours to the airport, along with her son Daniel's friend Will, and picked up her next set of house guests who would take over Betsy's room. They arrived on the early morning flight on whose return journey Betsy would depart. Betsy had been waved through to the departure lounge with gifts of local cheeses and honey deposited in her checked in case, many hugs and a warm invitation to return at some as yet unspecified, but definitely future time. Will had somewhat embarrassedly allowed himself to be hugged by Rebecca, who felt someone had to give him a fond farewell, as Daniel had only mumbled something indecipherable that morning before they left and he had turned over and gone back to sleep.

Rebecca just about had time to grab a *café con leche* before her long-standing friends Jenny and David Marlow burst through arrivals, excited to see her and to begin their holiday. Both were teachers and they had longed for that exhausting summer term to end, to complete their marking duties and to head off to guaranteed sunshine.

They had been friends since university. Rebecca had introduced them. Jenny had been in Rebecca's tutorial group and David one of the four other students with whom she was sharing a house. She had counted them as the first real friends of her post school adult life, and they were generally very easy around each other.

Rebecca spent the rest of her holiday shopping and cooking for her guests, with everyone mucking in and organising them out of the torpor of hot days spent in the large and beautiful municipal swimming pool to make the occasional trip out of her beloved mountains to Granada, making sure that any of the guests who had not seen the Alhambra had the opportunity to do so. They were never disappointed once they had made the effort.

David and Jenny were with her for a fortnight. They got up late, easily adopting Spanish time and habits and spent their days in different swimming pools in neighbouring villages. These were lazy days lying in the sun, against all sensible advice, reading and from time to time lapsing into to the occasional conversation that fizzled out when a swim became imperative. Some days they drove to the sea. It was a forty-five-minute drive to the nearest beaches which were stony and the sea was potentially clean enough in the morning but often grubby in the afternoon with the discarded debris of boats and local communities that was polluting the Mediterranean and making it less attractive as a prospect than it had been in their youths.

Longer conversations took place in the kitchen where they shared the cooking or over long suppers on the roof terrace, enjoying the local wine, waiting for the stars and the bats.

Here they caught up on each other's lives and put the world to rights, which with the passing years what had seemed straightforward and easy when they were young, they were finding increasingly difficult to get right.

Life seemed to be getting more complicated and options for positive change fewer – or maybe it was just them get older, loosing energy and conviction.

Sometimes they ate late, but used the few hours between the easing of the ferocious sun and the dark to walk in the hills.

There was something delicious about those balmy hours of cool when it was possible to climb up the hill and look back to the village. On a clear day it was possible to see the small boats on the sea over thirty kilometres away. It didn't happen often in August – the heat of the day did not lend itself to the crystalline air it requires to provide such a long view. This was more of thing of spring or autumn or winter, but on summer evenings the sharp contours of the mountains are softened in the early evening by a rosy light that re-shapes their harshness, conjures up subtle shadows upon them that make them seem benign and nurturing. Often, as the group made their way up the hillside, the old men would be making their way home on their mules laden with the produce from the *huerta* – the vegetable garden – for the supper table.

It was a dying way of life – most of the farmers, the younger generation, had four by fours and passing them was less pleasant as they raised a dust storm on the narrow paths through the hills that forced you to stand aside and cover your face until the cloud settled.

This cool of evening was Rebecca's favourite time of day. After showers and getting clean from the long day in the sun, washing the chlorine of the pool or the salt from the sea if there'd been a day at the beach, from hair and body and before the long evening rituals of the uncorking of the cold white wine, sitting on the roof terrace watching the hills turn their evening pink as the sun drew to a close.

She most enjoyed that lull between the harshness of the August sun by day and the lushness of a deep, dark Hispanic night, when there was still the supper to cook and the food to be shared with friends before the weariness of sleep overtook everyone and the time came to part.

A few nights before they would pack up the house to leave for home, there was a ring at the door in the early evening.

This was really unusual, as few people just called on the off chance and evenings were usually really peaceful. It was before supper time and the smells of the neighbours cooking wafted down the street. Rebecca went down to answer it, to find Lola standing outside.

Lola Gonzalez had sold her the house which had belonged to her mother. All four foot eight of Lola jumped up to grasp Rebecca round the neck and plant three kisses alternating her cheeks. She launched into her rapid Gatling gunfire, almost indecipherable Spanish: "Rebecca, you owe me money."

"Really Lola, I don't know how, but of course, if I owe you money I'm going to pay you."

At that point Rebecca lost the tenuous thread of understanding to Lola's guttural Andalucía dialect that still grated on her ears as the words were mangled and Lola just carried on. Her many hand gestures were not helping.

"Sorry Lola, I just don't understand what you're saying, can you slow down?"

But slowing down was not in Lola's range of responses.

She took Rebecca's hand: "*Vámonos*! Come with me," so Rebecca followed her.

They walked up the street and into the high *barrio*. They were getting uncomfortably close to Lucinda's house and Rebecca found herself hesitating .

"Oh," said Lola with a chuckle, "you think I'm taking you to Lucinda's house, don't you? But I'm not. I wouldn't do that."

So this was the point where Rebecca understood that everyone in the village knew about her spectacular falling out with Lucinda who had previously been a friend for over twenty years, and who was the person who had first invited her to the village and now hated her guts.

She felt a mixture of embarrassment that Lola knew the story and relief they were not on route to Lucinda's house.

Rebecca had told no one in the village the story of Lucinda so it could only have come from Lucinda herself.

Lola explained. "I'm taking you to the house of another English woman who speaks good Spanish. She will translate for us."

Up round the corner and down along another street, they stopped outside the Bed and Breakfast called Casa Alpujarra, where Lola rang the bell and a woman roughly Rebecca's age: middle aged that is, came to the door. She was dressed in shorts and hiking boots. She was tall and rangy and had long dark auburn hair with a few grey streaks. She clearly knew Lola, who after brief introductions had been made and more cheeks kissed continued her quick fire explanation.

"Ok Rebecca," said Joanna, "Lola here says that when they transferred the house into your name they also transferred responsibility for paying the tax to the *ayuntamiento* in the village that pays for water supply and rubbish collections."

"Yes, I pay that through the bank in the village by direct debit."

"Yes, but there is another tax that gets paid to the regional government and this wasn't transferred. So, for the last six year Lola and Manuel her husband has been paying."

"So I owe her six years of back regional tax?"

"Yes, and you'll also need to transfer that tax into your own name, once you've paid her. If you like you can come in and I'll take you through what you need to do to make the transfer."

So, Rebecca made an arrangement to meet Lola at the bank first thing the next morning to clear her debt. Lola said goodnight and started off for home and Rebecca went inside with Joanna and over a glass of wine and some nibbles learnt about yet another facet of impossible Spanish bureaucracy she would have to negotiate before the payment date next year.

Joanna asked her if she liked to walk, as she was always looking for people to go walking with. Her husband, Thomas no longer liked taking any kind of exercise so never went with her, even though he'd once been a keen walker. Equally Thomas was worried about her walking in the higher mountains alone. It turned out that some years ago she had fallen down a *barranco* when she got lost on one particular walk and had badly damaged her knee, and taken several hours to hobble to the road where she got a mobile signal and was able to phone him to pick her up. Since then she always sought a partner for the more adventurous walks, though happy to do the shorter, local walks alone. Rebecca said she'd be delighted to walk with her and asked if maybe they could fit a walk in before she left in a few days' time. She added that she would be back for a week in the Autumn, when the weather would be more conducive to long walks during the day.

When Rebecca left Casa Alpujarra she felt excited because she knew she had made a new friend in the village.

Rebecca always felt saddened when the time came to leave the house and get back to work and London. This village and her house were her sanctuary and her place of peace. The moment she arrived the heavy burdens of work commitments juggled with the practical arrangements for Daniel – let alone the responsibility for the wellbeing of her staff that she carried on her back – like the sins of Pilgrim, just fell away. Her otherwise constant neck ache ceased and time slowed. After a short time she felt mellow, more like a person she was happy to own up to being, rather than the irritable, tired wreck she found herself being much of the time in London.

As she went through the routine of leaving, scrubbing the house from top to bottom to discourage rodent and insect intruders and dealing with rubbish, she felt the usual cloud descend. It would last until she had been back at work a day or two and then she would affect successfully the transfer between her two lives. While she was finishing off mopping the floors and before the final tasks on the way out of disconnecting the gas, then turning off the electricity and water, Daniel was packing up the car.

She took her last look at the view of the mountains.

She knew she could never live in this small rural community, much as she loved visiting it. For her, it was too remote and introverted to sustain a life. She couldn't work from there and, even if she could have afforded not to work, London was her home and she loved its pace and vibrancy. She felt she would be bored living full time in the village. Most of her neighbours were elderly peasant farmers who were on the whole kind to her and pleased to see her when she arrived unannounced. They were pleased that she was struggling to learn Spanish and would from time to time stand and chat with her – though she found it so hard to understand their dialect, she could from time to time get the gist and from time to time had huge lapses of understanding. She doubted that she would do what many other foreigners with houses here were planning, which was to come to live or at least spend increasing periods of time when they retired. This was still quite a long way off for her – so not a decision she would have to make anytime soon.

But now, she reflected, she had met someone who would become a real friend. She was curious to discover why Joanna and Thomas so wanted to live in this village, in these mountains, in this country that was not theirs by birth.

But then, suddenly recalling the revelation about her almost non birth that Aunt Betsy had drunkenly revealed, she realised that what is ours by birth is for many just an accidental conjuncture of strange events and even stranger people, and suddenly she felt blessed.

Even though beneath her blessing was the guilty knowledge she would have to explain to Elena that this was yet another year in which she had failed to write the story of her life and she hoped it was because she was still too busy living it, and decided she was in fact just really curious to find out what would happen next.

JOANNA GETS NEW NEIGHBOURS

Elizabeth Grant was in the kitchen with Jo. She had brought a lemon meringue pie for pudding.

It was a miracle of snowy lemon perfection. Just looking at it you knew it would have just the right amount of goo and sharp sweetness on top of crisp, light pastry.

Making mouths water was something that Elizabeth could do. She was proud of her cooking and her food was good. Indeed many of her friends would say it was a joy to eat.

What they found curious, particularly as she had been cooking for many years, was that she was lost without a recipe book. She followed recipes meticulously. Some might say slavishly. If she didn't happen to have the right ingredient – maybe as the result of an oversight in her shopping list – she felt a sense of rising panic.

This was not something that happened often, because Elizabeth was also a meticulous maker of lists and, unlike some friends of her acquaintance who did make lists, but in the shop sometimes forgot even to look at them, she ticked off the items as they went into her basket. Also, her lists were grouped under sub-divided headings such as: 'Veg: Salad items, Root Veg, Greens'. Fruit had sub-headings like: 'Orchard, Berries, Exotic'.

Anyway, you get the idea. Elizabeth liked lists.

Sometimes if she found herself without an ingredient when it came time to prepare supper she might send her husband Toby down to the shop to get it, providing it was a simple, easily recognised thing like salt or garlic. If, however, it required a little more culinary knowledge to identify like asafoetida or za'tar, she might decide it wasn't worth it. She knew that Toby, who had that most common of male inadequacies: a total lack of peripheral vision, would never spot the missing ingredient in a shop packed with items. Also, though he had been studying Spanish for over ten years and could read fluently, he was still most reluctant to initiate even the most basic conversation to ask for assistance. Besides, there was every likelihood that the local shop would not have said ingredient.

To do the weekly shop they would drive the forty five minutes to the nearest largish supermarket, which had a surprisingly large stock of more esoteric cooking ingredients.

If they ever went to Granada she would visit the spice stalls in the Albaicín – but she worried about the dubious hygiene she felt she observed on the hands of the man who served on one of these stalls.

She much preferred to shop at the stall where the seller wore plastic gloves, and would probably have been happier still if these spices had been readily available all neatly pre-packaged in a proper shop.

On occasions where she couldn't face Toby's failure to arrive back clutching the right ingredient – and the probability that he would bring entirely the wrong ingredient recommending it as a suitable replacement – she might take something out of the freezer or replace her original plan, swapping it for a meal planned with equally meticulous care for later in the week for which she did have the ingredients.

Toby remained supremely unaware of his wife's consternation, though it might give her a nagging headache for the next few days. He thought the food department in their household was his wife's domain, and was always reasonably satisfied with the food she served him. Indeed, he would boast to his friends about his wife's prowess in the kitchen, declaring himself to be a lucky man.

Toby was occasionally urged by Elizabeth to cook a meal. She would feel a rising tide of frustration that she was chained overly to the kitchen's sink, and in a 'tools down' bid for freedom would demand he made supper.

This would worry Toby. He would give it much thought. Several times during the day he might stand in contemplation by the open door of the fridge sighing and failing to register what was sitting inside. It didn't really matter, however, as he had only one dish he might attempt: sausage and mash.

When complaining of his lack of culinary invention, Elizabeth had been heard by friends to iterate on occasion: "It's not bad, sausage and mash – but it is always sausage and mash."

Also, though one part of Elizabeth longed for Toby to take a more active role in the management and execution of their alimentary well-being, the other part hated losing control of her domain.

He did not do things the way she wanted them done. He didn't peel the potatoes properly. She liked a nice thin peel, leaving maximum potato for the mash. He would hack at the potatoes with a sharp nice, forgetting to use the Swiss precision peeler bought especially for the job. Often more peel came off the potato than went into the pot. Also, he made messes that he didn't properly clear up, though his deficiencies in this department might not have been visible to the naked eye.

Elizabeth knew that her fear of losing control and the need to exercise it quite so tightly was neurotic. On good days she could laugh at herself. On bad days she took to labelling everything in the kitchen on the basis that Toby, who was beginning to have a few problems with memory, would not be able to differentiate between the tea they drank in the morning, from their afternoon cuppa unless the packets had a clear label attached.

Elizabeth had not always been quite so tightly wound. In

her previous life she had been a Head Teacher of a large comprehensive school in the West Midlands. Running a meticulous time-table had always been in her blood. The trains in her network would always have run to time and she never accepted the educational equivalent of leaves on the line as adequate reason for sloppiness (for many years the train companies in the UK used the excuse of leaves on the line in autumn for slow running and lateness of trains, and it had become a national joke that seemed to explain why the country that had led the great industrial revolution of the Victorian age was now falling apart).

At the same time, as she was a great administrator, Elizabeth was also a completely inspirational teacher and it gave her great joy when the pupils from families without a single advantage did well and went on to university. She gloried in their success and she was generous with her time and with her praise.

There was no toleration of bullying in her school. The pupils were taught respect for themselves and each other and to aim as high as they could and then even a little more.

Given that her school had the highest proportion of free school meal, students in the area and some of the best exam results, everyone reckoned she'd done a fair old job.

She wasn't just interested in exam grades. There was music and art and drama and debating clubs as well as sporting success.

Word had it that if you got a place in Elizabeth Oliver's school you had lucked out and your future was assured, providing you put in a bit of effort.

The issues of burgeoning neurosis for Elizabeth had started when her working life stopped.

She and Toby had moved to the Alpujarra when she retired, because they loved the outdoor life of walking and bird watching.

Toby was a poet, from which there is no retirement but also, for the many, no equivalence to the professional success of his wife. He had been published occasionally, in obscure college magazines and had once had a poem in the weekly Guardian. He'd made a sort of a living teaching poetry to reluctant adolescents in a further education college. He remembered the agony of the weekly sessions of what was called a 'poetry taster' for the seventeen year old telecommunications apprentices insisted on by an aspirational College Principal that was meant to give these sons of toil some access to a wider culture.

They had left pairs of women's tights on his desks that were indescribably manky and congealed with substances he's rather not think about and when asked to put in poetry requests did so inevitably for *the Ballad of Eskimo Nell* or *the Shooting of Dan McGrew*.

Unlike Elizabeth's experience of retirement, Toby had had no problem leaving work. In fact, for him it had been a longed-for liberation.

Despite his vagueness in the cooking department he was an expert in orienteering. They loved nothing better than packing a picnic and going for long walks in the hills.

It is true that getting ready for these adventures took some time, because they both had to have the right equipment. Sometimes they took gaiters to wear over boots where they thought there would be mud or thistles or the terrain was rough. They both had to have the right hat for the occasion. There were different hats for different seasons, by weight and density and brim protection. Toby, who had thinning hair on top, needed particular protection, but then so did Elizabeth who had an elaborate and very expensive haircut with exceedingly expensive – but exquisite – streaks of colour.

Often boots needed to be cleaned before venturing out and a change of trousers in case, given the weather, they might progress from long trousers in the morning to shorts in the afternoon. They could have had the kind of walking trousers that have a removable lower leg via a zip, but they found these uncomfortable on the leg while walking.

Then there were maps and gloves and poles and a whistle each in case either of them lost the other.

When finally they were ready to rumble, they would spend the day walking in a paradise where it was rare to see another walker.

They'd see the farmers working the fields, and the shepherds with their mixed flocks of sheep and goats raising dust across the high paths in the opposite valley.

They'd enjoy the silence of the mountains, interrupted only by bird song and the accompanying low moan of the wind and maybe, if they were lucky, they'd see the occasional pair of eagles, kites or even once or twice a magnificent flock of buzzards catching the thermals to float lazily through an azure sky on a sharp eyed look out for lunch.

They'd seen the kill made by a screeching eagle with talons extended in a precision raid carry off a newly born baby goat.

Once, on a walk when their dog had been nosing in the undergrowth, they'd disturbed a whole tribe of wild boar that stampeded with their young down the hillside, forcing Toby and Elizabeth to hide behind a rock and hope the dog wouldn't be gored to death in the melee. It wasn't, and later they agreed that it had been a magnificent sight.

They got good at spotting the distinctive outline of the wild mountain goats where these rested on rocky out crops reached through their impossible climbs up the mountain side.

They learnt the difference between the breeds of snakes and lizards and even the poisonous pine caterpillars that cover the mountain in long deadly processions each spring.

There were a lot of compensations to living in the Alpujarra. One of them was having Joanna and Thomas as neighbours.

Jo and Elizabeth hit it off immediately. Jo had watched them arrive. Of course, she'd known for months that the house opposite their Bed and Breakfast had been bought. Like many of the empty houses in the village it had been on the market for a long time and she'd seen the several price revisions downwards in the estate agents office in the local market town over a two year period.

She and Thomas must have been away on their long planned three-day holiday to Seville when Elizabeth and Toby finalised the deal and commissioned the builders to make the renovations.

There had been months of building activity. Well, as is the way of things in the Alpujarra.

It's not just in London or Leeds where the builders would turn up, work for a couple of days then disappear for periods of time.

In the Alpujarra to boot they disappear leaving mounds of sand and stones in the middle of the roads, that neighbours would drive around or over as they manoeuvred the narrow, winding village streets to get access to parking and to get in to their front doors. Then more deliveries of tiles and kitchen equipment and bathroom taps would be made, and the builders would come back and gradually a house took shape.

Jo and Thomas had taken possession of their house after the previous owner had done a lot of the renovation work. They'd been able to move in and gradually, over years, put their own stamp on the property.

Jo thought it might be a nightmare to have to make all the decisions about a house in one go before you had even lived in it. These decisions would include things like where to put all the electric plugs in a kitchen, when you had no idea what appliance you wanted to go in what space. You'd have to decide whether the doors should open out or in and what kind of locks you wanted on the windows and doors.

Jo remembered a story she found hilarious that her friend Rebecca had told her.

Rebecca did not live in the village. She was still working and lived in London, but had had this process of having to make all decisions upfront with her house and had to trust the builder to get it right.

She said she'd chosen to have traditional red tiles on the floor and to have green and blue tiles on the kitchen walls to go with her blond wood kitchen cupboards that were edged in blue and green. At one point, Rebecca had an email from the builder to say that the chosen tiles had been discontinued, and to ask her to choose again and send him the details. This she did, which was not easy given Spain's backwardness in those days in putting products online.

There had been a mix up. Rebecca, who was only just learning Spanish, had thought the builder meant that the red floor tiles, meant for the floor, had been discontinued. She chose some beautiful, expensive and highly decorated floor tiles, also red, and told the builder what she wanted.

When she arrived to visit next, she found the original floor tiles on the floor, and her beautiful expensive and highly decorated red tiles, that she had meant to go on the floor, covering the kitchen walls.

"What did you think?" asked Jo.

"I thought: 'Fuck me, this kitchen is really red'. And then I laughed. I've come to love my exceptionally red kitchen over the years."

When Elizabeth and Toby arrived with their U-Haul truck in late July that year, Jo and Thomas were at home. Well, Jo was at home because she was waiting for some B&B guests to arrive, who had just phoned to say apologetically that their plane had arrived late and they had just picked up the hire car, would immediately be on their way and would expect to see her in three hours or so.

It was around four pm and Thomas was at the *cortijo* working in their small holding. Jo phoned him to ask what soft fruits they had as she would like to make up a basket to take to welcome their new neighbours. He said he'd see what he could find.

She let them get inside the house, then went and rang their new bell. When a weary Elizabeth came to the door, Jo introduced herself and asked if they'd like a cup of tea and a slice of cake before they got to work unloading.

"Oh, do you know, that would be just lovely. We've had a two-day drive from the ferry into Bilbao to get here and I'm parched and feeling like two penn'orth of God help me."

Jo had never heard what from the accent she guessed to be a Brummies' expression, but got the general drift and went to put the kettle on.

She hadn't been able to help them much that evening as she had to welcome her family of four when they arrived for their two night stay, but the following day she and Thomas gave a hand to unload the van and she delivered the basket of fruit from the *cortijo*.

Jo soon discovered that she and Elizabeth liked many of the same things like reading novels and listening to classical music. They had the teaching and educational experience as a uniting factor – both having fought for liberal values and resource for their pupils in a system that they both believed had become increasingly mean and elitist, reversing many of the educational gains that had been made for less privileged pupils.

Both Jo and Thomas were impressed with Toby's status as a poet, and Jo thought she'd never met a real, live one before, even though poetry was not exactly her thing.

Toby and Thomas got along, though and that helped cement a relationship that became a firm friendship. Poet he may be, but Toby liked all sport and could talk football like a what passes for a 'proper man' – so he and Thomas could happily chat for hours.

On the night of the lemon meringue pie success, Thomas and Toby were upstairs drinking beer on the roof terrace in Thomas's newly built enclosed bar area. This was Thomas's crowning achievement.

The structure was sturdy enough to withstand the biting winds of an Alpujenian winter and had enough glass to allow host and visitors a view of the drama of the mountains in all seasons.

While, downstairs, having delivered what she thought would be the star attraction of the meal, Elizabeth was sitting on one of the high bar stall seats in Jo's kitchen, while Jo was busy putting the final touches to a Thai beef Rendang curry that along with jasmine rice and pak choy would be their supper.

Jo, as was her wont, was putting dirty cooking utensils and plates in the dishwasher in a somewhat haphazard manner. Elizabeth tried not to, but couldn't help thinking to herself: *Well, really, there's a way to stack a dishwasher and that isn't it.* But she managed not to say anything.

Jo was blissfully unaware of Elizabeth's urge to teach her the art of dishwasher stacking. Elizabeth thought to herself, *I think maybe I'm getting worse,* and she smiled, recognising her own ridiculousness, even though in her heart she still remained convinced that standards really do matter and her way with a dishwasher was really the only efficient way.

By this time, they had been in their house for six months. They'd experienced their first mountain winter and had been pleasantly surprised. They had still swum in the sea in November. It had been tee shirt weather during the core daylight hours even in December, though morning and night had been cold and they'd really needed the wood burning stove that had been a major investment. Three weeks in January had been bitter with biting winds and snow, but that hadn't lasted long on the village streets and now it was February and though not quite tee shirts and shorts weather during the day it no longer felt unbearable to put a nose outside the door.

You could enjoy pleasant walks again in the hills but the weather was still unpredictable and you had to be alert to potential for sudden whiteouts that could obscure even paths you thought you knew well. Occasionally there had been torrential rain, which the Spanish called 'pyjama days', as on them they rarely climbed out of theirs.

There were days when the sea mist came in up to the roofs on the houses and you could sit on the roof terrace in the sun whilst looking at the white out below, and feeling the village as a world cut off and floating in time and space.

They had dined well. Jo was also a good cook, though perhaps not with Elizabeth's absolute precision. There had been declarations of delight over the pie and more than one portion had been devoured by all. There had been red wine to drink and a mellow brandy for those who wanted it. Thomas and Toby had disappeared to watch the roundup of the winter Olympics from Pyeong Chang, leaving the women upstairs to chat over another glass of wine.

"I've been meaning to ask you how you're doing in your post retirement life, here." Said Jo. "You seem to have adjusted really well, but it is a big change and a very different life to Brum."

"Well yes, it is, and I'm not sure how I'm doing if truth be told. I make a lot of lists."

"Really, what do you mean? Lists?"

"Yes, well, I have shopping lists, laundry lists, house snagging lists for the builder, meal planner lists, and garden planting lists. Then there's Toby's medicine list and times they have to be taken and of course, the calendar, which is really an events list and a list of potential dates for visits from friends and family and maybe it's also a list of any social events here, as we gradually get to meet people and get included in outings.

I don't know but I think I'm losing my grip on life a bit and the less in control I feel, the more lists I make.

Oh, and I've also taken to labelling things around the house. I justify it on the grounds I think Toby is having problems with his memory, but I'm not sure I'm not imagining that. He's always been a bit vague and maybe he's just feeling as disoriented as I am and it's not really the signs of early dementia setting in."

She paused and looked at Jo to see if she was undergoing a lunatic alert.

Jo smiled at her and said: "You know, Lizzy, in the last few months you've completely changed your life. You're living in a new house, in a new country, in a completely new environment from the one you're used to. You've stopped working after thirty odd years of being top dog in your field. You've left your kids behind, even though they're grown and supposed to be independent and neither of them lived with you. Is it any wonder you're having a few adjustment problems?"

"Was it like that for you when you first came here?"

"Yes it was, a bit, and a lot of those things applied to me. I think the difference was that both Thomas and I really wanted to change our lives. We'd never really lived in town, always outside in a village. Also, he kept his job when we moved, and I set up this business so we've been busy. You've been a really busy person all your working life, with a lot of recognition and status and here you're just another foreigner of a certain age trying to live a dream and having

82

to come to terms with its reality – the good and the disappointing. Were you happy when you were working?"

"Yes, really. I loved my job. I liked being busy. I liked the status of being in charge, and I was really good at it.

I think I was a good boss. People liked working for me. I was a good manager and I believed in developing and empowering the team. I was delighted when one of my staff members grew in confidence and skills and I really wanted them to fly.

Look, working gave me a huge sense of purpose. I may have had sleepless nights worrying about budgets and what the idiots in the council were going to do to us next: even worse the idiots in government, but I never stayed awake at night wondering what I was doing it for."

"And your relationship with Toby, how was that? I'm asking because you can't have had that much time together if you were so busy, and now you're thrown together all the time. That's another big change."

"Toby is a lovely man. Well, on the whole he is. He's quite gentle, if very stubborn.

He was a great father to the children. In fact, he was much better with them than I ever was, and the girls adore him. Truth is, I didn't really enjoy being a mother – I love them and I'm proud of them and I worry when their lives go awry, but I was very bored by the baby stage and yes, I'll admit it, by the toddler stage as well.

I liked them better when they grew a bit. I don't think I had the imagination to deal with their pre-logical, magical phase. I'm a very practical person and I like doing things. So, Toby was more a parent than me and he let his career take a back seat to mine. I would never do anything to hurt him, well, except I had a lot of lovers during those years."

"What?" Asked Jo, wide eyed and spluttering wine with her laughter. "You had lovers? Why?"

83

"I'd hate him to find out. It would hurt him so much and it was never a threat to him. Even though from time to time a lover would get a notion to push our thing further or make it permanent, I had strict demarcation lines. I would never have left Toby for anyone else. I guess I just had a lot more sexual energy than him. I also had a lot of opportunity. When you run a school there are a lot of evening events and it's very easy to invent a few more or not go to some that are in the diary. Also there were a lot of conferences and seminars that justify time away.

I hope this doesn't sound cold blooded. I was fond of them and some were around for many years. One dated back to my university days and that's now forty years ago. You see I've always been good at picking up on the signals of male desire, and when I was younger men used to tell me that I radiated sexual attraction. I liked that feeling of being desired. It made me excited. I guess it gave me energy when I responded to the desire for me I felt in a man."

"How many lovers did you have?"

"Well, I was twenty-four when we got married and I'm sixty-one now – that's thirty-six years. Give me a minute I'll have to do a recky." And Elizabeth started counting on her fingers.

Jo could tell Lizzy was quite enjoying this confession. As ever, Jo was fascinated by the complexities of people' lives; the unexpected nature of their adventures and the many paradoxes that a relationship – perhaps especially a marriage – could entail and hold.

"Well, eleven, if you count Adrian, but he pre-dated Toby, so I've never thought of him in the same way as the others. Really, it's not as cold bloodied as it may sound. I was fond of all my lovers and to some extent I got involved in their lives. I preferred an affair to last a year or so and fizzle out as they met someone new or the spark between us departed. Some were very persistent. Two got quite ill and needed support, which I gave as best I could, but thankfully they were separated by a few years, and one of them died and I was upset. I tried not to overlap lovers because that definitely made life far too complicated.

"Every now and again Adrian would turn up and I'd renew our connexion. He was maybe the only man who might have tempted me to leave my safe life with Toby – but I never really trusted him.

I don't mean I think he was using me or not consciously, nor that he didn't love me. I think in some dark recess of his soul he felt love, but with him it was pretty much out of sight, out of mind and he travelled a lot and any things, including me, spent a lot of time out of his line of sight.

Anyway, he was the constant, inconstant and the others were time to time distractions.

"Having all this adventure going on made me appreciate Toby even more. I think it was what kept our marriage alive. I said goodbye to my last lover the night before we drove the van to the ferry to drive here. That was six months ago, and I am still getting messages of regret from him. These are messages on my phone that I try not to leave lying around in any incriminating places for Toby to find. And, now as you might guess, I am unlikely to find any lover material in the immediate vicinity. I have never had and will never have an affair with any of my female friends' partners. I do have a moral code of sorts – though it may not be a conventional one. I would never do that, and I've ruled out Paco the goat herd: I'm told he gets fleas from the goats and that's really not my cup of tea. Not sure his personal hygiene would meet my requirements and standards."

Then she laughed, more schoolgirl like than headmistress.

Jo felt like she should push her chin up to close her mouth and stop gawping. She loved Lizzy's hidden depths and she realised that there might be many more stories to come over the course of their growing friendship.

"Well," she said, "I thought you were having an existential crisis linked to work, retirement and moving. I didn't realise it was also linked to the death of your interesting sex life. That's much more serious. Producing even perfect lemon meringue pies might not seem like an adequate substitute."

Occasionally Jo would wonder if over the course of the next few years Paco might seem to become a more attractive proposition to Elizabeth if her high hygiene standards dropped as a result of village life. Though she couldn't really envisage that happening. Perhaps her libido would be eroded by age and opportunity, or maybe her list making habit would just escalate.

Several times over the next few weeks Jo had it on the tip of her tongue to spill the beans to Thomas, but she didn't. She hadn't promised Elizabeth she wouldn't tell anyone but there are boundaries to protecting friendships between women about what can be told. Besides, there is an unwritten code of *omertà* amongst the women of the Alpujarra, where what happened in Brum gets to stay in Brum.

A TALE OF TWO SISTERS

Brenda ran a local bar in the village. She was there for a few years. Like many others before and since she turned up, brazenly or maybe bravely inserted herself into village life and then abruptly and under something of a cloud, she left.

Not everyone who left the village left under a cloud. There had been a delightful woman called Dee who ran a gift shop and whose daughter had become a Spanish speaking school-child. She had been married to a handsome local drunk. He had downed the profits of her business and ruined her. She had to leave and did so regretfully and with the good wishes of her neighbours who loved her.

Dee may well have been the exception as a leaver – but it was surprising just how many who left, did leave under a murky cloud.

Brenda did not arrive alone. She had John with her. Village gossip had it that she had met him somewhere on the costa and together they had hatched a plan to open a bar somewhere off the costa where the trade was not so satiated. God alone knows why they ended up in our village where there was not much trade to even begin to get excited about, apart from a brief period in the summer when everyone with even a remote connection goes back to the *pueblo* for their holiday and the village doubled in size.

There was only one main restaurant in the village: El Paraje had been there as long as anyone could remember. Occasionally – maybe only for the summer season – another little bar would open in a back street, but they were strictly spit and sawdust pokey places. None of them had had sticking power. To get a decent meal you had to be prepared to travel and even then the options weren't brilliant. So when Brenda and John turned up, everyone thought it would be good to have some competition and were prepared to give them a go.

The last time anyone had used the premises on the main road that they were taking over, it had been frequented by a group of druggies from outside the village. When what they considered to be their bar opened – albeit with new patron and name – they flocked back in. Brenda's first move, approved by all, was to ensure they knew how unwelcome they were. It was the first time, but certainly not the last, that she displayed just how ferocious she could be. At that time her actions were universally approved. She was after a family clientele and she wanted as many Spanish people to use her bar as foreigners.

Brenda was from Barnsley, or at least, as she informed everyone, the Metropolitan District of Barnsley in South Yorkshire. The family had lived in Goldthorpe in the Dearne Valley which was the last coal mine to close in the area in 1994. Its only real claim to fame was that the actor Brian Blessed had lived in Probert Avenue, just round the corner from her. She said they'd gone to school together, but given that he was in his late seventies and, at the time she came to the village, she was in her early fifties, this seemed a little farfetched.

In January 1986 Highgate and Goldthorpe pits had merged and were kept open on a 'care and maintenance' status. It was closed in 1988, with the shafts being filled and the site cleared between 1991 and 1994. She said her dad was a miner until 1988 when he'd got a caretaker job until the pit closed for good.

Then he was a layabout, in her words, poncing off the dole

in the period between the severance pay running out and his state pension kicking in. She said when she left school she'd worked in Goldthorpe Market in the town centre. But the market operated only on Tuesdays and Saturdays. She started working in a local bar to supplement income and secrete away enough money to run away – which she did as soon as she had enough to start a new life. She never talked about any other members of her family, although you could glean from time to time that there had been siblings.

So Brenda was initially given a fair wind and welcome, and she did gather a group of regulars around her. Spanish families came mainly at the weekends. She did chips with everything on the menu that one could occasionally fancy, particularly in Winter when it was definitely an egg and chips kind of day.

During the week it was mainly workmen drinking once the working day was done, in that period before they could no longer avoid going home. The kids came to play on the table football machine and initially teenagers would try our how lax she might prove to be on underage drinking – but the answer was not at all. Brenda knew trouble with the Guardia would deal a death blow to the business and was sure that one of her neighbours would denounce her, most likely the owner of El Paraje.

Rebecca, though not much given to going to bars often, made a beeline for Brenda's bar when she first arrived in the village to catch up on the news, because Brenda mainlined gossip and was a great source of it. As she had no discretion, you could get the latest from her whilst being exceedingly careful not to give her anything that might stoke the rumour mill about yourself. Rebecca often thought that all small village life was pretty much the same everywhere. There was always someone who was watching: who would see.

The thing that was difficult to escape was the malicious

edge around Brenda's personality which seemed to take a personal delight in the misfortunes of others. This became more apparent over time, when it became clear that Brenda was a holder of grudges. She had a sharp tongue and regularly dipped it in vinegar.

In fact, the reason she didn't speak about her birth family much was that she believed each and every one of them had done her down in some way. This one had stolen money from her; that one had stopped her getting a job she wanted. Her older sister had gone off with Brenda's husband, leaving her with two children to bring up and no money or support.

These stories may or may not have been true: what was obviously true was the level of her rancour against the people involved and the strength of her desire to do them harm if the opportunity ever came her way.

So Brenda was a person on the wrong side of whom you had no desire to find yourself. Rebecca always felt that finding yourself on that side might be both dangerous and all too easy to achieve. She believed Brenda had only one way of burying a hatchet, which was the most uncomfortable one for the recipient, and she trod as warily around her as did nearly everyone else.

Still, a bar was a bar. It was somewhere to meet people when El Paraje was full, or on Wednesdays when it was closed and no one else had opened a drinking outlet for the season. Besides, it had a decent outside space under a grape vine that gave shade on warm days, that made a very nice place to have a morning coffee with your breakfast *tostada y tomate.*

She may or may not have met John on the costa as the rumours had it; it didn't prevent him from having a very similar accent to her own, which was broad South Yorkshire. He was broad in other ways. Broad and squat with a tubby frame and a stomach weighed down with a lifetime's beer intake. He had a round face tending to fat with little piggy eyes covered by gold rimmed John Lennon glasses, and a receding hairline, which thankfully he did not try to cover with a comb over of longer side growth. He owned his baldness. It was about the only thing he did own. He was definitely a dominated man whom one felt had almost lost the will to live. Things between them only seemed to work if he made no resistance.

Whilst Rebecca would never advocate violence under any circumstances, she sometimes felt John might have been subject to it from time to time. Certainly she could envisage him taking the occasional slap for reasons that were probably never properly explained.

After a few years Brenda started talking about her daughter. She hadn't seen her for a long time and no one ever got the story of why she hadn't. It seemed she was now a young woman and pregnant and had asked her mother to visit her. When Brenda was telling Rebecca about this development, she actually seemed to have some tenderness in her and she glowed with the idea of the baby and a granddaughter. Though it seemed that a partner was not coming along as part of the package and Brenda, being Brenda, could not stop herself intimating that there might have been several candidates for that honour. Still, as she said, a baby is a baby and always welcome. She decided to make the trip.

While she was back in the UK visiting her daughter she had run into her younger sister Marian. This one had been too young to do any of the things that Brenda so bitterly held against the other siblings. On the spur of sisterly bonhomie she invited her sister to pay her a visit in the Alpujarra. She agreed and they'd set a date between Brenda's return and the grandchild's birth, which would necessitate a second trip.

The visit duly took place but had an unexpected outcome. One of the drinkers in the bar who occasionally missed the moment for going home was Pedro, one of the shepherds in the village.

He had a large mixed flock of sheep and goats and was often to be seen out on the hillsides with them during the walks Rebecca and her visitors took. You could hear the bells on his flock as they came through the village, and there were days when the sound resonated off the mountains. Whenever the flock went through the village there were steaming heaps of grape nugget poos which sometimes the old ladies collected up on shovels for their roses. It reminded Rebecca of her grandmother's tales of horse drawn carriages in London when gran was a child and being made to walk behind them with a dustpan to get the horses doings for her Nan's garden.

Rebecca would never have had Pedro down as a Romeo. He could scrub up after his day with the flock but all the animals had fleas and there was always a chance that some of these could be lurking in the seams of his trousers or shirt. This thought always made Rebecca move several seats down if Pedro came into the bar – which he did most nights, she had been told. On Marian's first night in the bar, their eyes met and the story went that she disappeared with him and was not seen again until the day she was meant to leave.

Marion did leave but only briefly. She went back to Barnsley to quit her job, to close up her flat and to arrange for her furniture to be shipped to these remote Spanish mountains.

When she went, Brenda went with her to be with her erstwhile estranged but now new bestie – her daughter – during the birth of her daughter.

In the meantime she left John in charge of the bar.

Perhaps she figured that he was competent enough not to run her business into the ground for the few days she was away, and loyal or cowed enough to act on her behalf. But if she did, she figured wrong. When she got back a week later John was long gone, taking with him the best part of her bar stock and all the takings from the bar and was never heard from again.

Rebecca had heard that Marion had come back with her sister and was ensconced in the shepherds' cottage that belonged to Pedro's mother. By all accounts, she was a bitter old woman who thoroughly resented her new, if informal, daughter in law for a wedding never took place. It was further said that she made life hard for Marion finding fault with every little thing she did. But Marion, who spoke no Spanish and still had love light burning in her eyes, told it differently. She called his mother her mother-in-law and swore that she was a sweet old lady who appreciated her company and treated her like a daughter she'd always wanted, unlike the daughters she actually had, who were, it seemed, bitches in person. According to Marion it was these other daughters, who were still living in the village married to local farmers, who were jealous of her and spread these malicious rumours. Well, anything is possible.

Rebecca happened to be on a visit to the village the day that Marion's furniture arrived some three months later. She went into the bar having noticed a huge mess outside on the street. It turned out to be the cardboard and packing that had come out of the removal van. Marion had truly burnt her boats by giving up her council flat for a life with her lover. Wiser heads might have told her to suck it and see, in a manner of speaking – but fools, and romance, and rushing in, and all that. Wiser heads did not prevail.

She'd booked a local Barnsley firm who claimed to be experts in moving abroad. The team had taken just one look at the narrow, twisting, steep village streets they were supposed to navigate their large van for door to door delivery and thought *not on your nelly*. They unpacked all her goods in the main street, which is more or less straight and on the level. Her things included a double bed and a rather enormous, exceedingly unattractive stuffed gorilla.

By the time Rebecca arrived, a mule driven cart had transported most of the belongings up to the shepherd's cottage, leaving the packing debris in the street for someone else to clear up. The gorilla, however, was enjoying a seat on the terrace of the cafe where it stayed for the next several months, becoming a feature of the bar.

Rebecca thought it was one of the uglier things she had come across and gave it a wide berth, but it proved oddly popular with the bar's other clientele.

Occasionally, when relatively harmless gangs of bikers came through the village, they might prop the gorilla up as if it were easy riding their bike and take a photo. Children climbed all over the gorilla adding to the wear and tear it was experiencing. Someone put a Mexican sombrero on its head, which stayed. It was said that regulars would, from time to time, buy it a beer and in their cups might even attempt a profound conversation with it as if it were their best mate.

What Rebecca also noticed was that Brenda had a new man behind the bar. At least she didn't think it could be John. She'd heard the story of his betrayal and Brenda was not the sort to forgive or forget.

She was however confused, because the new man looked just the same as John. He had the same square, fleshy appearance and beer gut. He wore similar glasses and was about the same height. Then she noticed he had slightly more hair in the right places, albeit cut militarily short and it was blond not brown.

"How do?" He said in the same accent as John. But, unlike John, he was Brian, as Rebecca discovered when Brenda finally introduced them. Rebecca thought to herself, *maybe there's a factory in Barnsley where they make this one model each slightly different, and Brenda just decided to get a replacement while she was visiting.* Brian's provenance never was explained, but he quickly fell into John's role of subservient servitude. After a while his shoulders, which had probably never been as militarily erect as his hair, started visibly to sag.

The next summer a new restaurant opened up two doors further down the street from Brenda's bar. It was an immediate success. It served almost decent food, had a real chef and gave service with a smile. They hired a delightful woman from the village to serve behind the bar. She was never surly or abrupt and would greet you with a warm welcome. There was no contest. For a while Brenda tried pub quizzes, curry nights, fish 'n chip nights, live music – but old vinegar tongue couldn't compete with her neighbour's conviviality.

During this time the gorilla, whilst maintaining his sentinel post, became shabbier and shabbier: much like the bar itself. Whenever anyone went in all Brenda could do was moan about the success of the new bar and restaurant, claiming unfair competition and skulduggery. She had become a conspiracy theorist, spreading any scurrilous rumour she ran across or could plausibly make up about the new bar's owner and his family. Not even his children were exempt from her ire. It became an obsession and a visit to her bar – always on a knife edge of social tension – became a fully-fledged unpleasant experience. Naturally people stopped going and word spread and her business slowly died.

During this time she also fell out with her daughter for reasons that were never revealed, and with her sister, whom she'd seen sneaking into the new restaurant for a rare night out with Pedro, who appeared otherwise to be starting to neglect her.

Brenda, never one to turn her back on a grudge if a grudge was to be had, banned them from her pub. It was said that in the best tradition of Barbara Windsor as Peggy Mitchell on EastEnders she had ordered them to "get out of my pub".

From that point on the enmity between the two sisters was as fulsome and as time consuming as ever had been their previous amity. It was the beginning of the end. The takings went downhill fast and it was said that Brenda was in financial difficulty.

The next time Rebecca came back to the village the bar was closed, locked and bolted. The scandal was that Brenda had absconded late one night, owing the rent on the bar, and money to several people in the village and having loaded all the remaining stock and Brian into her van. For him it seemed like there would be no escape as he was now a fully-fledged partner in crime.

She did, however, leave the gorilla who sat outside lonely and forlorn all through a winter of rain, sleet and snow and fierce winds that buffeted him around his padlocked enclosure until the stuffing was literally knocked out of him.

Marion had decided to stay with her shepherd and his saintly or dastardly – depending to whom you spoke – mother-in-law. She always denied any knowledge of her sister's whereabouts. It was not the first time she had seen her sister start a feud or do a flit but more than that she was not saying.

There were all sorts of rumours that Brenda had opened another bar, probably with a John/Brian equivalent, in this or that part of Spain, but this time always on the Costa. The rumours were neither confirmed nor denied, but she was never seen in the village again.

A COACH JOURNEY IN SEARCH
OF A LOST PATH

In a local town at a lower altitude than the village where Joanna ran her bed and breakfast business, there was a market twice a month. All the little villages had two market days per month, but most of these only had a few stalls selling vegetables and maybe a few clothes stalls. These mainly sold outsized knickers and bras and the *batas*, or housedresses that the grandmothers of the villages wore every day over the habitual black of the widow. Often Joanna forgot to go to market days in her own village, but she always tried to get to the market day in town. It was the biggest market in the area and had many stalls. As well as vegetables there were sweet stalls selling *turón* and other traditional Spanish sweets, as well as seeds and candied peels of grapefruit and limes. There were shoes stalls and hats stalls and clothes stalls and occasionally there would be an artisan jeweller selling their handmade earrings and bracelets. You could buy a barbecued chicken and take it home for lunch, or break the morning preamble through the market with a coffee with a friend too long absent from your life. There was enough there to make a diversion from the daily rhythms of village life, a must, and besides people came from all over the hills and seeing people emerge from their daily seclusion working in their *huertas* – vegetable gardens – always gave the day a holiday air.

The market was mainly run by the gitanos from further south, but there were growing numbers of Africans seeking a better life than home could offer.

One or two had stalls, others took patches of ground and opened out their blankets to reveal fake and imitation goods – knock off Gucci handbags and Nike trainers, or bootleg films and albums. Like immigrants everywhere, they were trying to move on and claim a part of the new life to which they had escaped, from who knows what danger or hardship, to find.

Most had originally come to work in the *campo* for farmers who had once been peasants tending their own fields daily on mule back, but who now owned vast tracts of land, drove four by fours and sent their children to university.

Some of the local farmers had their own stalls selling home grown and pressed olive oil. Sometimes the vineyards took stalls to promote their own wines.

Increasingly there were stalls that were the product of the small holdings of environmentalists from other European nations, as well as those of Spanish origin – they were seeking an alternative, a reduced environmental footprint and a more organically based life.

It was towards these stalls that Joanna gravitated. In season she would offer these stalls the raspberries or chestnuts from her own *cortijo* to sell or barter for loaves of the delicious wholemeal breads their owners baked. It was at these stalls that Joanna got a lot of the news about what was going on in the distinct communities around the mountains.

On this particular day there was a poster on her favourite stall advertising a trip to a festival to celebrate a Lorca anniversary. It would take place late in the evening in the Generalife – the summer palace – in the Alhambra.

The event was organised by '*El Sendero Perdido*', or 'The Lost Path'. Joanna had never heard of the organisation, but it turned out to be a local women's group who arranged a lot of trips and cultural events. They also organised things like classes to teach lost arts, such as basket weaving using the raw esparto grasses that grew in the valleys. They even made espadrilles from the dried and crushed variety.

Joanna thought their name was just a bit on the sad side, but felt this outing might bring her delight, so she bought a ticket. There would be a coach to take the participants – all women, it later turned out – to Granada, a three hour journey on the regional buses that went three times per day, but likely to be less on a bus not stopping to pick up passengers on route, as the public buses had to. It would be a late night but she hadn't been to a theatre presentation – apart from the occasional performance by an amateur dramatic group – in the whole ten years she had lived in her village. This was a big deal. It was a professional company and sponsored by the Granada *Ayuntamiento*, or town hall. She felt excited at the prospect but knew that if they had bookings for guests she would have to ask Thomas to lend a hand and make the breakfast. She was sure he would.

So, the day of the journey came. It was a seasonally hot day in late July. The coach was to leave from the local town at four pm. She drove the jeep down. There were twenty women going. She'd cut the journey fine and just made it, parking the jeep and having to run for the coach; so didn't get to choose her travelling companion.

She had dressed up for the outing. Wearing a new dress for the occasion and some newish sandals she had judged capable of managing the cobbled streets around the Albaicín in Granada, where they were first going for a couple of hours to eat and rest and maybe even shop before moving on up the hill to the Alhambra.

As she climbed into the coach she could sense the excitement from the women gathered on board. It wasn't that they didn't like their lives, but outings like this were rare in what some considered such a remote place to live. Most of the people she knew on the coach had chosen to live in this part of the world from wherever they once called home and were making their way, some singly, others in couples. Most of the women lived with men, but some with female partners.

She looked around the coach. There were women she knew on the coach; there were excited conversations animated by slightly hysterical laughter. These women did not get out that often and certainly a trip to the big city in such a group and for such a prestigious purpose was an unusual event. Most had scrubbed up well for it.

There was only one aisle seat left on the coach. Jo sat down next to a woman she hadn't seen before. The woman gave her a wary smile as Jo examined a face that was ageing with a delicate lined beauty.

She had strong, thick black eyebrows framing the darkest of brown eyes set wide apart. Her eyes were lightly rimmed with kohl, making them look huge. Her face was elfin shaped and her bow mouth painted a vivid scarlet. Her hair was long, black with a few grey streaks and caught up on one side in a clip with a flower attached. Jo thought to herself that only a Spanish woman could get away with such a look. She held out her hand and introduced herself.

"Ah, I know who you are you run the posada in the village and when I tell you I am Dolores, you may have heard of me," the stranger said in competent enough English.

Jo realised she had indeed heard of Dolores.

She always marvelled at the names the Spanish gave their girls. These were names of the middle-aged and elderly, now dying out to be replaced by those of more fashionable celebrities and pop stars.

They were redolent of the dark mystery of the Catholic Church, steeped in original sin and pain and suffering. Dolores or sorrows; Remedios after 'our Lady of the Remedies'; Encarna, 'to be made flesh' and Consuela, or 'consolation'.

Certainly, in the life their parents had envisaged for them, there would be more to endure than enjoy.

This Dolores was the legendary cruel and by repute bitter woman who had been married to the *dueño* and cook of one of the restaurants in the village El Paraje. As the story went she had walked out on her husband Miguel, leaving also two teenage sons and a baby of two years old.

"Well," said Jo with a wry smile, "I expect there is another side to the story. By the way we can speak in Spanish if you prefer. If you don't mind I could use the practice."

Jo settled down and they shared a few pleasantries, moving at first awkwardly and, as the miles passed, more easily between the two languages.

Jo asked Dolores if she had visited the village often in the ten years she herself had lived there, she had not seen her around.

"I have lived in Granada for more than thirteen years. I run a bar in the Albaicín. I live alone in a flat over the bar. It's quite a successful business. I'll be going back there after the performance this evening and not returning to the village on the bus."

"So what brought you for a visit?" asked Jo.

Dolores regarded Jo for a minute trying to decide whether she would make up a plausible reason, but decided, as if it was part of the path she was trying to find, to acknowledge her real reasons. After all, this woman appeared to understand that there was more than one side.

"I went to the village, as I find I increasingly have to, to try to get my sons to talk to me. I have made progress with my eldest, Dani, but the middle one, Pedro, remains prickly and my baby refuses even to look at me. You will know that years ago I left my husband and my children. It gave the old hags in the village something to talk about – and I don't just mean the old women; some of the old men are worse and can be even more vicious. You will have seen those men. Every day they sit from morning to night on the benches in the Plaza Vieja, gossiping and playing cards, while the wives are at home cleaning and cooking. I don't know if they still talk about it, but I'm sure someone will have mentioned it in conversation at some stage. I'm not sure there's much to choose between them in their level of vitriol, particularly when the object of ridicule is a young and, as I believe I was then, beautiful woman."

Jo butted in. "I have a friend who says she thinks that the women starch their men every morning and put them on those benches to dry."

Dolores laughed, and paused for a moment – but she had warmed to this stranger in starting to tell her side and found she wanted to continue.

"When I first left I just wanted to cut myself off complete-ly. I think I had a nervous breakdown. I had stayed too long. I really tried to make it work. I loved Miguel when we mar-ried. He was handsome and I thought he was gentle and he adored me. I was naïve and very young – nineteen when we married. He was ten years older. He had promised me that we would live in the city after our marriage, where he would open a restaurant and I would manage the front of house and the bar. I was lively. I wanted to go out dancing. I wanted a life. Miguel's father had owned the restaurant in the village and that was where Miguel had learned to cook. It was a fam-ily business. His father had a massive heart attack and died soon after our marriage and Miguel felt he had to take it over and run it to support his mother who was a depressive and a reclusive character who never left the house. He promised me that we would be able to move in a few years' time but I think I knew we would not escape the village. I hated the vil-lage. I hated the narrow mindedness and superstitious ways of the peasants. I didn't come to live there until I was ten years old and I had known a totally different life as a child.

"My father came here as the school teacher in the village school. You know that in Spain you don't get to choose where you are posted for work if you are lucky enough to work for a public authority. It was a shock to have to move to the village. My father was grateful to have a teaching job. Like many Spaniards from the south my father had escaped to work in Germany during the years of the *dictadura* when in 1960 Spain and Germany signed a bilateral agreement allowing gastarbeiters in. Franco severely punished Andalucía for having opposed him in the Civil War. The people here were poor; deliberately kept poor and politically squashed. My father had been a socialist and a bit of a student activist, yes, but it didn't take much activity to be branded a traitor and to be denounced. I don't know that much about my father's sufferings under the regime, because he never really spoke about it – but as he was still a young man he made his escape when he was warned that he might otherwise end up as one of the disappeared. He had qualified as a language teacher but could only get manual work in Germany. He worked in the chemical factory on the Wolfgang Industrial Park in Hanau, twenty five kilometres from Frankfurt. It was where the Grimm Brothers were born and was a pretty town with a beautiful medieval centre.

"My dad met and married my mother there. She was a German citizen and their marriage meant that he could stay in Germany beyond the two years usually allowed for gastarbeiters. My mother died from breast cancer when I was nine. Franco died the same year and my father who was then finally free to come home, brought me back to Spain. We lived in Granada for a year while he got his teaching applications sorted out and qualified though public examination to work as a teacher. We ended up in the village and I went to school here.

"I always felt like an outsider in the village – though I did make some friends. Much of the time I was lonely. I was shy and very young, but I'm told I was beautiful and very different compared to the other girls around who were mostly the daughters of peasant farmers. I think I was always seen as stuck up and, I suppose, I was. I met Miguel when I was seventeen. My father had wanted me to stay on at school and go to university. He encouraged me to go and I got good grades at school and could have gone – but dad got ill when I was eighteen. He had a cancer that was maybe from his years of contact with chemicals at the plant in Germany. He died six months later. Medical treatments in Spain in those years were still primitive, way behind the rest of Europe. I was lost and alone and when Miguel asked me to marry him I don't think I really had the courage to do anything else. Besides, I was in love and foolish and he had promised me we would open our business in Granada.

Well, anyway we got married and it was ok for a few years. I didn't mind his mother. She was not a bad person. On the whole she was kind to me – just difficult when the depressions overcame her. Still, she was company and counted as my only friend. I didn't get pregnant for the first five years of our marriage and then I did and had Dani and Pedro just two years apart. I was busy with two young children, and the dream of leaving for Granada kept receding. I felt like Irina in the *Three Sisters*, forever dreaming of Moscow.

"Miguel had always liked to drink alcohol. I can't quite remember when it began to get out of hand. If you are inclined to be a drinker, then working in a restaurant with a bar constantly on tap is the worst place to be. I suppose in his way Miguel was as frustrated as I was. There was no way we would have moved his mother and the restaurant was hard work, but as Miguel descended further into alcoholism, I took over more and more responsibility for the bar. On many nights I would also be the cook and run the bar and take care of the children and his mother and then him. Eventually I took over the business completely and hired staff in to help me. Financially we were doing ok, but in every other way we were falling apart.

I did that classic thing that the partners of alcoholics do when they try to cover the social embarrassments of drunken behaviour. I think these days we would call it co-dependence. At the time you think you are winning enough space for your partner to be able to recover their social position without having lost all their dignity. Above all, alcoholics have no dignity. They strip themselves of it and then they strip you of yours, and because you are emotionally paralysed and have lost all your self-respect, you let them do it.

"During this period I had become very fat," Jo looked sideways as the svelte, elegant woman sitting beside her and found it hard to believe, "I was fat from child bearing and comfort eating in the kitchen of the restaurant. I was tired from working too hard and I was full of self-loathing. I wanted to be happy. I did ridiculous things to make myself beautiful again which I thought would make me happy. I had liposuction to dissolve the fat from my system. I had plastic surgery on my nose. I took a lover to make myself feel attractive and wanted. I was ridiculous. My affair was a series of passionless, crude fumbles in a shepherd's hut on the outskirts of town, where I was observed by one of the *vecinos* who delighted in telling Miguel.

"That same night was the first of the drunken beatings I took over the next couple of years. On that occasion there was a black eye, and of course I told people I had walked into an open cupboard door. Later, as his self-loathing grew, there were broken ribs. On one occasion he busted my very expensive new nose and it took a long time to mend. Of course he would be sorry as all hell when he had sobered up the following day. Oh, we had many conversations about his dreadful regrets and how he was going to change and be different, but if you have many conversations with a drunk when they are deep in their cups, you learn over time that all the earnestness and the heartache is for nothing. In the morning they don't remember and the drinking starts again by late afternoon, and on bad days quite early in the morning.

"I had made up my mind to leave him: just take the kids and go. Later, when I had time to think about it, it felt to me as if at that point he had sensed that I was making plans to leave him. One day he told he still loved me and that if I would work with him he would give up the booze – and he did. He sobered up. He started to work in the restaurant again rather than just prop up the bar. As he cleaned up I began to see again the man I remembered the man I fell in love with: the same gentle person. I was happy. Bit by bit I began to trust him. Bit by bit I was able to be physically affectionate. We started sleeping together again and the inevitable happened. I got pregnant with baby Miguel. Our baby was, I thought so stupidly, the fruit of our renewal. I was still so naïve – so innocent – so hopeful. Then, bang! Almost at the moment I told him I was pregnant I saw the wolf in his eye. He had got me. The drinking started again. He didn't hit me while I was still pregnant; though once the baby was born and I was breastfeeding he became so jealous of this child that he could no longer contain his anger. Sometimes I would wake in the night, choking, to find he was trying to strangle me; other times he just lashed out with no warning.

"I stood it until the baby was two, nearly three and I really thought that maybe Miguel would kill me. I didn't have a plan anymore. I was just scared and desperate. I thought that maybe I could come back for the kids later. One night I broke. I was shaking and couldn't speak. I crept out of our bedroom, grabbing some clothes as I went and took the car key and all the takings from the restaurant that hadn't been banked, and ran. I drove through the night. I went to a women's refuge in Granada.

"It took me six months before my brokenness mended enough for me to take stock. I discovered Miguel had got a court order for the custody of the children and I had been cut out of their lives.".

At this point they were on the outskirts of Granada. Dolores realised that Jo had taken her hand at some stage of her confession and she smiled at her.

"Thank you for listening to me. Even though all this happened more than ten years ago, going back to the village over the past few days has been upsetting. I have huge guilt about my sons – particularly my youngest. I feel guilty I didn't try to see them sooner. I didn't know if they would believe me and didn't want to tell them those things about their father. I was scared to in case even knowing them, they would take his side."

"What will you do now?" asked Jo.

Without hesitation Dolores replied: "I'll keep on trying. The older boys agreed to see me this time and maybe over time my youngest will soften. I know that as I get older the need to see them only grows in me. I don't think I could give up. In my saner moments I know there was nothing else I could have done. If I had stayed I think I would be dead now, either by his hand or mine, and I love myself enough to know I deserved a better life. But not every day is a sane day. On some days sanity is outweighed by the weight of my guilt. But tonight we will put these sad things away and have fun."

"Do you know anything about the organisers of this trip?"

"You mean the 'Lost Path' group?"

"Well, yes."

"I knew some of the women who formed the group and I still get news from one or two. It's odd, isn't it, that this group could almost have been named for me? So, I wonder how many of them are still lost, because I think that finally I am finding my path."

"Dolores, maybe I could visit you sometime when I'm next in Granada."

"I would like that Jo. We can practise your Spanish and I promise no more sad stories. But thank you for this evening. I don't often tell my story, but for some reason I didn't want you to think too badly of me. I wanted you to know. I hope I haven't ruined your evening."

They were almost the last to get off the coach. The last was Doris. Seeing Doris made Jo feel she would have liked some light relief after the unsettling things Dolores had told her. Doris always made her laugh. They agreed to go to the tapas bar together, all three of them; slowing their pace, as these days Doris nearly always had to walk leaning on a walking stick for support.

Jo thought Doris had to be over eighty, though she had more energy than most fifty-year olds. She had once asked her how she carried on being as active as she was. Doris has told her that she lived on a permanent diet of pain killers and adrenalin. Doris was remarkable for any age. She was an American who had fallen out of love with the American new right morality – or, as she said 'so-called morality' and in love with European culture, though she retained a wild frontier spirit. Her hair almost reached her waist. Mostly she wore it up in a classic, tidy French chignon. She was so elegant. Her clothes were beautiful; slightly Mexican peasant style with vivid blues and greens on white backgrounds. Today she was wearing a voluminous caftan in a silky red paisley with a white floppy jacket over it. Her only concession to age was a pair of sturdy walking sandals. She always wore large chunky necklaces of exotic beads and metals. Some of these she made herself. She called herself an artisan, a maker of things.

Doris was a painter and a potter and an occasional sculptor.

She lived in a cottage on the path of the GR7, a major European walking route overlooking a part of the Contraviesa, where on clear days you could see down to the sea.

Her garden was a profusion of bright flowers with a whole section of sunflowers that gradually turned their faces as they traced the progress of the Sun throughout the day. Her small house was full of crude ceramics of moons and stars and planets. She made her own mugs and water pitchers. There were dream catchers hanging up on her door frames, because as she said in this vale of tears you had to catch and hold on to dreams or they slipped through your fingers, and you too easily forgot you had ever had any.

There was always music in her house. She had a particular penchant for opera and when you walked past her house, which Jo did at least a couple of times a week when taking the dog for a walk, you would often hear ethereal soprano voices rendering an aria or two through the open doors and windows.

Sometimes she made tapes for Jo who was trying to develop her own musical education, which she feared she'd sadly neglected. Last time she'd heard the divine Maria Callas and *Casta Diva*.

Jo didn't like to disturb Doris while she was working, but was always really glad when Doris spotted her and invited her in for a cup of tea.

They left the dog outside where it would run to and fro picking up the scent of the ibex it loved to chase and never caught in these mountains.

Doris was the oldest student in the local yoga class. She still practised every day. Said she had once been a dancer with a body that was as supple and lithe as it was strong and desirable, but now she had a dodgy right hip that hurt a lot of the time and there were many yoga poses that she could no longer do.

"It is agony now to stretch" she'd say, "but if I don't do it every day I will seize up and then probably cease up and die."

She said this cheerfully and would laugh at her own pre-sentiment of the shade to come.

"So, what were you two talking about on the way here?" she asked as they made slow progress to the tapas bar.

Jo, wanting to protect Dolores, said: "Just the things that brought us here."

"I thought the thing that brought us here was 'The Lost Path'. Bloody silly name!" said Doris.

"Do you think so?"

"Yes, I think it's just an excuse for a whinge fest."

Doris was not much given to whinging. She didn't do it herself and she took it ill from those who did. "I've been to some of the meetings and I've heard it: all the excuses for no action because life has been unkind. Sure, life throws you curved balls, I don't know anyone whose life has been without pain, and I do accept that in some unfortunate lives there is more pain than any person should be expected to handle, but I think the only person who can find a path for you is you, yourself. Sure, everyone loses their path from time to time. It's what happens when the facts of living over-whelm you, but I don't think anyone should glorify the state of being lost. You have to get to those open spaces where you can see clearly who you are. I know it happens rarely in life and, believe me, I know how quickly you can lose that self-knowledge and confidence, but you have to try your damnedest to cling on to yourself and prolong those amaz-ing periods of knowing who you are. I'd rather they called themselves 'The Path Found'. Maybe I'll suggest that at the next meeting of the group."

"Doris," said Jo, "I think you are the most positive person I know, but maybe," she added for Dolores' sake, "You need to cut the less fortunate a bit more slack."

They'd arrived at the oldest tapas bar in Granada where they served huge platters of delicious cured meats and cheese and fish. There were other members of their group there but not everyone in the group had stayed together. Having said their hellos, they got the last table for three in the crowded interior. They ordered a bottle of a gorgeous *tempranillo* and a mixed platter of *tapas* and a salad to share. For the next hour and a half they shared some village gossip and drank their wine and mellowed out in the back streets of Granada.

They were not due to get the coach up to the Generalife until nine pm, as the performance wasn't due to start until after ten. So, after they'd eaten, Jo left Doris and Dolores chatting and made a quick trip through the Alcaicería market, where in a few narrow steep cobbled streets all kinds of Moroccan goods and spices are sold. Its original was built in the fifteenth century, when bazaars of this kind were common. It is now one of the few remaining tastes of such markets. The Moorish tradition is still deeply embedded throughout southern Spain in mudéjar architecture, of which the Nasrid Palace in the Alhambra is perhaps the most exquisite example. Other examples are in the acequias and drainage systems of the *campo* and in the food and beverages of the people, but there are few such traditional markets left.

Jo needed to get some Ras-el-Hanout, which she and Thomas loved in stews and which was not available in their local village shop. Whenever she was in Granada she liked to stock up. She also loved the rose scented green teas available from the huge array of teas available on the merchants' stands around and she wanted to get Thomas a white soft cotton Arab style shirt as a kind of consolation for not being female and eligible for this trip. Jo managed her purchases and got back to the restaurant just as the members of their group were leaving for the coach.

They arrived at the Alhambra where other coach parties and groups were converging. They took the short walk from the entrance to the Generalife. It was exciting to be there in the evening. Their tickets gave them access to numbered seats and they were several rows back but still had a good view of the stage. The concert was in the garden of the Generalife, which was lit up behind them. The garden was fragrant in the summer evening.

Jo realised the significance of Lorca to this southern Spanish culture. She had read that on a spring afternoon, a month before his thirty-first birthday, Lorca had stood before a crowd of friends and family who had gathered in his hometown to honour him. It had been a triumphant year for him professionally. "If by the grace of God I become famous," he told the crowd, "half of that fame will belong to Granada, which formed me and made me what I am: a poet from birth and unable to help it."

This was in 1929. Seven years later – thought to be on 19th August 1936 – he was shot dead, assassinated by Nationalist soldiers in the first months of the Spanish Civil War.

In the decades that followed under Franco's rule, Lorca's books were banned and the circumstances of his death obscured. So in the post Franco era his countrymen had adopted him not just as a poetic genius but as a symbol of freedom and modernity. He had been an outspoken socialist, a Republican and a gay man. His remains have never been found although several attempts have now been made to find them.

This concert to honour him had become an annual event originally started by the Government of Andalusia Ministry for Culture. This year they would see a performance by the Flamenco Ballet of Andalusia.

It was a wonderful night of colour and proud movement and images created on stage, and the poetry read in a Spanish with such a thick Andalusian accent that Jo found it hard to understand. Still, it didn't matter. It was the ambiance in the Alhambra after dark as the night sky grew inkier blue and the air cooler. By the time the concert was over even the warm shawl that Jo had brought with her wasn't enough to keep her warm and she longed for the comfort of the coach.

When they got up to leave she lost Dolores in the crowd, so didn't get to say goodbye.

She hoped she had enjoyed the evening as much as Jo herself had done. She had been sitting next to Doris who declared herself stiff from sitting outside in the cool night air and in need of a stiff brandy, which alas they hadn't had the foresight to bring. She held Doris's left arm and between Jo supporting on one side and Doris's stick on the other they made their way to where the coach would pick them up. When they got on the coach they naturally sat together.

"What a wonderful night. It is really the only thing I miss about living here. Not having easy access to the theatre and opera. Films I can still see on Netflix, although later than I would like."

"Is there nothing else you miss?"

"Well, there's my wonderful Charlie but as he died on me he wouldn't exactly be available anywhere I yet want to go; but that is the main reasons I came to live here. I was sixty nine and people told me it was a ridiculous time of life to move to a Spanish mountain, but I think it saved my life."

As the coach pulled away on their journey home, Jo figured out that Doris had been living in the Alpujarra a few years longer than she and Thomas had been. "I've often wondered what brought you here."

"Well, it was Charlie. Shall I tell you about him? I like talking about him. He was the love of my life"

"I'd love to hear about Charlie," said Jo and settled down for another story, thinking about what an eventful day that had turned into, and how also shared journeys that took you out of the everyday norms opened up space like this, for greater intimacy.

At times like these people told you their secrets.

She'd often noticed that she got to know people when she went walking with them.

There was something about not having to look at each other or make eye contact while walking side by side, or one behind another up on mountain paths. It made it easier – as if it made it somehow more impersonal – to open up. Sometimes it worked better than face to face – except where opening the bottle and pouring the wine eased the embarrassment of revealing yourself to another. Both took time and trust, but she had no doubt there was some need in women to explore otherwise hidden selves that men, or most men in Jo's experience, shied away from or just didn't have. Maybe it was just the need for recognition and affirmation, and women often still got less of it in their lives, or men made up for it through action, giving them their positive reinforcement and self-confidence.

In her view – and maybe this was just another of the overgeneralisations to which she was prone – women live better with their ambiguities than men do.

There was no doubt that, sitting side by side on a coach created the same comforting cocoon.

"So, tell me about Charlie then," she said as they settled into their comfortable seats for the journey home.

"Well I can't tell you about Charlie unless I tell you a bit about me. I think you know I trained as a ballet dancer. We lived in New York when I was a child. We had an apartment on the Upper East Side of Manhattan, with a view over Central Park. My mother came from old money and my father from new. I was a Jewish princess. We weren't very religious – just high days and holidays at Shul, a scattering of Yiddish words and an occasional longing for lux and bagels

– oh, and a tendency to humour balanced by tribal guilt. I was protected. I went to school in a chauffeur driven car. We had holidays in the Catskills and I went to ballet camp in the summer. I wasn't as spoilt a brat as this might have made me. I was very shy and a lonely child. My mother was not warm. She had her charities and her good works and a million cultural pursuits, but no great intention of spending much time with me. I was brought up by a succession of maids and nannies and nearly all my memories of my childhood and youth are of feeling lonely and unwanted. As I grew up I immersed myself more and more in the world of ballet, and I begged to go to a specialist school. I wore my mother down and eventually she let me. It was the School of American Ballet, founded by George Balanchine in 1948. I was a weekly boarder there from the age of fourteen. I didn't have to board. It was only twenty minutes or so from home by subway – but it neatly solved both my mother's problems and, I thought at the time, my own. I was wrong. True, it got me away from home, but it just increased my sense of isolation.

"Since 1948 the SAB has been the official training academy of New York City Ballet.

That was my dream; of one day to go into the ballet, and I did. First I went into the corps and then later the touring company. If I remember right, I was on the first tour in 1961 to Ohio, North Carolina and Vancouver International Festival. I watched wonderful dancers like Patricia McBride and Conrad Ludlow get promoted to Principal Dancers. I remember Patricia in particular because she was kind to me. She was the youngest principal and spent thirty years dancing with the ballet. She had such a delicate beauty. I thought she looked like Audrey Hepburn. She had that same sort of glamour and refinement. I remember her particularly in Balanchine's Jewels, but people like Jerome Robbins created roles for her. I think she's still alive and living somewhere in South Carolina. She was five years younger than me and I tried not to be jealous of her, but I finally accepted when she made principal that I never would see a promotion.

"In 1961 I was twenty four. The following year we did tours to Germany to celebrate Stravinsky's 80th birthday and after that in the summer we went to Seattle for the World Fair. It was an amazing life and my big secret was that whilst everyone around me was fucking like rabbits I was still a virgin, and I was twenty five and vaguely embarrassed about my status.

I now have no idea why I had remained a virgin. You know dancers have so much flesh action going on. There's the adrenalin and excitement of performance; there's the arrogance of the body and the stirrings of youth – and I was the only virgin in the room. I hid it well. You know that song *Seventeen* where Janis Ian sings: 'I invented lovers on the phone who said come dance with me'? Well, something like that, anyway that was me, but I had no excuse," she chuckled, "I was way beyond seventeen. It wasn't too difficult to hide because so many of the boys only liked other boys – but my virginity hung on me like the proverbial millstone round my neck. I think I was very scared of sex- and then Charlie happened.

"We met at the World's Fair in Seattle one afternoon between the matinée and evening performances.

I was coming out of the theatre and I actually bumped into him, covering him in the coffee he'd been carrying while he stood in line to get tickets for the show. To cover my embarrassment, I offered to get him a complimentary and he said he'd accept providing I let him buy me dinner after the show. Sometime later he told me that that was the boldest he had ever been with a woman. I think I said yes because he had these eyes like Paul Newman that crinkled when he laughed and I immediately felt a benign presence. Charlie was beautiful and sexy and oddly he became mine.".

"...and did you live happily ever after?"

"Not quite, Jo. Charlie was not Prince Charming, but we did live and the longer we lived together the more I realised that with all his faults he was a prince amongst men. I may have been a virgin until I was nearly twenty five but once there was Charlie there was no looking back for me. He was my whirlwind and he set me free. He was a free thinker and he lived in the fast lane. He looked like a frontiersman, but blond, and bearded. He could have been an advert for Marlborough man. Well, he was also a lifelong smoker which I hated and which, in the end, did for him."

"Did he live in Seattle?"

"No. He was there to work the World's Fair. He was working in an amusement park in the Fair that ridiculously was called the Gayway, which even in 1962 made those in the know titter. After the Fair they changed the name to 'The Fun Forest', which I guess was a sort of message for the growing West Coast gay community. Charlie was running a ride called the 'Flight to Mars'. It had a load of space pirates running around Mars and a lot of black lights and glow paint.

"Charlie had worked as a writer. He came from San Francisco. As a younger man he'd been an assistant on a series of TV shows for an actor called Lionel Standar, who had been in films like Frank Capra's *Mr Deeds Goes to Hollywood* and the original *A Star is Born*.

Standar got denounced to the House Un-American Activities Committee by two actors: Larry Parks and Marc Lawrence. Lawrence claimed Stander had introduced him to the communist party line and told him that if he joined the communist party he'd get to know more women. Standar contested this and sued Lawrence, but from 1951 he was banned from TV, though he got some parts in theatre. Standar was a hero. He made a brave, amazing statement to HUAC when he was subpoenaed in 1953. He said he did know a group of fanatics who were undermining the American Constitution; these were ex-fascists and anti-Semites who hated everyone including Negroes and who were actively part of a conspiracy outside of the law to undermine the concepts on which American democracy was based. Of course, he meant the committee itself. Well, his career was toast after that and when he went down so did Charlie. Even knowing Standar was enough to get you banned from the studio.

Standar went to live in London but he kept in touch with Charlie because he never forgot his friends. I met him in 1966 when Charlie and I went travelling. He was making a film with Roman Polanski called *Cul de Sac*. It was a weird film and we all know – well think we know just how weird is Polanski – but in those days who knew? They were filming in a place called Lindisfarne, on the Northumberland coast of the UK. I remember it was beautiful and bleak and very cold, but Standar was warm and charming and he welcomed me as Charlie's wife, which I was by then. He was a giant of a man. Anyway, you know how easily I get side tracked."

But Joanna loved Doris's side tracks. They made her feel that her own life had been sheltered and uneventful against the technicolour and glamour of Doris's own. She admired people with strong personalities and opinions, although her own were, she felt on a good day, just as liberal in the tradition of live and let live, but perhaps a little milder and more open minded, and on a bad day just more characterless and insipid.

"Now where was I... Oh, I know, there is a point to this ramble. We met up again with Standar in 1968 when he was filming one of the Spaghetti Westerns with Serge Leonie...I think it was *Once Upon a Time in the West*, but it could have been *The Good, the Bad and the Ugly*, who in hell can tell them apart? Anyway, they were filming the outdoor location in Spain. They were in La Calahorra, near Guadix. We saw Lionel and then we drove through mountains and discovered the Alpujarra. We fell in love with the area and we promised ourselves we would come back. In 1968 it took a long time to get anywhere. The roads over the mountains were mostly tracks and the driving was scary. But Charlie hadn't been the *dueño* of a Flight to Mars for nothing.".

"When did you come back?"

"Oh, I'll get to that, but first let me tell you about our life in the States. We went back.

After that time I'd showered Charlie with coffee and he'd swept me off my feet we didn't emerge from a bedroom for several days. I went from virginity to sexual heaven in one easy step and our sex life was always good.

I finished the tour with the ballet and then I quit. I had found my path and I was determined to walk it.

"Over the years we did some crazy shit.

There was a time we had a ranch in Arizona near a place called Cave Creek. Charlie bred Palominos and he took tourists on horse trail routes through the Black Mountains and the Sonoran dessert. They'd dress up in cowboy gear and play a part- but they learnt something about the ecology, too.

I ran a dance school in Scottsdale, about thirty miles away. I'd also started to paint and make my own jewellery. We had a nice life. We did regret not having children. Well we regretted it for a while and never really understood why. But Charlie was a dreamer and he needed all my attention. It's true that he set me free from all my Jewish upper middle class shtick and my prison of sexlessness, but in other ways he could smother my enthusiasms in his lust for life.

There were times when I felt overwhelmed by him. His need to swallow oxygen sucked up all my air.

A couple of times I left him. I even took a lover from time

to time just to have a space of my own that had another story going on inside it. I think he probably did the same but we never had a confession session.

I always went back to him. He'd give me some space and time and then he'd reel me in".

"So when did you come back to Spain?"

"Well, I was getting to that. You know things in America started to go sour with Nixon. We had some periods of hope along the way, like Carter and Clinton but when George W was elected we'd had enough. For a few years we'd been coming to Europe not every year, but we found ourselves coming back to the Alpujarra and in 2001 we bought our little house. We thought of it as a summer house and knew we'd only visit at most once a year- but we loved in. In the meantime back in the States, the Koch brother were launching 'Americans For Prosperity' and the shifts of wealth and the selling out of the middle classes had already started. The popularity of Hockey Mums was already guaranteed, you know those women who are like pit bulls but with lipstick.

Poverty was growing apace. Abortion clinics were being bombed. I didn't like it.

Mind you I would probably have stuck it out if Charlie hadn't died on me in 2005. It was the smoking and he had a massive coronary and died in the ambulance on the way to hospital.

I sold up the ranch and came to our house here early 2006 to come to terms with the pain and I never left."

"Did it take you long, coming to terms with the pain?"

"Honey, the truth is I'm not sure I ever really have. Of course the sharpness diminishes but that dull ache can still overwhelm me when I least expect it. But I keep busy and I'm not sure if nature made me an optimist, but I know damn well that Charlie did.

Now I've been here eleven years or more. I have friends

and a full life. I'm determined to try to grow as much as I can and to learn as much as I can, even though my body is doing its best to slow me down and I know time is not going to roll backwards any time soon."

If Doris was ever capable of looking wistful, it would have been then.

"Doris, you are my inspiration. Do you want a lift home?"

"Thanks Jo, I'd love one."

THE WEDDING OF HEAVEN AND HELL

Rebecca flew in to Gibraltar on a Tuesday morning.

The wedding was to take place on the Wednesday in the poshest hotel in Gibraltar that boasted having played host in its time to luminaries like Errol Flynn and Winston Churchill. She had little time for the machist derring-do of the one but a grudging admiration for the inclination for beach fighting of the other, although at the time she learned of his stay, she had no inkling of how relevant his experience might become. Karen and James were staying in this hotel as a special treat and Rebecca was keen to see it.

She had got an early morning flight. She preferred to travel early because airports were less crowded at that time and she'd never been to Gibraltar before, so she was keen to explore a bit and see a monkey or two on the rock before settling down into being a serious guest at what was likely to be the village's wedding of the century.

Jo and Thomas weren't arriving until the morning of the wedding, but would stay on Thursday as well, so that they got a day of recovery before tackling their journeys home. They'd all booked in the same hostel in La Linea, on the Spanish side of the border.

Jo had decided that hotels on the British side were just too expensive. Rebecca had allowed her to choose where they stayed and then she'd booked in to the same hostel: Hostal La Roma.

It was only a two star, so Rebecca had no great hopes of it, but she was appalled when, having completed the double border crossing transaction and a leisurely walk in the sunshine, she finally found the hostel in a remarkably unprepossessing side street beyond the Plaza de La Iglesia, with its ridiculously kitsch, but strangely attractive monument to the three graces by sculptor Nacho Falgueras. The statue represented them in traditional flamenco costumes.

On her way in she had passed another Falgueras statue, the monument to the extraordinary Cameroon De La Isla who had lived much of his life in the town.

Rebecca hoped for his sake he had never had to live in Hostal La Roma. It was a fleapit.

Her room was a slightly extended broom cupboard with just room for a bed and a sink and a mini cupboard, with nails hammered into the wall at the back to take a few steel hangers. The walls were the flimsiest she had ever experienced, except perhaps for that disgusting student hostel where she had stayed one night as a student traveller in Tel Aviv once, where the shower was full of cockroaches and had what appeared to be human excrement smeared on the walls. Maybe La Roma was not that bad, she thought as she dumped her bag, carefully extracting all valuables to keep on her person.

The walk had been further than she had anticipated and the early morning start was beginning to tell – but she couldn't bring herself to lie down on the bed just in case she disturbed more wild life than she thought she could cope with at that moment.

She texted Karen to say she'd arrive and got one back saying just: "Please, come. We need you."

"Ok. Are you at the hotel?"

"We will be in half an hour."

It was coming up to English, not Spanish lunchtime, but as Rebecca had only had time for minimal breakfast she felt that, on this occasion, she would be content to settle for once for British customs on the other side of the border.

She walked back to the border, circumnavigated the passport obstacle course and on entering Gibraltar discovered there was a bus that would drop her nearer to the luxury hotel.

Indeed the hotel was luxurious. The contrast between their and her own accommodation made her laugh. The Rock was elegantly framed against the hills behind it and the sea around. It was five stories of luxury, with handsome, secluded balconies on the more expensive floors. The entrance was undeniably grand and led on to a Hall of Fame showing pictures of the many famous people, who stayed since it had been open for business in 1932.

The very polite receptionist directed Rebecca up to the appropriate room, having first checked that she was expected. They were staying in a suite of two large rooms with a magnificent bathroom where the shower was larger than her room in La Roma.

They greeted her with huge hugs and kisses.

"We're just so pleased to see someone sane," said Karen, while James just nodded his agreement. They both looked tense and drained.

"What's been going on?"

"You won't believe it."

"Try me?"

"First, a drink," said James, who under the best of circumstances needed little prompting. James was one of those exceedingly generous drink pourers who only produce enormous glasses and proceeded to fill them to the brim. Rebecca knew she would have to pace herself and was relieved to see they'd ordered sandwiches as, she dreaded the consequences of the bottle of champagne he was opening on her empty stomach and during the day, when as a rule she never drank alcohol. But then she noticed it was a bottle of vintage Dom Perignon and all her possible objections fell away.

They settled down on the luxury silk sofas while she bolted down a sandwich or two to fortify for the attack on her senses that was about to arrive with many very small golden bubbles.

Rebecca had first met Karen six years before and via Joanna. Karen had had a house just outside the village for about eight years by the time Rebecca first met her. She was a large woman with blond hair that clearly had been naturally blond, but probably needed a bit of help from a bottle by this stage. She had those startlingly clear blue eyes set in ultra-white sclera that go so well with blond and she would, Rebecca had judged, have been really pretty except that her face seemed set with a mouth in permanent downturn. Rebecca had her down as a whinger and Rebecca disliked whingers on principle – but she found that she did not dislike Karen. The first thing she really noted about her, however, was that wherever she went she was accompanied by two small, white, furry dogs of indeterminate breed. With little prompting Karen would declare that she had always liked animals far more than she liked people. So, Rebecca, exercising all her cod psychology knowledge, knew immediately that Karen had trust issues.

The summer after she had met Karen, in the autumn, Rebecca's lifelong friend Elena was staying with her. They decided they'd invite Karen out for *tapas* as Rebecca had formed a theory that she was just lonely and had a yen to know more about her. It turned out to be an hysterical evening.

They discovered that Karen had a wonderful life affirming sense of humour. Admittedly it took a while to warm her up, but it became clear she was a wicked raconteur with a fund of fascinating and often funny stories to tell. After about half an hour of what was quite hard work, Karen had just suddenly relaxed and started telling them about her life.

It turned out she was from the Welsh borders but had moved to London to seek adventure in her early twenties.

They listened mirthfully as she told them about her life as a postwoman in London, whilst she was living with a rich boyfriend in luxury in Hampstead who paid for her upmarket sports car and her exotic holidays around the world as a deep sea diver. This rather satisfactory arrangement went on for a few years until she discovered, coming home from one such adventure earlier than expected, another woman in what, if they had been married, which they weren't, would have been the marital bed.

Her revenge on his hugely expensive sports car was what paint stripper was made for. Meanwhile, she packed her diving gear and other belongings and made off in her still intact sports car.

For years she had worked as a postie, making enough money to go travelling and travel she did.

She went all through Latin America on her own without a word of Spanish, compensating with a winning smile and travelling as the people travelled on trains, coaches and buses and, from time to time, on mules.

When her money ran out she returned to trudging the London streets until she'd saved enough for her next adventure.

From time to time there had been a lover but no one of comparable significance to the rich boy.

She'd taken redundancy from the Post Office in her mid-forties, and bought a traveller caravan and set off round Europe.

On the particular trip where she'd discovered the village her half-sister Eva had been with her.

They'd stopped in the village because they had seen the house just outside it with a 'For Sale' notice and spotted the estates agent name on the main road opposite the town hall. It was the same estate agent who had sold Jo and Thomas their place before she skipped town owing them the electricity bills. She gave Karen the keys to the house, and the half-sisters drove back to look it over. What Karen thought she wanted in those days was the seclusion of being near but not in a village, and what she saw from the back terraces of the house were fabulous views over totally unspoilt rolling hills down to a valley where a river glinted below in the afternoon light. It was a two-bedrooms house, which she figured would be just right for her needs with a generous living space.

She bought the house on the spot, clinching the sale some months later. She had reckoned on a peaceful life where she could have her dogs and encourage the wildlife around her.

She had been told that every morning and evening a small herd of ibex came through her land on their way down to the river to drink, and she looked forward to the magic of these visits.

What she hadn't taken into account was that the house was just too far for someone like her, who only took exercise if she was attached to a compression tank and floating in a benign teaming sea, to walk to and from for evenings out, and that without visiting local restaurants and events it was hard to make friends.

She hadn't figured on the loneliness this would bring in its wake.

Over a period of years, she lost her enthusiasm for life and was low level depressed most of the time. The more she whinged the less likely people were to put her on their visiting list.

At the end of her evening with Rebecca and Elena, Karen was on fire. Her face was animated and she looked really beautiful. They told her this and she told them she hadn't enjoyed herself so much in a long time.

Elena, who always spoke her mind in ways that could be deeply uncomfortable for the recipient, except for Rebecca, who was very used to her directness after years of exposure, said: "Karen, your trouble is that you are lonely. You should sell your house and move closer in to the village."

As they said good night, the hour was late but a new friendship had been made and the evening ended with hugs and kisses all round.

Later, as events unfolded, Rebecca thought that Elena's blunt comment might have been the start of a process: either that, or a recognition and acknowledgement of a process that had already started. Karen didn't want to move in the village – but she did acknowledge that she didn't want to live on her own any longer, so she had a better idea of how to solve the problem. Some six months later Karen travelled back to the UK to sort out the details of her late mother's estate and when she came back James was with her.

Karen always said that James was a BOGOFF, the Buy-One-Get-One-Free that she'd got on an internet dating site. This site had advertised a two for one offer. Karen had not liked her paid for date but she had liked her freebie, and apparently it had been mutual. James had moved back with her to the village and here they were, a couple of years down the line, about to get married.

What Rebecca had learnt about James was that he had a hugely kind heart. He actively practised kindness, but along with this came an unbelievable number of exceedingly bad jokes. Well, Rebecca supposed that by the law of averages a percentage had to be funny, and to be fair some were. They were just outweighed by the sum of the ones that weren't.

Rebecca had some personal experience of hiding behind being a joker – sometimes she thought that her ability to hold the amused attention of a crowd was the only thing that had saved her from innumerable beating ups behind the bike shed at school. So she recognised a soul that was more vulnerable than it wanted to let on. James was one of the people who gave her that shock of recognition that it was not easy to grow up as a male. Mostly she was not inclined to give this thought much house room, because men should just try how awful it can be being a girl growing into womanhood in a male-biased world. But she had sympathy for the sensitive boys who had had to contort themselves into rugger buggers to survive: providing, of course, they were only pretending.

Still, she and James got along fine and she had no doubt that Karen would house train him as she did her dogs: with infinite patience and love underneath which there was steely and obstinate determination. Rebecca thought that though they were very different people, they each had something the other needed, and might turn out to be well suited. Besides, who from the outside ever knows why a marriage – well maybe any relationship – works, or even gets close to understanding why it falls apart?

As a family solicitor Rebecca was more familiar with failed than successful marriages, but constantly saw the impact of hope over experience as her clients and friends embarked on second or even third attempts to get it right.

These reflections were being gently overwhelmed by the alcoholic weight of a really good champagne. She urged them to tell her why they were so wound up, and needed an injection of sanity, and so began the story of the arrival of disparate parts of Karen's family.

It had been very easy for James. He had a son from his previous marriage- long over and as bitter in its dissolution as were so many. His son was perfectly presentable, if, according to Karen, a little self-centred.

He had arrived on schedule the previous day to serve as his papa's best man. Karen's family was a bit of a different story.

Karen had told Rebecca the gist of her family's story one long evening when they'd shared a night out together. Over the years they had known each other, more bits of the story had emerged. Rebecca was fascinated by the story in the way that rubberneckers at a car crash site are glued to the view, with equal parts of salacious morbidity and wide eyed horror at the fragility of human life.

Listening to that story was like getting a regular episode of her very own television soap. It felt like an endless round of people driven by ill understood passion, and the need for revenge, and the acting out of long held grudges. Secretly, Rebecca thought about them as tales from the underclass. It was a milieu from which university had rescued Rebecca and introduced her to others in transit as she was.

Whilst she never felt she had arrived for a comfortable sojourn in the middle class, she had found her tribe of fellow travellers. These were the ones who knew where they had come from and who they had been, and were glad to have escaped both but did not ever really want to arrive or have to live in the stifling atmosphere of middle class respectability.

The sister with whom Karen had been travelling when she first bought the house had become a Jehovah's Witness. She had seven children and they had all at one time been part of that church.

This sister, Karen had explained to her, had been their father's favourite. There were only two daughters. He was apparently always very affectionate to this child who had been adopted, though Karen always spoke of her as a full sister. As a child Karen had been jealous of her sister and didn't understand why her father should so favour Eva over her. As adults they had become friends, though Karen did not share her sister's religious leanings at all.

Rebecca supposed that the strange church Eva had joined had given her a sort of structure for living.

Over time, some of the children had left and relinquished their faith – or at least the practices of the Jehovah's. It was this break in their religious solidarity that was going to cause a problem for Karen's wedding. She desperately wanted her sister to be with her.

She and James had offered to pay the air fares and hotel accommodation for her and the remaining six children. Eva had consulted the male elders of the church who had at first said that she could attend – providing she made no acknowledgement of the disfellowed, or those who left the church. She would not be allowed to speak or even look at them as they had to be shunned by all believers.

Initially she thought it would be ok if she could sit on a different side of the congregation, because it would be fine for her to talk to unbelievers, providing she obeyed strictly the rules with the disfellowed. Later, as she was also increasingly physically disabled, she decided she couldn't deal with the stress and the children still in the church followed suit.

On the whole, Rebecca had thought she'd do better at a party with the sinners than the saved. So, the unsaved were coming to the wedding. Three of the girls whose family relationships Rebecca was never to figure out beyond "it's complicated" were to be maids of honour.

Rebecca was keen to know the reasons for disfellowshipping.

She'd looked up on Wikipedia the serious sins that could lead to it. It was a list that was long enough to appear in alphabetical order and included things like bestiality, alongside drug abuse, drunkenness, extortion, fornication, fraud, gambling, gluttony and homosexuality.

She figured maybe they had just left, and that was enough and though she was keen to know, she had determined not to ask if she had a conversation with any of them during the wedding party.

Karen had done a meticulous job of organising the wedding from a small rural location in a far flung bit of Spain. This had involved accommodating the wishes of someone who from the photos was clearly a size fourteen – if not larger – insisting she was a size ten.

Karen had come up with an ingenious plan of ordering a size sixteen and asking a bemused but compliant dress maker somewhere in a seemingly equally far flung bit of China to put a size ten label in it. As time had gone by, the plans had seemed to become more rather than less complicated.

So, there were three maids of honour and a flower girl to kit out. These were all staying in decent hotels down to the ever flexible credit card of Karen and James.

Karen herself had two wedding dresses: one to get married in, natch, and one to wear for the party that would follow. She even had a pair of genuine Jimmy Choo's to wear walking up the aisle.

As she said: they might cripple her and she might only be capable of wearing them for the twenty minutes of the ceremony, but she was going to wear Jimmy Choo's up the aisle at her wedding if they killed her.

She admitted she'd brought them on EBay and that they'd go back on EBay for re-sale or bid as soon as the honeymoon was out of the way.

There were the morning suits for James and his son. There were the flowers for the bride and the flower girl and corsages for everyone else, the catering and the music for the party and the photographer and the bar and the cake. Then there was the accommodation for the rest of the family on a posh campsite with cabins and tents and the posh kennels for the – by now – three dogs.

Rebecca had already figured that this wedding was costing at least a medium sized fortune, and it was all lovely.

In itself, the spiralling cornucopia of complexity would have been enough to create stress for most people – but there were additional factors.

The unsaved had arrived in small groups at Malaga airport and all had had to be picked up from the airport and transported to overnight accommodation outside Malaga. Then they were to be transported to Gibraltar the following day when all had assembled in a single minibus, but they had refused to stay put. Karen and James, practised at herding sheeps, finally had got them all rounded up in the bar at the camp site where they were drinking beer and chillaxing, till James said he'd pick up the bar tab when they started ordering rounds of serious cocktails.

They were fairly pissed at the end of the evening and decided that a party was in order, on a campsite that had a 'no noise past midnight' rule. At two thirty am the gay couple staying in the next cabin gently remonstrated with them, and one of the boys, Jacob – whose attitude towards homosexuality was not what you might call enlightened, so that was probably not the reason for his disfellowship –had offered to take them out, and he didn't mean on a date.

There was apparently a bit of a scuffle, but Jacob passed out and order was restored.

The following morning, when James arrived in the minibus to pick them up, he heard the story and in his nervousness over the possible consequences, he managed to back into the gay guys' hire car. He thought he hadn't done much damage, but he knew he had to do the right thing and he knocked on their cabin door.

This was at seven am, the morning after a drunken crowd of ex Jehovah's witnesses had kept them up till three am. James introduced himself as unfortunately about to be related by marriage to the hooligans they had encountered the night before and also, by the way, the idiot who had just smashed into their hire car – but who would of course pay if the hire company tried to charge them for the damage.

Silent tears of suppressed laughter were already running down Rebecca's face. She was trying her best to be sympathetic, but the champagne on top of her early start was getting the better of her.

It turned out that just before she had arrived, James had had a call from his new gay friends to tell him the hire company had charged them a thousand pounds for the damage.

There was a stunned silence as they all looked at each other and then they all laughed, hard and long and the tension was broken.

Karen and James talked over and interrupted each other with other tales of family awfulness, none of which they could complete without being overcome by giggles.

It turned out to be a great afternoon.

Karen and James had a kind of return to sanity and Rebecca got to use their hotel entrance to the fabulously huge swimming pool, while they went off to herd cats and do last minute chores. They invited her to meet the family for pizzas that night, but she thought she might give it a miss.

She was still keen to see something of the Rock that was not the hotel. So, after a swim and a bit of novel reading in the sun, she walked to the cable car and took it to the top.

By the time she'd finished on the Rock enjoying the views out to sea, she walked back through Gibraltar, taking in the twee ambiance of a place that seemed to her a 1950s England preserved in aspic, though she was not aware of seeing virgins on bicycles or hearing the sound thwack of leather on willow – to misquote one well known British Prime Minister.

She walked down to the commercial harbour and stopped for tea at a point when the Brits in evidence were starting on the cocktail hour. She decided that Gibraltar was full of fat vulgar cockneys and re-crossed into La Linea, a place she was prepared now to like better by contrast.

The following day Thomas and Jo arrived around midday.

It was around a five hour drive from the village and they had done it in two, bits having set off the evening before and slept in the van overnight on a deserted beach past Malaga.

They were clearly in need of showers, but they had time as the wedding was scheduled for late afternoon. They dumped their stuff and went off for coffee and snacks.

They were a little taken aback by the lack of charm offered by La Roma, but their room at least had its own shower, and besides they'd spent the previous night sleeping on a mattress in a van and were unlikely to be entirely sober on their return from the wedding.

Rebecca had had the foresight to buy a large towel in the Marks and Spencer that was the pride of Gibraltar, so she had put it over the mattress on what she assumed was a fairly busy bed on her first night – though she didn't have any bites, so it might have been a case of over-active imagination – and would also use the next day when they recovered on the beach from what she accepted was likely to be a hangover.

There were other people from the village who were coming as guests to the wedding and Rebecca knew most of them by sight and others quite well. She was looking forward to meeting and maybe getting to know those she with whom she wasn't yet on speaking terms.

When they were finally showered and dressed up fine enough for a wedding, they set off, walked to the border, and got a taxi on the other side to the hotel.

Rebecca had told them about her champagne fuelled hysteria of the previous day and the party mood amongst Karen's family. They'd concluded they might be in for a bumpy ride and agreed they might need to hang on to each other but expected to have an adventure.

They were not wrong.

The wedding took place in an enclosed terrace. It was beautiful.

There was crisp cream linen on tables, with light streaming through long golden gossamer curtains that gently undulated as they let a slight breeze into the room. The long room was divided into two. What would normally be groom's and bride's sides of the church were in this instance divided into family and friends. Alongside what Rebecca laughingly told herself were the village people were some friends of Karen's from a previous life who looked like they might be fun and turned out to be precisely so.

Rebecca was keen to get a look at the family. Her first impression was of skinny men with large women. They had scrubbed up; some better than others. Rebecca was transfixed by a particular young woman dressed in a translucent white sausage skin elongated boob tube dress that revealed every line of underwear and bulge in the thighs. She had clearly needed a best friend at the right time to just say "no" or at least to remind her about who is meant to wear white at a wedding, but now was far too late to rescue such a large sartorial disaster. Rebecca did wonder if this was the polish mother of the flower girl. It seemed appropriate for a white sausage to be Polish, but she seemed a little young. No one had introduced the guests to each other so guessing was essential. She had been told this mother was very large.

Then a huge, whale-like presence in a massive tent dress entered the room and Rebecca whispered: "Bingo." She was particularly interested in this woman.

She had been separated from the child's father Luke, who was one of the seven siblings, and the girl had lived with her father and his new girlfriend. Just a few months previously, in the early summer of that year, he had an argument with the new girlfriend and left the house having had a bellyful of beer "and the rest", Karen had added when telling her the story. According to his aunt he was a loveable, hapless kind of fellow with too ready a temper and a drinking issue. What had worried the girlfriend was that he had taken his fast car and set off down the motorway. The girlfriend had phoned the police hoping, or so she said, that they could track him down and stop him before he hurt himself or possibly someone else. The police did track his car and they set up a sting operation to slow him down and divert him off the motorway.

The plan went badly wrong; he didn't slow down and then he collided with a Range Rover which was a write off, unlike its driver who miraculously survived unscathed, unlike Luke whose fast car turned over several times and exploded, lighting up the night sky and sending him to the Maker in whom he apparently had once believed.

This story had left a completely shocked silence when Rebecca had first heard it, but in its wake a sort of morbid fascination in the messiness of some people's lives. What she couldn't quite get her head around was the strange contradictions of uncontrollable alcohol fuelled temper with a life as a Jehovah – lapsed or not.

Anyway, the upshot of this terrible event was that the flower girl was back living with the mother who didn't want her. Over the course of the next many hours Rebecca had a chance to see the interaction between mother and daughter and would have sworn there was none. The mother did not look at, pay attention to, or touch the child. Lots of other members of the family did spend time with her. She was not without cuddles and encouragement, but from the mother, *nada*. It made Rebecca's heart ache and she wondered vaguely if she should put in a call to social services – but perhaps today was not the day.

Finally the assembled guests sat down on their assigned sides of this secular kirk. The groom and his best man took their places and the grand doors at the back of the room opened and, one by one, the flower girl – a golden child of seven years with a wide, attractively gapped tooth smile – came slowly down the aisle followed by three very attractive maids of honour dressed in exquisite deep purple gauzy dresses. Then, walking slowly so that she might not fall off her Jimmy Choo's, came the bride herself in a long wedding dress with a traditional veil. She looked exquisite, and there were more than a few tears in the eyes of her friends as she came to a rest at the side of her bog off who twenty minutes later became her husband.

Rebecca took loads of photos as Karen had asked her to do.

Whilst bride, groom and their attendants went off with the professional photographer to the hotel gardens, Rebecca blagged a glass of champagne before the bar officially opened to keep her going.

The official bits of a wedding, like signing stuff and having photos taken always seem to take interminable amounts of time, but eventually they sat down for a wedding supper. Then there was the cake and then the disco and the party started.

The family didn't seem interested in meeting the village.

Rebecca did try a couple of time to initiate conversations but the only taker she got were the maids of honour with whom she had perfectly civilised stranger to stranger talk. The boys of the family seemed a bit surly and were unresponsive, though the boy accompanying what she had taken initially to be the Polish sausage did smile sweetly at her.

Most of the evening, the members of the family stuck together in a secluded space while the village danced. The next day Rebecca worked out that she and Jo had danced for over six hours. They were determined to give Karen and James a wedding party they would remember with pleasure.

Karen had disappeared to change and come back in her second weeding dress – also white but with a waist and reminiscent of the famous dress worn by Marylyn Monroe standing on the grid of the wind blowing. She looked amazing. For about an hour there was party bliss and the village people did their thing with bride, groom and maids of honour joining in.

It was later in the evening the trouble started.

One of the surly boys. To be precise Jacob - that is the same Jacob, who had threatened their gay neighbours on the campsite a few nights previously, also had something of a drink problem combined with a bad temper. It did seem to run through the male line of this family. He had been unable to find the toilets. Instead of asking at the reception desk, which most normal people would have thought to do, he merely staggered into the Hall of Fame and pissed on the carpet, under the fixed photo gaze of Antonio Banderas, who did not bat an eyelid and, less fortunately, within eyeshot of a hotel guest who did, and somewhat shocked remonstrated with him, and whom he punched.

James had heard the kerfuffle and also went to restrain his new nephew who then punched him as well. The receptionist called the police. James went off to dress what would be a very sore eye and Jacob lurched off into the night and the rest of the party, which had been attracted by the noise, stood looking aghast at what, in every sense, was a mess.

It was a party that had ended with a bang as well as a few whimpers.

"Well," said one of the village people to the rest of them, who were in something of a state of shock, as they all made their way out of the hotel and before they dispersed to their different hotels, "I never think it's been a real wedding, unless it ends in a good fight."

ALINE AND HER SAINTLY FATHER FELIX

"Your father... he seems like an amazing man," Joanna enthused.

"Yes," said Aline, hesitating briefly as she searched for a descriptor with which she felt comfortable. "Mmmh. He is certainly a piece of work."

Joanna caught the whiff of a story that might, or might not, emerge over the course of the next few days. Aline had been staying at the B&B with her father and two of her four siblings. They were spending up to five days in all, and were two days into their visit when the initial exchange had taken place between the two women. Aline was the eldest of the siblings. She was thirty at this time. The family had had a strange mission to accomplish and Joanna, easily moved and endlessly resourceful, had elected to help them.

Some two months before Joanna had received a phone call from the father – Felix. The family was Scottish. Felix lived somewhere near the borders between England and Scotland, in a small village near the town of Dumfries. Most of his children lived in and around Edinburgh, though one, Clare, had moved as far away as London where she enjoyed life in the big city. Joanna had known none of this at the time of the first call. All she had been told was that the family's strange mission was to deal with the ashes of the mother who had recently died.

Felix McMurdston spoke with a soft Scottish burgh accent that made him sound deeply attractive. In that first call he had startled Joanna by requesting that they be allowed to release these ashes on a plot of land behind her house. Even Joanna, used to odd requests from guests, was taken aback.

"Well I'm not sure about that," she had said to Felix on the phone. Then, caught by her own curiosity, she had asked: "Why here in the Alpujarra and why in my backyard?"

Recognising that technically she did not have a back yard, but a hillside behind her house, and wondering why he supposed that she did have one and would lend it for these purposes. They had a desultory conversation with many bits of miscommunication on both sides. She supposed he was still gripped by grief for his recently dead wife. Could she have had some previous connection with the house? No, he didn't think so, although she had travelled throughout the Alpujarra as a walker and a bird watcher in her younger days, just post being a student, and had stayed for longer than she planned and found work in some towns and villages in the area as a waitress and sometime children's nanny. She had been happy there. She had learned Spanish. She had loved the region and its culture and she had felt free and always longed to go back, but then, after her marriage to Felix, when her own children had come along in quick succession, despite her best intentions the opportunity to return had never arisen.

When she had realised she would die from the breast cancer for which she had been treated over the previous few years, she had expressed a wish, he said.

"What, she wanted to be scattered over my back yard?" she asked him.

"No," he said, "not specifically over your back yard, but somewhere in the Alpujarra. She left it to us, to her family to decide the place."

"What made you choose my back yard?"

"Well, we were looking on the Booking website and we saw your place. It looked from the photos as if you had ample space around your house."

"Well, we live in a wide open space, but unfortunately we don't have a back yard to the house. We do have a small *cortijo* up in the hills. That might do for you. It is quiet, about a mile above the village. It has its own water channel so there is always the sound of running water and the wind is often in the trees."

"That sounds perfect," he said, then added: "...and you wouldn't mind?"

"No," she had replied, "I don't think so. It sounds like such a wonderful thing to do. You might even plant a tree on the *cortijo* grounds, and we could put a small plaque on it so than in future you and your children could have a place to visit if you wanted."

She was letting her enthusiasm get the better of her. Thomas was always telling her she too easily got involved in other people's plans and she should more effectively curb her enthusiasm, but she could not. Being Joanna, she was already planning in her mind the kind of ceremony that the family might hold to honour the mother as they released the ashes and planted the tree.

"That is so generous of you Joanna," said Felix, for by now they were on first name terms. She could tell he was moved, that he had a lump in his throat and that his voice was catching in his throat. She didn't want to upset him further.

"Please, call me Jo..." she said, "...everybody does. Well, just think about it," she concluded, "...and phone me back when you have decided what you want to do."

She put the phone down and hurried off to tell Thomas about the strange phone call and the even stranger offer she had made so spontaneously, though she knew she needed to consult him. She wondered briefly if he would be irritated, but thought he probably wouldn't be. Thomas was laid back by nature, and over the last ten years they had lived in their mountain retreat he was also laid back by a growing daily intake of beer. Not enough to give her major concern, but enough to have given him a little bit of a paunch and an increasing reluctance to venture up into the mountains as he had once loved to do.

"Really?" said Thomas when she had told him. "Why the hell did you offer him our *cortijo*?"

He was spooked by the idea in a way she hadn't expected.

"I'm sorry Tom. I realise I should have checked with you first. I really didn't think you'd mind. But I don't see how I can un-offer it now."

"No. I don't suppose you can. But maybe we won't hear any more about it. Maybe they'll just disappear."

But they did hear, and by the time they did, Felix and his family were getting ready to appear in short order.

Felix phoned back one month later to say he had now talked to the children and three of the five were prepared to make the trip with him to lay the ashes of the mother. Their plan was to travel to Granada, the city she had loved, to stay the night before entering the Alpujarra at the western side making their way to Lanjaron, where she had worked as a children's nanny. They might, he thought, make a further stop on their way to Joanna's. They planned to spend a couple of days, would get a room on the way in one of places the mother had stayed in; maybe they would do some of the walks she had recorded in her diaries from that period. It was a kind of pilgrimage in her honour and they would finish their trip in the village staying for three or four days at Joanna's place. On the way or maybe when they arrived, if it was possible, they would buy a tree to plant. They had already had a plaque made that could be eventually attached to the tree as it grew to act as a kind of shrine as Joanna had so kindly suggested.

Felix was already something of a saint in Joanna's eyes. So clearly dedicated to the wife he had so recently lost that he had organised a pilgrimage and a vigil to honour her and who knew, even maybe a wake as well. She talked to him over a number of sessions about the kind of tree that might grow well. He wanted a weeping willow. She was unsure whether or not there would be enough water to give such a tree the constant nourishment it needed.

Summers in the mountains could be so harsh and hot and every few years there were droughts. At these times the *acequias* would dry up – these were water channels constructed by the moors in the ninth and tenth centuries, when they ruled this part of Spain and which were still, on the whole, functioning efficiently to provide villages and farmers with water for most of the year. When the *acequias* dried up, farmers feared for their crops and water was severely rationed. Joanna reckoned that such a delicate tree might not survive these conditions.

In the end they decided that a black poplar would be best, although that too would require a lot of water. It was native to the area and known for encouraging abundant butterfly and moth populations which depended upon its catkins for nectar and sustenance. It would also provide much shade in summer and would turn bright gold in autumn.

In the village they would spend the first day or two working out the details of the ceremony to be held and making their purchases. Day three was to be the scattering of the ashes and they would perhaps spend a fourth day recovering from their trip and what might prove to be an emotional and draining adventure before setting off back to the airport to catch their various flights, after which they would separate and go their own ways.

Joanna did not know what to expect, except a family that seemed united in its grief. She stood by, ready to provide the kind of breakfast that would fortify them and the large glasses of wine or the beers that would help them relax after possibly arduous days of planning and executing their possibly grim but seemingly romantic task. She did not expect to have massive amounts of fun, but was very interested in how their trip and its mission would pan out. She did expect to get a story she could tell into the future. As it turned out, she was right on both fronts.

Felix and his three older children turned up on a Tuesday evening in June. They had explored the Alhambra in Granada and spent a night in a small hotel in the Albaicín. They had stayed in Lanjaron, where she had worked as a nanny and according to her diaries, and for some time in a bar. They had got lost and on a walk through La Taha, somewhere between Pitres, and Capillera above it.

It was growing dark by the time they reached the village. They were all tired and seemed tense, so Joanna offered them a quick supper and showers before an early night. They were all quiet and spent. Felix had referred to 'the children' but it became apparent that they were all mostly grown up and independent.

Aline, the oldest, was a social worker in Edinburgh. Benjy came next. He was twenty eight and a barrister at the Scottish Bar. Clare worked in the art department of a fashion magazine in London. She was twenty five. The younger girls were identical twins in their early twenties. They were finishing off degrees of some sort of scientific bent at Scottish Universities, where higher education fees were still free for Scottish students. They had elected not to come for reasons that remained unexplained.

For the next couple of days they explored a bit of the area; Felix was keen for them to stay together but the three siblings kept wandering off without him.

From the observation that Joanna could make of them, the children seemed far closer to each other than to their father. They were polite to him, but no more, and she couldn't discern any deep affection for him. She thought it was a bit odd, but perhaps this was because they were still all experiencing the grief of a mother's death – but even so she thought it was a little cold, when he was clearly such a caring individual.

The family was together to buy the tree and they were together when they visited Joanna and Thomas's *cortijo* to choose the spot for the scattering of the mother's ashes. Then they were ready. On the appointed day Thomas carried the tree and Felix and two of the siblings up to the *cortijo* in the four by four. Aline had chosen to walk up to the *cortijo* with Joanna and her dog.

It was possible to drive other vehicles up the steep track leading up the mountainside to the *cortijo* and many of the farmers had just about roadworthy vans and cars that belched smoke out of dirty exhausts that they used to get to their bit of *campo* to farm. These were nearly all in battered state.

This was not a place where a car remained pristine for long. The village streets were so narrow in places that a single car could scarcely get through, with a narrow margin of error on either side. The all white houses were built at odd angles, jutting out from the hillsides. There were sudden sharp bends in the streets with lopsided dips and ramps where if a driver didn't pay attention a car could get scraped or fall down a massive, unprotected bank. Most cars had white scratches down their flanks from an unanticipated meeting with a neighbours' wall. You never knew what was going to come round a corner and sometimes a hapless driver would have to back up uphill round a sharp bend with a sheer drop on one side. It had taken Joanna and Thomas a long time to acclimatise to driving through the village. They only really relaxed when they gave up caring about the appearance of their vehicles.

The only one they really cared about was the minibus with their business's name and logo that they sometimes used to transport guests to and from airports where this was requested. For daily use they had eventually opted for a four by four they bought cheap from a neighbour, that had already had its fair share of pre-existing battering and bruising when they took delivery of it.

When they first came to the village they were enchanted by the spectacle of the mules that most of the farmers had used to get up to the *campo*. These often had highly decorated and embroidered bridles and carried huge panniers either side to carry farming tools up the mountains and to bring back crops for the family table. In all the *cortijos* that sparsely lined the hills there would be a mule under the shade of a tree, whilst nibbling coarse grass and brush around them and flicking away the black flies that sought them out during the heat of the day for torture.

They also loved the sound of the mixed herds of sheep and goats whose neck bells could be heard occasionally all over the hillsides. Flocks were driven by motley crews of ragged dogs with a single shepherd who would wander with the flock from early morning to sundown, moving them further and further up the mountain to find pasture as the summer progressed.

They had been entranced when the herds passed through the village on their way back to the enclosures where they spent the night. The mules were mostly gone. A few old men who had never learnt to drive still used them, and it was still a delight to hear the clip-clop of their hooves on the roughly cobbled street in the morning, but they were disappearing fast and had become a ghostly and nostalgic reminder of the time before. The flocks, however, were still very much in evidence.

One of the ironies of the internet age where prosperous elite customers in urban settings hankered after artisan products was that it had saved the cheese producers in high Alpujenian villages and hence preserved the flocks that provided the milk.

Joanna was explaining some of this to Aline on the walk. By the time they arrived at the *cortijo* they were laughing about the sad ironies of modern life and their impact on even such a small community as the village.

Joanna realised that Aline's shoulders, which had been up around her neck obscuring the gracefulness of her movements, had just relaxed and dropped. Only then did she understand how tense Aline and her siblings had been, in contrast to the more relaxed behaviour that Felix had exhibited over the past few days.

If she had thought about it all, Joanna had assumed that the children's grief was responsible for their exhibited desire for isolation and the sudden gaps in the conversation between Felix and his children that Joanna had noticed when she was with them. Felix had managed these gaps with grace and charm, skilfully changing the subject with his hostess so that her awareness of the occasional coldness between them was a slow, cumulative dawning.

They arrived at the *cortijo*, dusty and thirsty and stopped before joining the others to take a drink from a perfectly pure natural spring that ran constantly through the grounds.

It was a glorious day: still too early in the year for the burning sun of mid-summer to keep people indoors at its height, but late enough for the spring flowers to be in vibrant bloom and for the butterflies to be dancing in and around each other. The perfume of wild lavender and thyme added to a heady mix, and the wind gently rustled the leaves in the nearby poplars so that they appeared silvery green. It sighed in the capacious sweet chestnuts that grew on either side of dirt road and up into the hillsides and that would give their perfect burnished copper nuts come autumn. Across the valley the last of the pink almond blossom clung to the trees.

Aline took Joanna's hand in hers: "Thank you so much Jo. This is the perfect spot. Mum would love it."

Joanna was making a 'no sweat' shrug of her shoulders, when Felix said: "Can we all gather round? I think we are ready."

The hole for the planting of the tree that they had all come to call Hannah's remembrance tree had been dug the day before. Despite his scepticism, Thomas had offered his help and it was now neatly finished and looking like a baby's sized grave with the earth piled up on one side. The idea was that Felix would say a few words and offer the space to the children to say anything they wanted. He had discussed with them the reading of a favourite poem, either of theirs or one they knew had been a favourite of Hannah. The children had opted for a Quaker-like period of silence in which they could focus on their mother in a sort of meditation, but keep their thoughts about her to themselves.

The ceremony began. It was brief. Felix said his few words. Joanna could barely remember them afterwards, though he had spoken strongly throughout his voice only cracking slightly towards the end. She was absorbing the atmosphere of this balmy day and hearing more of his tone than his words as they rose above the constant drone of wild honeybees seeking out the wild lavender that was scattered over these hills. There was something about his joy when they were first married and the children arrived, their life together during her illness, her fortitude and strength and his guilt that he had not always behaved well. He finished with a poem.

"Love and Death
Shall we, too, rise forgetful from our sleep,
And shall my soul that lies within your hand
Remember nothing, as the blowing sand

Forgets the palm where long blue shadows creep
When winds along the darkened desert sweep?
Or would it still remember, tho' it spanned
A thousand heavens, while the planets fanned
The vacant ether with their voices deep?
Soul of my soul, no word shall be forgot,
Nor yet alone, beloved, shall we see
The desolation of extinguished suns,
Nor fear the void wherethro' our planet runs,
For still together shall we go and not
Fare forth alone to front eternity."

She had heard it all and thought it beautiful and deeply touching. She asked him later who had written it, and some days later in a rather less sentimental and more enlightened mood looked up Sara Teasdale, the 19th century poet from Missouri who had committed suicide at the age of forty eight. This time she recognised the real significance of the poem to everyone gathered round that tree and sighed at what she now saw as her own wishful thinking naivety.

The children had seemed less sanguine with the poem than she. There had been tears. Then the tree was planted with each of them throwing handfuls of dirt into the hole mixed with the ashes they had so dutifully carried on their pilgrimage to bring Hannah around the place where she had been happy. The remembrance plaque had been given to Joanna for safekeeping until the tree was large enough to attach it. They threw the remaining ashes in the branches of the immature black ash and watched the breeze carry its lighter components away whilst the rest sank into the earth which now contained her spirit. They then all sat down around the tree in silence. They sat for perhaps twenty or thirty minutes. The Benjy stood up brushing dirt from his khaki trousers. The others followed suit. It was peaceful.

On the way back in the four by four it was clear to Thomas that Felix was now drained. Benjy and Clare in the back spoke in soft whispers to each other and their words could not be heard over the drone of the engine. Felix sat with his head bent forward and his hand covering his eyes as if to hide a tear, or maybe just to wipe some road dust from his eyes.

Aline walked back with Joanna. It would be the family's last night at the guesthouse. Joanna noticed that Aline was digging her nails of her left hand into the palm of her right. When the four by four was out of sight, she turned to Joanna and said: "How dare he? How the fuck dare he? I thought even he had more self-knowledge than to do that. That's why we agreed to come on this trip, to his plan. We thought he might have changed. We thought he might have been genuinely sorry."

Joanna said: "Aline, I don't understand. I thought the ceremony was lovely, didn't you?"

They stopped on the dirt road and Aline turned to look at her.

"No Jo you don't understand. My father is not the great guy he pretends to be.

"The first time my mum had cancer was twenty years ago. The twins were a year old. I was ten. I didn't know it at the time – adults never tell kids anything. They think they're protecting you as if you didn't instinctively know something was terribly wrong. My mum was given a few weeks to live. Turned out that my dad had been having an affair with someone at work for a long time and he chose that moment to walk out on us.

My mum couldn't cope; of course she couldn't. She was in hospital and had horrible, radical surgery as the cancer was so advanced. She was having radiotherapy which burned her skin and she was in agony because her husband had left her.

There was talk that we would have to go into care or to foster parents, but my gran came to stay with us, and mum's sister Diana lent a hand. Mum was a real fighter and – amazing this, against all the odds – she survived. We stayed together and we've had her on our side. We were poor, although he let her keep the house. I think he occasionally gave her money, but it wasn't consistent. He had a child with the woman he lived with and eventually married once he and mum were divorced. We saw him a few times a year for a while, but the occasions got fewer and fewer over the years."

Joanna was deeply shocked, though of course it explained the strange silences between the children and their father. What it didn't explain was Felix's relaxed charm and self-assurance.

"What happened Aline? How did you all come to be on this trip with him? Why would you?"

"His second wife left him a couple of years ago. It sort of coincided with the return of our mum's cancer. By then Clare, Benjy and I had left home and only the twins were left living with mum. We had all done well at school. Mind you, if we hadn't lived in Scotland we would never have been able to afford university, but we got by with free fees and jobs in bars and restaurants in the evening and shop work between terms. As kids we all had to have free school meals and could never go on school trips, but at least we were together and a lot luckier than some. I think the younger ones, the twins, really resented the fact that the child of his second family went to fee-paying schools and they all had regular family holidays.

"I think we all knew that this time mum wouldn't be so lucky with her health. She was tired out. She'd had a hard life getting by. Felix got back in contact with her. I guess he was lonely and I tried to believe that genuinely there was a part of him that wanted to make reparation to her for the way he'd deserted her – and us – first time round. He had money and he made her last few months more comfortable than they might have been. Our mum was a wonder. She forgave him. I don't know why or how. I did ask her before she died. All she said was that she had always been the stronger one. She had known he was weak when she married him but she was in love and thought her strength would be enough to see them through.

When she got ill that first time, she knew deep inside that she would lose him, although she had hoped for better. She had thought about it much over the years; at first with great bitterness but increasingly, with time as her emotional scars faded, with more understanding. She believed that the thought of her death had scared him so much he ran away from his pain. He wanted an easy life and that was what he had chosen. I still don't know why she took him back – but we all tried hard for her sake not to resent him too much.

The twins never knew him, and they more or less ignore him. They refused to come on this trip. Clare and Benjy have some memory of him but were too young when he went to carry too much resentment – and as for me, I'm confused. We agreed to come for mum's sake, and he's paid for this so-called pilgrimage, but a part of me hates him with a venge-ance. Another part sees that mum being able to forgive him was good for her soul, but I am so not as generous as her. I've held my contempt for him in throughout this trip. It was the choice of the poem. How dare he claim her for eternity? She is ours – not his. How dare he claim any part of her? He will never deserve her…never." This last was delivered in a whisper.

Joanna took Aline in her arms and the tears started slowly and quietly at first, then with huge sucking sobs.

Joanna could feel her own throat constrict. She felt in her arms the frail but steely form of this woman who from the age of ten had clearly taken care of her mother and her younger siblings, albeit helped by gran and mum's sister. She felt rather than knew that Aline had intuitively felt it her task all her life to keep her mother alive and hopeful and reflected on what a huge burden that must have been for the girl.

Now, here she had to cope with the selfishness of an abandoning father who, because he had returned to be forgiven, felt he had the right to take her mother away and claim her for himself.

No wonder, she thought, that Aline had not been able to hold back those explosive emotions any longer. How could anyone?

No doubt Felix had his own pain and deep regrets, but, Joanna thought, there are some boundaries in life that cannot be overcome. She gave Aline a tissue when the sobbing subsided and their embrace had ended. They walked back in silence and when they got back Joanna cracked open a bottle of her best wine and they shared it to the dregs and went of tipsily to their beds, firm friends.

The following day the family packed away their things in the hire car and prepared to leave.

The pilgrimage was over and their mission accomplished.

Thomas was on hand to say goodbye. Both he and Joanna gave them all kisses on both cheeks in the Spanish style. She gave Aline an extra hug. She made a feeble joke about hoping they would give her guest house five star rating on the website, though in reality she had no doubt that they would.

In farewell to them Joanna made it clear that they would be welcome back and that she hoped they would want to visit their remembrance tree, and certainly at least to revisit for the attachment of the plaque in Hannah's name in a few years' time.

As they drove away with waves and shouted farewells, she wondered if any of them would ever return, and if they did, if they would do it together. She felt the latter would be unlikely – but whoever could predict in life the actions of others?

BOUNCING BABS THE BABY BELLE

"G'day," came a slightly raucous call from below. "Anyone 'ome?"

Thomas glanced up from reading the paper left by previous guests, where he was seeking some detail of a recent cricket match, even though it was by now out of date, to share with Toby. Immediacy and instant news had less relevance in the Alpujarra.

He and Jo were on the terrace. They'd invited their neighbours Liz and Toby in for tea, on the basis that their paying guests weren't meant to arrive for several hours.

"Blimey, " said Thomas with unaccustomed humour, "tie my digeridoo down, sport, I think the Aussies have arrived."

Joanna was hushing him "Shush; they might hear you," she said as she hurried to the edge of the roof terrace and peered over its safety wall down to the street below, where indeed two substantial figures, with sturdy legs firmly planted, were gazing upwards at her.

"You must be Babs and Bobbie" she said with the sweetest smile she could muster, that had rapidly replaced the smirk she had been wearing in response to one of Thomas's rare jokes. As they nodded assent she told them she'd be right down to let them in.

It turned out they had parked their car down by the church from which there was a steeply sloping road upwards to the high *barrio* where the bed and breakfast was to be found. In the little map she had sent them, there was a note suggesting they might park at the top of this road rather than by the church, as visitors often misjudged the steepness of the climb and it was perfectly possible to park beside the rubbish bins situated at the top. She did not suggest they tried to drive any further through the village because she didn't want their first experiences of the village to be a collision between their hire car and any of the walls of houses that too closely bordered the narrow, twisty roads round to the B&B. There was an alternative and much safer way to drive to her house, but experience had taught her that most guests were too nervous to attempt it when they first arrived, given that at its start it looked steeper than it was, or they were unable to locate it as it was up a concealed entrance.

"Please," she said, "come join us for a cup of tea and then we'll give you a hand with the luggage and we can re-park your car in a more convenient place."

Poor things were clearly not used to walking much and there was little roundabout this village that was not up, unless of course you were facing the other way when it was decidedly just as down. They were a little hot and more than a little sweaty. In fact, Joanna felt quite alarmed by Bobbie's face. It was puce. Jo wondered whether or not he was about to have a heart attack. He hadn't said anything about having a heart condition when they had made the booking- but apart from his colour his breathing was a little laboured.

"Are you all right?"

"I'll be fine," he said, taking a pill box from his pocket. "Just need to take one of these little 'bueats'," he popped one in his mouth.

Barb lent forward and explained: "Beta-blocker. He's got AFib and he forgot to take his pill this morning. I told him you'd said in your note not to walk up from the church- but what can you do? Men, eh?" she said as if that explained everything.

Joanna was looking into a face that, though slightly ravished by the fierce Australian sun, had clearly once been very beautiful. Her round face was punctuated with a button nose, sparkly blue eyes and a generous mouth that, from the lines around, it was clearly easily given to laughter. "AFib?" Asked Jo.

"Oh, Atrial Fibrillation, it's a heart condition where the heart races out of control and makes you breathless and kinda tired. He used to faint too, but he's taking the beta-blockers now and they've stopped the fainting. Doc says he might need a pace maker. Age, eh? It's awful when the bits start to drop off," and with that Babs smiled broadly at Jo revealing a deep dimple in each cheek that made her even more attractive and somehow shiny.

"Is he in any danger?" she asked whilst Bobbie was clearly struggling for breath.

"Don't think so. It's his own stupid fault for forgetting to take his meds." Barb replied robustly and then turned to him enunciating clearly and loudly "I said it's your own stupid fault for not taking your meds this morning." Explaining to Jo: "He's also a bit deaf, and it's murder when he doesn't wear his hearing aid." Bobbie just shrugged in response.

Joanna decided she couldn't possibly ask Bobbie to climb up to the roof terrace for his tea. This would entail climbing two sets of fairly perilous, steep stairs. She sat them down on the bench outside her house and went to get them their tea and a slice of the perfect lemon drizzle cake that neighbour Liz had brought with her as a gift.

It was autumn – a mellow mid – October when the trees in the Alpujarra turn golden and the vines a dark purple that stands out starkly on the hillsides. It is the season when the sweet chestnuts that populate the area are harvested. In the village there is a chestnut walk to celebrate the harvest, where a procession of villagers weaves its way through the trees and a *fiesta* takes place with a dance in the evening in the Plaza Vieja along the top road of the village.

Fireworks are set off, but these are fireworks with a difference. They are not pretty, but they are extremely noisy. They are huge rockets that go up with a whoosh when the touch paper is lit, and then follows a crash-bang-wallop-mega-banger-like explosion in the sky.

Jo hated them, but they were beloved by all the Spanish, though every dog and animal in a five mile radius was cringing under a bed, if they were domestic, and who knows where if they weren't. These rocket-bangers left a trail of black vapour in the sky, and the smell of cordite at least until the following day polluted the otherwise pure air.

There were good things about this autumn festival. For example, all the elderly people in the village were given a sack of chestnuts – which were a real treat – and there was a special meal put on by the town hall for a whole village celebration. For foreigners like Jo it was a great treat to get the toasting pan out for the first crop, but, by the end of the season, when all were satiated, no one ever wanted to see another chestnut, which, of course, they forgot long before the next autumn rolled by.

Jo had a spread of chestnut trees on her *cortijo* that for some reason grew chestnuts at twice the size of trees elsewhere, so she was able to harvest and get a good price for them in the twice monthly market in the local town.

Somehow, Bobbie and Barb had heard of this autumn ceremony and wanted to be part of it. Jo had looked it up and sure enough it was now covered on the '10 Best Things to Do in the Alpujarra' on TripAdvisor. It came in well under the number one which was the celebration of New Year in August that was held every year in the neighbouring village. This had been running for several years, since, legend had it, the year when the village church clock had broken on the very cold night of New Year's Eve, and the village had missed midnight arriving whilst the villagers had hung around waiting to consume their grapes or *'Las doce uvas de la suerte'*.

The twelve grapes of luck is a Spanish tradition that consists of eating a grape with each clock bell strike at midnight on December 31, to welcome the New Year. It is meant to bring luck and prosperity and has been celebrated since at least 1895: but not that year, and not in that village. Many of the villagers were superstitious and so decided they could not let the New Year pass without at some point getting to eat their grapes.

What they realised, however, was that once the close association with the calendar had been broken; they could have their celebration at any time of year. After much deliberation they voted on several options as to when they should celebrate New Year's Eve and the first weekend in August was judged the most pleasant of the options, and hands down won the vote.

It has become a huge event with busloads of tourist turning up. Joanna had been once early on when they first arrived to live and had enjoyed the madness of the fake snow and the too many people in the too narrow streets – until, that is, it felt positively dangerous and fearing getting crushed she had to get out – and the mad discos in all the bars with glitter balls a glowing and Sister Sledge belting out their high hopes for the future of having all your sisters with you. But once, as they say, had been enough.

Jo remembered Rebecca telling her how one year Daniel, Rebecca's son had gone to this *fiesta* with some Spanish mates from their village. Thinking he'd get a lift back she'd gone to bed, but woken up and sat bolt upright at around five thirty a.m. with her heart pounding. She couldn't get back to sleep and had made a tea and gone to sit on her roof terrace, occasionally glancing down the road anxiously. She'd phoned his mobile several times, but it had gone straight to voice mail. Eventually Daniel had appeared, hobbling down the road, bloody, scratched and bruised.

It turned out he was leaving the disco to walk home, an eight kilometre walk, and got a way down the hill out of the village when he started texting his girlfriend who was in London. Not looking where he was going and with a skinful of whisky still sloshing inside of him, he tripped and staggered and then fell down the left side of the road, where a small bridge hid a gully thirty feet deep. He and his phone had gone flying in different directions. The phone was never seen again. Daniel had to climb out over the huge but well established bramble that blocked his path and that tore into his bare legs and arms. Whilst he was recovering sitting on the bridge, a *guardia* car had come by.

It turned out they were looking for an arsonist who had chosen this busy night to set a few fires going in the hills. At first when they took one look at Daniel they thought they might have found their man, but as he told them in his halting Spanish about his adventure, they believed him, even shone their torches down the gully on the side of the road where he'd fallen to see if they could locate his mobile. When they shone their torches down on the other side of the gully they revealed it was a huge depth of over one hundred and fifty feet.

As Rebecca said later it was a good job that Daniel was for once uncharacteristically obeying the rules of the road by walking on the side of oncoming traffic: otherwise he would have broken his neck. When she asked him what time he had fallen, he said he had left the party at about ten past five, so it would have been twenty minutes later. Rebecca, though not given much to superstition, always thought this was a perfect illustration of the intuition of a mother and the ever vigilant antennae they keep alert for erring children.

By now Barb and Bobbie had finished their tea. Jo whistled up Thomas, and Toby also came to help. They found the hire car down by the church, drove it, possibly illegally, through the village and parked it outside the B&B. Thomas extracted the luggage and took it to the room where Bobbie and Barb were getting comfortable. Bobbie's colour was far less livid than it had been, but he was still a little too pink – but maybe that was just a case of too much sun.

They hadn't booked supper as part of the deal, intending to eat in the village, but Jo took pity on them and defrosted a casserole for them to share with her and Thomas, and they were grateful.

Despite his many ailments, Bobbie was fond of a beer and put away one or two in deep conversation with Thomas during the course of the evening, while Barb talked to Jo about the things they had done in Spain.

They had been travelling through Europe for a while. As Barb said, if you were going to come from the other side of the world a trip had to be worthwhile and for the last several years they had made a long trip each year to avoid the worst of the Australian winter, which neither of them liked at all.

This year they started in Venice – which, according to Barb, was one of the few places you get to see, places like the Taj Mahal, that are even better close up than anyone leads you to expect. She had loved travelling by Gondola down the Grand Canal. They'd visited Peggy Guggenheim's house.

Turned out Bobbie, who in his professional life had been a quantity surveyor since retirement, as a hobby had become an expert on Jackson Pollock and Lee Krasner and ardently wished he had played some sort of role in getting her recognised as one of the foremost abstract painters of her time. This seemed unlikely, but Jo knew of many stranger things that had happened. More likely was their trip to Murano, where Barb had bought up a storm of glass. Jo knew that many people adore Murano glass but she had always thought it vulgar – not that she would have dreamed of saying so – if for no other reason that that it might lessen her chances of getting a perfect five on their assessment of their booking on customer feedback.

After Venice, they'd been to Florence and Sienna and Rome and spent some time recovering in Pietrasanta on the Northern Tuscan coast, visited Lucca and then from Bologna did the train journey to Paris, where they spent a week living in a hotel Barb described as gorgeous.

From Paris they got a train to Barcelona, visited all the Gaudi houses (apparently another of Bobbie's obsessions) and the Sagrada Familia and picked up a car.

They stopped in Madrid, where they'd visited the Prado and seen the Velazquez Las Meninas, and made one further stop in Granada, taking in the Alhambra and other sights.

By now Jo's head was reeling. She hadn't done that much travelling because they just didn't have the money, since Thomas had been made redundant from his job as an industrial design draughtsman a couple of years before. They were entirely reliant on the proceeds of the business until getting their pensions, which were still some years away. But all the places that Barb had mentioned were magic to her ears. She figured life in Australia had been good to them – particularly when Barb mentioned that when they travelled long haul, they always travelled business class.

Jo and Thomas had managed a couple of days in Madrid before this season had begun, but Venice, Florence and Lucca remained a dream for her.

She went to bed that night trying not to feel envious.

The following day Joanna was serving a substantial but healthy breakfast. She baked her own wholemeal bread and had preserves made from the raspberries and blackcurrants grown in their own *cortijo*. There were cereals and fresh organic eggs from her friend Pedro's chickens. There was the air dried, serrano ham, freshly cut from the huge cured leg that hung in the pantry. There was a bowl of fruits and freshly pressed orange juice. Barb ate well, but Bobbie merely picked at his food and this morning he was as white as last afternoon he had been puce.

"Bobbie, what's wrong?" asked Jo.

"Truth told Jo, I'm feeling crook." It turned out that Bobbie was feeling a bit dizzy and sick and when he stood up, a little light headed.

"Do you think you're going to faint?"

"I'd really like to go back to bed and lie down."

"Barb," Jo said turning to her, "I think we should take Bobbie down to the clinic in the local market Town for some tests – particularly given what you told me about his heart condition. There is a thing that some people get here as a result of the altitude. It's a bit like labyrinthitis; you know that thing you get in the inner ear that affects your balance. It seems to particularly affect some men with heart conditions. I've known the doc to give medication that can ease the nausea."

"Well," said Bobbie "I don't think I'm in danger of corking it, but I do feel rough."

"He means he doesn't think he's on the point of dying," Barb helpfully explained. She had finished her breakfast. Leaving Thomas to clear up, Jo went for the car keys and came back to grab a jacket.

"Ok, let's go," and they did.

The drive was uneventful and downhill but very bendy, and Bobbie was clutching a plastic bag tightly on the way, just in case. Thy arrived at the clinic fifteen minutes later, but found a bit of a queue in front of them. Judging they had at least half an hour before their turn, Jo went to get some fresh milk and local goat's cheese at the supermarket on the main road, that had a much better selection than the shop in the village, which only had long life milk. She got back just in time to manage the translation with the doctor who examined Bobbie.

Jo explained to him that the doctor's diagnosis was that he was indeed feeling the effects of the altitude and gave him some anti-nausea medication to ease the symptoms, saying: "You'll probably adjust in a day or so."

As they were only staying a day or so, this was not enormously helpful.

After a further wait in the *farmacia* to buy the medicine, they drove back and Bobbie took a dose and went for a lie down. This clearly left Barb at a loose end.

"Are you up for a bit of a walk?" Jo asked her a little dubiously as Barb was herself a little stout, and didn't immediately look as if walking was her thing.

"I'd be stoked," she said, and then explained she meant she'd love to. "I may not look it, but I'm good for a walk, even uphill".

Jo prepared some sandwiches for lunch and they set off from the house, walking in the direction of the *cortijo* where she thought they could always take a rest if Barb found it too much. She'd given Bobbie her mobile number in case he took a turn for the worse, gave Barb her spare set of walking poles, and they set off.

At first they walked slowly up the initially steep climb from the B&B up to the dirt road that then runs through the undulating hills. It was a forty minute or so walk to the *cortijo* and Jo didn't want to tire her guest by forcing the pace. Besides, they were in no hurry. Thomas was doing sterling work clearing up and tidying and as Bobbie was occupying the bed, no one needed to make it. Jo decided that if Barb needed it, she could get Thomas to drive up in the jeep to meet them to bring them back down.

When Barb had got her breath back as they reached flatter ground, she said: "Well maybe I am a little out pf practice. Mind you, when I was younger I was fighting fit, but back then I was known as 'Bouncing Babs the Baby Belle'."

"What?" said Jo, thinking she must have misheard.

"Yes, I know it sounds far-fetched, but it's true. Me and my sisters, we toured Oz as the Belle Sisters. When we were younger we did a singing and acrobatic act, a bit like Gypsy Rose Lee started out, where as the baby of the troupe I would end the act with a perfect set of cartwheels that ended in the splits. Well, it was Gypsy Rose Lee without the strip-tease," she giggled.

"See, dad thought of himself as something of an impresario. I don't think he would ever have actually prostituted his daughters, but with that old bugger who could tell?" Looking at Jo's still open mouth and clearly enjoying the impact she was having, she continued.

"As we grew and times changed so Vaudeville was no longer as popular. We'd always sung in the act. Awful things like *Keep Your Sunny Side Up* while we tap danced, and even worse we actually sang *Let me Entertain You*, the end of which was the cue for my big finale. Anyway, after Vaudeville died, Dad turned us into a girl singing group and he managed us until he dumped mum and went off with a secretary half his age. There was me, Ailis, Brigid, Colleen and Caitlín. I think we were given those names because originally dad had a long term plan and was going to call us the ABC sisters.

"His family was originally from a little place just outside Cork, called Killbrittain. It used to crack me and my sisters up during the troubles in Northern Ireland that our family came from a place called Killbrittain, but it means "Britton's church". It's about five miles southwest of Bandon, and near Clonakilty and Kinsale. All these places are beautiful. Bobbie and I paid a visit a few years ago and I fell in love with Clonakilty black pudding, which may have something to do with my weight gain since then.

Anyway, dad had met my mum Sheila in Sydney, where he went to live as a young man, there being few prospects for a young man in rural Ireland back then. Mum fell in love with him and loved him for the rest of her life – no matter what he did."

Jo's head was reeling from this most unexpected of tales, but she was really intrigued to hear more about the world in which Barb had grown up.

"I think I need more information. Why Vaudeville?" she asked to kick start Barb out of the reverie into which she appeared to have fallen.

"As my dad told it there wasn't much music hall in Cork, but Dublin was another matter. As a boy in the 1930s, he'd seen variety acts at the Queen's Theatre in Dublin which later also became a cinema. He fell in love with the greasepaint, roar of the crowd kinda thing.

"When he got to Oz, there was a still famous circuit called The Tivoli Circuit, that had been popular in Australia since the 1890s, and we only appeared in it towards its dying days in the mid 1960s. It had been set up by an English music hall comedian called Harry Rickards. The Tivoli became the major outlet for variety theatre and Vaudeville in Australia for over seventy years. The circuit grew to include Melbourne, Adelaide, Brisbane and Perth in their tours by the turn of the century. It promoted a lot of local acts, but occasionally had international musical, variety and comedy acts. Its acts included dancers, acrobats, comedians and ventriloquists, and it was famous for its scantily-clad chorus girls, who were called "Tivoli Tappers". Me and my sisters appeared early in the shows and weren't allowed to see the Tappers' perform. Dad had us travelling round the circuit like a band of gypsies. Our act didn't change much, but it really interfered with schooling. None of my sisters ever really recovered from it. Then, as Vaudeville died out, dad made us give up the acrobatic tricks and kicks and got us to stick with the singing. There were loads of girl bands in the 1970s all over the world. Sister acts were always a good gimmick in Oz. We even had some success and recorded some songs in that made it into the hit parade. We did a version of *He's Sure the Boy I love* and another of *Why won't they let us fall in love*. These both got into the Australian charts, albeit not so very high up. We never had a number one hit.

"It looked like we might make a breakthrough, but then dad, who was then in his sixties, went off with a woman in her thirties called Lindy who worked as a secretary in the record producer's office.

When he left our mum we broke off any contact with him and the band broke up. There was no one to promote us and our heart wasn't in it anymore.

I think we'd only really gone along with it as dad was a dreamer, a really driven man with a dream that his daughters would make his fortune for him – though we never did. I don't remember us seeing any money from our hit records, so maybe he did get a bob or two out of it that he kept from us.

So then dad and Lindy had a child, a little girl they called Sheila. We didn't know if he was taking the piss or it was some kind of tribute. When little Sheila was born my oldest sister was in her late twenties and I was a teenager.

Then Lindy got really ill. It was tragic, really. She was still in her thirties when she died from womb cancer. Dad was left with a small child and nowhere to go. He brought her home to us and Sheila met Sheila. Our mum was the soul of generosity and she took Sheila in. She took my dad back because she had always loved him, though whether she ever really forgave him, I don't know. I don't think us sisters ever really did, though she wanted us to.

By this stage he was not a well man, though he hung on with mum looking after him till he was in his late seventies and then died of a massive coronary.

"By this time only me and our Caitlin were still living at home at this stage. The rest of my sisters were scattered around and about. Caitlin was training to be a physio, so she was staying at college a fair bit of the time. After the band split I had also gone back to school and done some exams and eventually did a shorthand typing course. So I got to see a lot of little Sheila growing up.

In my first job, at the age of eighteen, I met Bobbie and we fell in love and we've been together ever since.

"Ailis, Brigid, and Colleen haven't done so well.

Ailis married a brute who beat her; Brigid couldn't ever settle to any proper job and never got married; Colleen couldn't let the fame business go. She craved it all of the rest of her life, and tried many different ways to break into the business, always failing, and then she hit the turps big time – became a drinker and ended up a few years ago dying from cirrhosis.

"Bobbie and I had two sons of our own. He was qualified as a quantity surveyor and we've had a good life and can now travel as much as we like.

When mum died, little Sheila was at college so she came to live with us in her holidays. I'm still very close to her and she's done us proud. When we go back we're going to a celebration for the publication of her PHD. She's a historian and her thesis subject was the history of Vaudeville in Australia.

It still makes me laugh that she turned what we lived into an academic study, but good on ya is what I say to her."

They had arrived at the *cortijo* and stopped just outside the gate before going in.

"Barb, what an amazing life you have lived. What a story. You should write a book."

"You know you're not the first person to tell me that," smiled Barb and those generous dimples appeared once more. Jo thought to herself: "I have to remember the details of this story right. This is one Thomas would definitely want to hear."

They never did get to go to the chestnut festival celebrations. Poor Bobbie's nausea didn't improve much and they decided to cut their losses and head back to sea level where he had been assured his condition would return to normal. If he recovered enough when they hit sea level, they planned to spend some days in Malaga seeing the sites before flying to London where they were to spend a week before heading back to Sydney for little Sheila's party.

Before they left, Jo took Barb's hand in hers and she told her that in her whole time running the business she had heard some very interesting tales, but that Barb's had been, she thought, the most fascinating of all. Although, when later when they had left, Jo looked up the Belle Sisters online and could find no trace of either them or any of their hit records. It made her think to check her bank statement, but their payment had definitely gone through, and some days when she checked the rating, they had given her a five star one.

She felt ashamed of herself for ever doubting Barb's story – but you would, wouldn't you?

JUST SURVIVING

"When were you diagnosed?" asked Joanna.

"Are you sure you really want to know all this?" Sarah asked her in return.

Joanna replied: "I do. I know you've told me bits over the last year, but knowing you I suspect you've also left a lot out and now you're here, I want the whole story."

"Even if it's a long one?"

"Even then."

Sarah and Joanna had met at university. Sarah was studying English when Jo was in the Languages Department. They both had rooms in a large shared house where there were the usual fights over who had eaten all the Greek yogurt in the fridge and who had left the mouldering spoilt milk to fester.

After uni Sarah had taken a job in publishing and moved back to London and she and Jo had kept in touch for a few years – spent a few weekends at each other's flats catching up until the business of living, partners and children had caught up with them. They had gradually lost touch apart from the regular Christmas card exchange where Sarah would let her know how she, Max and the girls were doing.

Jo knew that the divorce from Max had happened some eight years ago and that a few years after that Sarah had started a relationship with a new man called Jonathan – but she had never met him. In this year's Christmas card there had been a short note to say that Sarah had been really ill and out of communication most of that year, but that she missed Jo and would try to be a better correspondent.

This triggered off an email exchange which had culminated in this visit six months later. Jo had offered her a period of recuperation and she had chosen to come when her strength had returned enough for her to do walks in the hills.

So, here they were, enjoying the late afternoon sun on the roof terrace, drinking endless cups of tea; relaxing, while Thomas had gone to the *cortijo* to do some work and bring back the vegetables for supper.

"I kept a diary. For the first time in my life I kept a diary. Maybe I should have brought it and let you read it.

So, where to start? The diagnosis? Well it was long and drawn out. One day in March last year I found a small lump on my back. I went to the doctor who had some kind of toy like ultrasound machine. He told me it was a cyst and not a problem. A week later I found a lump in my armpit and went back to the surgery, insisted on seeing another doctor who felt it and immediately sent me for a blood test. I remember it was a Friday afternoon and I got in for the last phlebotomy appointment of the day. Within a week I was called to the hospital for more tests. I saw a woman consultant, Dr. Hannah, who treated me throughout the year. She told me upfront that in her opinion I had a blood cancer, but that they would do the tests that she felt sure would confirm what she had seen.

"By this stage glands all over my body were swelling up, including in the groin. So, I had my first biopsy. When I went to get the results my friend Anne, who is a nurse, came with me.

I was really glad she had because they had lost my results in the lab. We waited for an hour of growing tension whilst Dr. Hannah pressurised the lab to find them. In the end they did. She told me they confirmed ninety per cent that what I had was low grade lymphoma but that I would need a bone marrow biopsy.

"Anne told me she thought Dr. Hannah should get a gold star for the way she had dealt with all this and communicated with me. 'I think this is a woman you can trust,' she said and she was so right.

Sometime later I was called back for a liver function test. I found Dr. Hannah waiting for me in the clinic where I was to have the test because, she said, she knew I would be anxious and she hadn't been able to speak to me earlier, but just wanted me to know the test was to see if I could be part of a medical trial and was nothing to otherwise worry about.

I have to say she was straight and considerate like that all the way through my treatment. She would tell me when things got complicated that she had reached the edge of her competence, and needed guidance from more experienced or knowledgeable colleagues. So, I knew from the first day I was in the very good hands of the best kind of clinician.

"Where was I? Oh, yes. On the day before that appointed for the biopsy, I was in Birmingham chairing a book fair. I had to get a train back to London the night before and stayed with my sister, who drove me to the hospital the following day. I sat on the train coming back to Birmingham in a state of shock and in pain.

The bone marrow biopsy had been the most painful, invasive thing that had ever happened to me whilst I was awake and conscious. It went on for fifteen minutes only but it felt so much longer. I had not realised that although the skin and tissue can be numbed, the bone cannot be. It hurt like fuck.

Afterwards I acted as if everything was normal and dashed from the hospital to catch the train. It was only when I sat down in my train seat that I realised my jaw was still clenched and my spine held in a strange fixed tension. I did not unclench or unfix for two days.

That night I took the team out to dinner. It was hard to string a whole sentence together. I felt dazed and somewhat spaced out by the pain, or the memory of the pain, that I couldn't shake. The following day I chaired a discussion between three of our authors in a mental haze.

"When I got the results of the test it confirmed Dr. Hannah's diagnosis and I was put on to a 'watch and wait' regime.

"Low grade lymphoma was not such a bad result. It is a chronic condition you die with rather than from, but it can sap your energy and from time to time treatment may be necessary, depending on the staging.

Mine turned out to be stage four non-Hodgkin's follicular grade B.

It took me some time to absorb this information. What is interesting when you have bad news is how quickly but by grudging degrees you adjust to it. Whilst it wasn't welcome, it was not the worst news.

My main worry had been the girls. They had just had their eighteenth birthdays. They are the same age I was when my mum got the breast cancer that killed her three years later. I so did not want them to go through what I had experienced in the horror of her death."

Jo remembered Sarah going home immediately after her finals to look after her mum. Her dad had died at the end of their second year at university and Sarah had struggled through her final year, somehow keeping her poor mum afloat from afar with the help of an aunt and a niece. Sarah had seen her mother through a deeply unpleasant, drawn out death and had re-built her life afterwards through periods of deep depression and a mourning she didn't seem able to escape for years, so hard did the experience hit her. Jo understood entirely why she had wanted to protect her own girls from going through something similar.

In a routine visit to Dr. Hannah in June the previous year – almost exactly a year ago – Sarah had reminded the doctor that they had agreed she should have a further biopsy on the lump on her back that had taken her to her family GP in the first place. So it happened. Then things started to get complicated. It appeared from this biopsy that her cancer might be changing its nature. It was the worst that might happen. Apparently when low grade lymphoma transforms into high grade it gets dangerous and dying from it rather than with it becomes a real possibility.

"At that point I got scared. I recognised that in the space of two months I had gone from being an unconcerned well person through being diagnosed as having cancer with an expectancy of surviving at least ten years with low grade lymphoma to, at minimum, to a grade four with death as a possible outcome. I had a cousin who had died aged thirty-four with high grade lymphoma and at that stage I knew of another eight people who had the high-grade form of the disease of whom only three are still living. That's a less than fifty per cent chance of survival.

"I felt calm on the surface talking to Dr. Hannah because she managed giving me the information I needed straight, and I tell her that I appreciate the pro-active way she is managing my case and my disease. But deep inside I had this nagging, growing fear like a toothache threatening to flare up, knowing that my condition is potentially now life threatening. I already feel as if I have been through some hard transitions and know in my gut that there may well be more to come.

"Dr. Hannah transferred me to King's College Hospital where my mother had been treated. On my first appointment there my memory was taken straight back to my mother's last appointment with her consultant just shy of thirty seven years earlier.

My father had died since mum's last appointment with the consultant. Her very kindly consultant asked me in to his office after mum had gone to get dressed. He told me what I already feared, that she might now give up fighting her disease. She was fifty one. Five years younger than I am now.

'Is something wrong?'

He said: 'Your mother does not seem her usual lively self.'

'My father died a few months ago. She is locked in pain.' So was I.

He took my hand and looked into my eyes and said slowly. 'I am very sorry': and he was. 'Your mother seemed to me to get much of her will to live from your father's strength.'

'I know.'

'It is hard to say this to you, but you do realise...'

I heard the rest dimly as if the sound was muffled by cotton wool in my ears, but I already knew what he was going to say and with tears straining at the back of my eyes I was struggling not to cry in front of this man with his kindly concern but oh, so professional distance from the raw pain in my heart.

"Feeling locked in this unwelcome nostalgia, I met my new consultant. I was kept waiting for over an hour at Kings College Hospital this morning. I guess it was bad news day for someone else before I got my turn at bad news.

The professor was a slightly built, almost petite man with an open, intelligent face. He was sympathetic without being maudlin and talked me through all the treatment options. Early on in the conversation it became clear that he did not think no treatment was an option, but he had not seen my full set of results as in a somewhat absent minded professors way he had lost the password for his computer and could not get the records up on screen.

He offered CVPR, a lesser chemotherapy regime than the CHOP and rituximab mix but only if the epidemiological conclusion was that the lymphoma had not transformed into high grade.

It turned out that his lab people had sent my tests to another colleague at the Royal Marsden to help with the diagnosis, as it is such a complicated case. That colleague eventually called with his considered opinion.

They conferred and agreed that, yes, my cancer was transforming. They would now have to consider it as high grade and treat appropriately

"The problem now is that the treatment for high-grade lymphoma deals only with the high-grade lymphoma and will leave some low-level disease behind that could well become even more resistant to treatment itself as a result.

It appears I am in worst of all possible worlds, not the best. This, in my book, counted as bad news.

"At this point I had another threshold change. I had gone to this appointment hoping that I would need no treatment. During its course I had already got my head round the idea of a lower toxicity chemotherapy treatment, but was now adjusting to the idea of R-CHOP starting shortly.

Even I was not quite ready, however, for the tumult that came next of options on bone marrow transplants and tissue typing any willing relatives and me for a match.

I remained unprepared for such a risky medical procedure options, for which I was truly unprepared. I was however, fixated in horror by the knowledge I would lose my hair.

Oh, vanity – and all that. It was the next threshold to move through.

"I started the treatment in September. The first cycle took all day as the Rituximab is put in very slowly like oil into the egg yolk when making mayonnaise.

I think it took over four hours but had a pre-med so was a bit dozy. Then the rest of the cocktail follows.

It was OK. I had no adverse reactions to the drugs going in and spent quite a busy day arranging therapeutic massages, blood tests and wig fittings.

I came out feeling quite cheerful and the girls and I got

lots of videos out and settled down that evening to watch them. I even ate reasonably.

If the day had been bearable, the night was not. My body was like an inferno of chemical reaction with little geysers of strange pains and gasses going off all over it. I felt like one of those scenes from a garish cartoon of the mad scientist in the laboratory except my body was the lab.

I was far too busy to sleep. I was also nauseous, but not sick, although I was deeply uncomfortable with twitchy limbs.

"I had set up a weekly conversation with a therapist in my bid not to overburden the girls. I wanted somewhere I could offload and be open about my fear. Going to our first session I felt fine and strong but the moment I walked through his door I started cracking up.

He was a tall, gaunt man with the slight stoop that self-consciously tall people get. In his case I suspected this to be arthritis or some difficult physical disabling condition.

It was only when I was shaking his hand did I discovered it was bent over like a hook and deeply disabled and this was a shock. He did not resist the handshake but could not reciprocate and I wondered if shaking hands is part of the etiquette of therapy or not, having had no previous experience of it.

He had a slight, barely grown beard and moustache, mostly grey but with a hint of the red that might once have been vigorous but could have been pale ginger. It is always hard to tell with an ageing red head.

"We sat on opposite sides of his bright but austere consulting room.

His eyes, a twinkle in his long face were gazing at me, waiting for me to begin, to express my needs and wants. He did kick start me, for which I was grateful.

Once started there was almost no stopping me. I gave the broad brush of my illness, its history, diagnosis and options for prognosis and how I think I feel about it.

Of my girls, and how fearful I was that I would let them down.

Of my mother and the horror of her death and of my role in life since the age of five of keeping her alive; of my fears that in working things through with the girls I will be re-working things through about her, my role in her death and all the things I thought I had dealt with over the years.

Of my life as a carer for others with never enough time for me and of not even knowing what I need. I talked about my work and the greatness and solidarity of my team and the richness of support and love from friends, of good friend-ships and being a private person.

Of being poised between total despair and equal positiv-ity. Of being someone who copes who has always coped and does not know how not to cope and does not want not to cope or be vulnerable to rejection. Of fearing that I will die and knowing that I may have to face this but feeling immortal and knowing that if anyone can beat this illness it will be me.

Finally, I told him about Jonathan, and knowing in my gut that I will lose him as a result of the illness, but desperately hoping not to.

It may have been the steroids gabbling, but I ended up feeling grateful that this man was being paid to be on the receiving end of my diatribe.

"He was good. Whenever I reached a pocket of pain that required tears he gave me space to re-group and a tissue. Whenever I ran dry he kick started me again.

At one stage, when I told him about my control freak ten-dencies and how I am working those through with my team at work, hopefully like a grown up, he gave a wry smile and suggested there might be a message in that for him about the relationship we will develop.

It made me laugh, because he was right, of course.

"He agreed to work with me. It was as if he was offering me a place of safety in the current chaos that my life had become.

I felt relieved. I can lean on this man in a way that I hope means I will not lean too heavily on any of my friends or my beloved girls.

With his support, perhaps, I thought, I can turn this experience into something positive that will enrich us all. That is what I wanted to do if it was possible, because at that moment – if only for that moment – I felt very much alive and perversely perhaps was counting my many blessings.

"I started losing my lovely long hair after treatment one. At first it made me tearful and I started doing the 'why me' number followed shortly by the 'why not me', that is the only logical response. I lost the rest of it after treatment two, when I started to get nauseous. I lost Jonathan shortly thereafter. It seemed somehow appropriate in a list of losses: hair, appetite, and lover.

"He had been avoiding contact with me through the diagnosis stage but had come to see me on the Sunday six days after my first treatment.

I made him walk with me through the local park so we could talk without having to look at each other.

We walked for an hour while I told him everything I needed to say about his behaviour and his denial. When I asked him why he was the only person who had not phoned over last weekend to see how I was surviving the chemo experience, he replied that given that he now understood what it was like for me to be on the receiving end of such silence there was nothing that could excuse it.

I talked him through the possibility of me dying and the options for him to think through about the role he might want to play in my treatment and either recovery or death and told him that denial and running away was not one of those options.

I told him I was not prepared for him to be a passenger on this trip and that I would not allow his inadequacies to drain my energy in managing my illness.

"He responded like a grown up and engaged with me and talked, but then he often does when he is with me. It is only when he goes back to that other life of his behind the fabric of lies and evasions that he hides away.

My demands were few. I asked that he phones me every few days and demonstrates that he is involved and supporting me in my efforts to fight this illness. I knew that if he could do it, it would make him a better and stronger man.

"I thought we had a pact.

We spent the rest of the afternoon in bed because the girls were out and I felt that we had so broken down the barriers of anger and resentment that we could be close. It was very loving and warm, if not – given my general energy levels and slight remaining traces of nausea, deeply passionate but we both needed that intimacy and closeness.

"Still, I had my doubts that he would come through, and these proved correct.

The last eight years with him had meant a lot to me, but I realised I might need to cut him out of my life in order to concentrate on saving it.

In short order it came to pass. I don't want to dwell on the details. They are too pathetic.

"I continued with the treatment. Meanwhile I was managing to work, going into the office a couple of time a week and working remotely the rest of the time.

It worked until the Staff Christmas lunch. I had my final round of chemotherapy on the 15th December and was feeling grim but on the 23nd went to the Christmas lunch at a great Indian restaurant where the food was lovely but too spicy for my system. I just about made it home by taxi before my system decided to explode at both ends. I had to crawl up the stairs and couldn't quite believe it when I crawled into the bathroom and heard a mighty crack as the cistern of my loo cracked and water poured out onto the floor.

It was one of those 'someone up there really doesn't like me' moments.

A friend persuaded a plumber to come out the following day when shops were shutting for Christmas, who persuaded his supplier to sell him a new toilet system which he put in for me.

I was in bed sick and collapsed and in that chaos Jonathan turned up after I had had not a word from him in over three months. He turned up with Christmas presents. I was too sick to see him and instructed the girls to tell him so. He left. I had no idea what he thought might happen.

"I felt a deep loathing that erupted into a murderous rage that I had not expected to feel.

That night I had a dream that scared me. I was trying to sleep without sleeping tablets and failing miserably. My sleep was light and uneasy.

I dreamt that I had agreed to meet Jonathan somewhere in central London. The dreamscape had all the characteristics of a 1930s film noir set. I told him I would never see him again. He turned into a crazed and wild looking man who said he would dog my footsteps and that I would never be free of him. By now it was dark and drizzling with rain and no cab would pick me up.

I got a bus and saw his mad face reflected in the bus window. When I eventually got home he was waiting for me. I just about got though the front door, but he put his foot inside it and was clearly going to hurt me. Somehow, I found something that looked like a medieval ball and chain (on waking and when calmer I realised it had been a metal version of the porcelain toilet ball and socket from my broken loo! This gave me a laugh). In the dream I bashed and bashed his hand with it so that he would let go of my door and I could close it, until his hand was bloody and broken, and I wanted to go on and on doing this to exact the maximum pain, but still I could not get him to loosen his grip on the door.

At the same time I was scared of his murderous rage.

I woke up breathless and sweaty and feeling terrified and could not go back to sleep.

"In my next session with my therapist I told him about this dream and he put it in place for me when he said: "You know that the stalker, although it may also be Jonathan, is really the cancer."

In my mind I had put Jonathan on the same side as my disease. I think this was just because I think this is where in my mind at least he had chosen to be.

"I recovered from my physical collapse after about ten days during which my system had rebooted itself. I had finished my treatment and needed the full panoply of tests, like CT and PET scans. These came back showing I was in remission. I had only the final bone marrow biopsy and a throat lump biopsy to go for the one lump that hadn't gone away. I remembered the pain of my first bone marrow biopsy and I negotiated with the doctor who was going to do it, that she would do it while I was under sedation for the throat lumpectomy. Instead I had a completely farcical day. I ended up not having the operation as the head ENT honcho declared the lump was not a node but a gland, was unlikely to have anything to do with the disease, but that if it did and needed to come out it would be major, not day surgery and require a week in hospital. So, he demanded ultra-sound and needle biopsy before he was prepared to operate.

"This was clearly the right thing as he had saved me from

a 'never event' in NHS parlance a thing that was meant never to happen and was someone's cock up.

It left me wondering why this had only been discovered five minutes before I was due to go under the knife.

It also left me with no general anaesthetic under which to have the bone marrow biopsy.

"We then had the complete farce of me in the recovery room surrounded by six hospital clinicians (one of whom was my doctor, who had temporarily left her clinic to do the biopsy) and the operating theatre admin people, none of whom knew what the right clinical protocols were for administering sedation in that setting.

I, with drip in one arm and the other, wired for blood pressure monitoring and chest armed with heart monitoring paraphernalia for what seemed like an age whilst they argued amongst themselves.

The theatre manager suggested that I should divest myself of all equipment, get dressed and walk over to main hospital where we could begin again, re-inserting my tubes and then have the biopsy under sedation.

My haematology doc made the observation through gritted teeth that this might not be in my best interest. She also observed to her colleagues that I was showing remarkable sense of humour in the circumstances, as I was still laughing about the whole situation when most other patients would have worked themselves into a suing hysteria.

At this point the senior nurse looked down at me – I was still lying on an operating theatre transport trolley and said: 'Sarah, you are seeing us at our very worst. I'm so ashamed of us.'

By this time I had had enough and asked them to get a grip and get on with it – and I suggested they give me a sedative and just do it.

Oddly, they all agreed and gave me the sedative and got

on with the procedure. I stayed in the recovery room for a couple of hours and my aunt picked me up and took me home."

"What was the treatment like?" asked Jo.

"You really want to know?"

"Well, yes, or I wouldn't have asked."

"Well, chemotherapy is a really rough, tough treatment. It gets progressively more potent over time. It takes away your hair and your taste buds. It destroys the nerve endings in fingers and toes. It impacts upon your memory and information, and your thoughts go into a black hole never to re-emerge, or, at least, not at convenient points, like when you need them in a hurry and in a corner probably at work.

It makes you nauseous, weak and faint. It destroys your digestion and gives you terminal, really painful, wind and, eventually, in order to make you well, it makes you really ill.

In order to survive the treatment you have to treat lots of different parts of your system – like strict oral hygiene, cleaning teeth and gums five times per day. You take up to forty different kinds of tablets most days of the three week cycle, but not in the same ratios or combinations at all stages.

If you get a cold sore or a mouth ulcer, they just don't stop growing and you can end up with a serious infection unless you take huge doses of drugs to reverse the process.

I do not know how people with little discipline or will or even with a modicum of confusion manage to get through it.

Throughout the treatment you feel physically uncomfortable the whole time at every stage of your day, and it destroys your sleep at night. Even when this is not entirely unbearable it is only just bearable and sometimes not quite that.

But the really good news, at the end of the six months, was that I didn't need the bone marrow transplant. That second bone marrow biopsy came back clear. The chemo was enough to put me in what the consultant called full remission and I was so relieved because my system was by then so frail and I was thin like a stick insect, and I don't think I would have survived the rigours of a bone marrow transplant. I felt incredibly lucky.

"To celebrate my good fortune I arranged a trip to Cuba with a friend. I was still very weak and I weighed ridiculously little but my hair was beginning to grow. I had a kind of bum fluff all over my scalp. It felt like a start.

"I spent a week in Havana with my friend Jackie, which was great.

We both loved Cuba and the graciousness and generosity of the people.

There is a terrible equality of poverty across the country. It is crumbling to ruin and you end up feeling that whatever the original logic may have been from the US perspective for the economic blockade when the soviet bloc still existed, it has now degenerated into the politics of spite.

Jackie kept getting frustrated that they could not pull themselves up by their own bootstraps and wanted to organise their urban regeneration programme.

We were both amazed by how personally secure it feels, In the end, despite the poverty and the fact that nothing seems to work on the surface – we both agreed that something quite profound does work as people have time for life even though they are working hard at making life work.

We also did lots of things and I had more energy than Jacks when it came to it, as she needed lots of sleep and to rest. We went to the ballet, saw a concert in the church of St. Francis of Assisi, heard music everywhere, walked miles every day, went to the Museo de Bellas Artes and Arte Moderno (all beautiful spaces) and to the Museo de la Revolución, which looks like a crude 1950s exhibition long past its sell by date from which I have a very silly photo of Jackie posing with a mannequin of Che that is wearing an exceptionally bad wig, that reminded me of my chemo period wig.

"We went out in a jeep one day, visited Veradero, swam in underground caves, and had lunch (horrible) at an ex-coffee plantation.

There was a point towards the end of the day, as we were surfing the waves down a river on the back of strange aquatic motor bikes when feeling the sun on my neck and hearing the song of birds along the river bank and feeling the speed and power of the bikes, I felt for the first time in a year the full joy of being alive and having hope of remaining so for a while, when the chemo seemed entirely worthwhile and I felt so very grateful to the universe for allowing me to survive it and hopefully have the rest of my life to live."

It was dark on the terrace by then. The solar lights had come on gradually as day had turned through dusk to night.

"I've spent the months since that trip recovering and just feeling grateful to everyone and everything that kept me alive."

Jo sat close to Sarah and ran her hands through the hair still short that had grown back curly, as apparently it often does after such treatment.

Sarah looked at her and said: "Thank you Jo. Thank you for listening. This isn't a story I've told that often. I love you, my friend."

Jo replied: "And I love you. You are a born survivor Sarah. I guess it's what we've always been good at the both of us – we are good at just surviving."

SOMETIMES GOOD THINGS HAPPEN

Early in her school life, Rebecca met Elena. This was a soul mate.

It had been at the end of her second year of school. She was not yet twelve. They had been on a school journey to the Isle of Man, staying in a boarding school.

Many of the kids had never been out of London before. She remembered a scrawny boy staring in amazement at the sea crashing against rocks below the cliff on which we were standing, which he was seeing for the first time – saying: "Fuck," then, "fuuck... fuuuck," over and over, with each repetition of the forbidden word elongating the vowels as his awe grew, as if intoning some sacred prayer.

The Religious Knowledge teacher who was leading the group had not been impressed with this inarticulate appreciation of the world's wonders, clipping him round the ear with a curt: "That'll do, Fergusson."

On the first night in the girls' dormitory, a short while after the lights had been turned out by the austere matron, a giggling came from one particular bed.

A voice called out: "Miss. Sue Bates is in Elena Laurenti's bed."

Rebecca recognised the voice as Maureen Driscoll: a strangely masculine, semi-autistic girl with few friends but much teenage acne. Then she heard the padding of footsteps and some rustlings, followed by a shout. At that moment the irate Matron switched on the light and there, where previously Maureen Driscoll had lain, was an upside down bed with Maureen underneath it. Standing beside it, caught red handed as she raised herself to her full height, was a defiant Elena Laurenti.

A sharp intake of breath went round the room. Whilst no one else was breathing Rebecca started to laugh, found she couldn't stop and got quite hysterical. Elena came to stand at the end of her bed and looked at this smaller girl, crying with laughter.

"Mmm", she said, "you might just be alright."

It was the auspicious start of a lifelong friendship.

It grew slowly, this friendship. Elena did not open up all at once and nor did Rebecca. They spent more and more time together at school as time went on.

This was not encouraged, because they were in different school years and there was eighteen months in age between them. Also they were both inclined to a naughtiness that simply got reinforced and exaggerated when together and rather alarmed their teachers.

Rebecca looked forward to meeting Elena at lunchtimes when they would go to the local café for beans, or sometimes egg on toast and then to the local park where they would light up fags and talk and laugh until it was time to head back to school.

Some days they talked so intensely about politics and human conflict they lost track of time and were late and once or twice they never made it back at all.

Sometimes they spent morning assemblies together, including one occasion on which they had misbehaved so badly, they spent the whole assembly standing in disgrace with their backs to the school and their faces pressed into the stage curtains, trying – and failing badly – not to snicker inappropriately.

Also they were also no strangers to the headmaster's study. They spent many break times standing outside it waiting to be seen for punishment either separately or together.

Rebecca remembered the Albrecht Durer painting of The Hands of the Apostle, known as the 'Praying Hands', that had been on the wall outside his study. She remembered the painting with distaste as she had ceased to see its genius in the many hours she had spent with only it to look at as she awaited her punishment at the hands of the bully that was the headmaster.

She had hated what, at the time, she saw as false piety, not of the print itself but of the man who displayed it, who would scream and rage for what seemed to her like minor offences.

Her sense of outraged injustice had transferred itself onto her feelings for poor Durer's painting.

At the time she had not known that Durer had painted it in tribute to the brother who in their exceedingly poor family of eighteen children had worked in the mines for four years to fund Durer's art studies. Nor did she know these were the very hands broken and maimed by their years in the mine that made it impossible for brother Albert to take his turn studying art.

Had she known, she might have made more common cause with the painting, acknowledging the cruel ironies of life.

In fact, she didn't know any of this until many years later, when Elena herself was finally studying art and had told her the story.

Theirs was not the kind of school that offered that kind of education.

Then, she had only known that her headmaster would eventually turn up to shout at her until his face turned blood red against the stark white of his eyebrows and neat moustache. Mostly she wondered if he had a volume control, or better still an off switch, and at times she fantasised that those gaunt and spectral hands might imperceptibly come to life and find and activate the control or, on really bad days when he surpassed himself in splenetic glory, wrap themselves gently but firmly around that scrawny neck and just squeeze.

What they did to get into trouble often passed them by. Sometimes it seemed, whatever they were doing, trouble found them with ease. All they wanted to do was have a laugh using up their excess energies. It was only ever small wickedness, yet they were never sneaky or really mean.

Except that once perhaps, where in the art room they had each of them loaded paint onto fat round brushes, crept either side of the obnoxious, nose picking Fergusson, and on an agreed signal, stuffed these into his wide, flapping ears. There had been much guilty pleasure in the laughs this had given them. For days afterwards one of them would only have to whisper 'ears' or 'paintbrush' to convulse them both. They knew there was more than a tinge of unacceptability to this behaviour, but its call was siren.

Rebecca remembered one occasion in which an irate and extremely nervous male religious education teacher had thrown her out of his class for blasphemy.

True, she had been baiting him, but reckoned that if he was going to so publicly espouse his faith, he ought to be willing and able to defend it in what she considered to be a fair, if bare knuckle, contest.

He had irritated her with his pomposity, so she had pushed and pushed to see how far she could go before he broke and break he did. He had pushed her before him to the senior religious education teacher's class: altogether a much more muscular Christian who would have enjoyed the contest but did not approve of her taking advantage of the lesser man.

Mr Loughton had looked at her and rolled his eyes.

"Ok Rosen," he said, "you can sit next to Elena Laurenti."

In her feigned boredom, Rebecca had not even noticed whose classroom she had so unceremoniously been thrown into. A smile sudden as spring showers had lit up her face. Now this was a punishment she felt she fully deserved.

She and Elena exchanged a wicked grin. It was true, heaven did come to those who persevered.

Their friendship allowed both of them to resist the pull of growing up. Neither wanted to grow up if growing up meant having to have endless conversations about who they might or might not fancy and make up and dancing round your handbag at the Palais waiting to be asked to dance.

They wanted to discuss music and art and politics and the greatness they secretly felt, but could not quite admit should, but hoped, would be theirs.

Neither wanted to have the life the girls growing up around them craved, like marriage and babies, but neither knew how to get a different kind of life and, to boot, both were working class girls with no social connections to ease their passage on the way.

Strangely, even though they loved each other, Elena and Rebecca did not see each other much outside school. The age difference, so unimportant in the daily space they shared, felt more significant outside it. Besides, outside school Elena had a boyfriend. He was boring. He was called Brian. He went to a different school, where he was sporting captain of this and that. Rugby and golf: GOLF? Rebecca would silently repeat the word to herself, as if the term itself would unravel a mystery.

Rebecca accepted Brian like you accept rain stopping play in cricket match. She felt he was a temporary blip on their friendship horizon. When she saw Elena out with Brian as she did on the streets of Brixton from time to time, there was this wholly other person, who barely acknowledged her and moved swiftly on.

On these encounters Elena wore neat little dresses, carried neat little handbags and smiled at Brian's jokes. He was a stupid, big, stocky sportsman who would in time run to fat, but he was benign.

Many years later, over a bottle of wine when they usually got in to reminiscing about the past and sometimes gently explored it, she had asked Elena: "And Brian. What the hell was he about?"

Without hesitation Elena replied: "I needed him to rescue me from the meat market that we used to be exposed to. I was too scared of a real bloke and I didn't want to grow up".

Brian had demanded little in return for his protection: an occasional snog, perhaps, which she felt protected her from being vulnerable to the male gazes and approaches that she did not yet want to come her way.

Secretly, Rebecca had a half yen for a Brian figure in her own life, if she could have had a less boring one – but she was never able to be anything other than herself, and boys sensed this.

She was oddly, in some ways, the more ferocious and sure of herself of the two of them. This had come as a surprise to her, because her teenage self had felt so raw and vulnerable and needy, but underneath that dislocation of unconfidently not knowing who you are there was an underpinning to Rebecca she could not escape.

At the time she had seen Elena's acquisition of Brian as a trophy that made her seem more grown up, and although she wouldn't in practice have wanted Brian in real life, in her secret heart she had longed for and feared having a lover who would introduce passion into her life, and because she knew she was not ready for this she kept boys away. She had not known that Elena wanted him to avoid having to grow up and face more challenging male prospects.

It was during this phase of her life that Rebecca had adopted her practice of finding unobtainable love objects, who were always forbidden or dangerous, and cherishing them passionately in private, whilst ignoring them and pushing them away in the real world.

After their 'Brian conversation', Rebecca had appreciated that she had loved Elena because in her company she felt strong and clear about the person she wanted to be, if still too little confident in the person she was.

Their shared laughter had been spontaneous and soul nourishing.

It made them whole.

Above all, Rebecca believed in Elena. She knew she would be a great artist. The only proof she really had of this huge artistic talent was a constant stream of doodles that Elena did on every surface and every piece of paper that came within her grasp. They were good, but there were others who could draw (Rebecca was not one of them).

In Elena's heart was the conviction of an artist with an unconventional but enormously perceptive and rich way of seeing.

It was this huge, unpredictable dynamism in her friend that Rebecca loved.

It took over thirty years for Rebecca's total belief in Elena to be realised.

Elena had left school with no qualifications to speak of, but did get a job in advertising.

Then, like so many women's lives, hers had been deflected from its course by marriage and children.

She found her way back to study late, got into college even later and eventually into the Royal College of Art where she got a Master's Degree. At the final show for her first degree, Rebecca had wept with relief and gratitude that her friend had made it.

Elena had not wept, though she had been moved and perhaps a little embarrassed by her pal's obvious emotion.

Rebecca understood later that this was because, as well as coping with her tears, Elena was simultaneously experiencing the sexual tension of having her newly acquired lover nearby (his final degree show was a few feet from hers) and trying to hide this visceral passion from the husband she would shortly leave, but who was on the point of taking them all out to dinner to celebrate Elena's success in being awarded a first class honours for her B.A.

There had been a difficult moment earlier in the evening. Elena's marriage to Andrew was already on the rocks. He was a controlling kind of man, who when they were first married in their early twenties had made a concerted effort to separate Elena from her friends, and most of them had complied, but Rebecca was nothing if not tenacious. So she had hung around and in time, particularly when she had achieved a modicum of fame as a champion of vulnerable groups and appeared on television, he had come to accept and occasionally welcome her into their home.

He was not a bad man, even interesting, and not without a brain. He was a film buff and he read a lot, always a recommendation in a man. He was a successful commercial artist who earnt loads of money, so their home was a very nice one in a small village in the West Country.

When they were first married, Elena had been convinced they would live as equal partners – even if babies came along, they would do equal shares in their care.

How wrong could you be? A few years into the marriage, when a child did come along, he was the one earning the money and all childcare was done by Elena.

His world view was cynical and he was often churlish about other human beings. He was also prone to being cold and remote and Rebecca always felt there was a deep well spring of anger in him that for many years he managed to suppress.

Over time, this anger emerged. It emerged primarily in his relationship with, and attitude to, Elena.

If you looked you could see it emerge in direct ratio to her diminishing independence as a person and her increasing reliance on him for pay and rations. It also emerged attendant upon the increase in his expensive top-quality red wine imbibing which grew prodigiously with each passing year.

Rebecca's abiding memory of arriving to spend a few days at their house was of his disembodied voice calling from his upstairs studio: "Kettle," as she watched her ferocious friend running to put the said kettle on the inevitable Aga. It was a beautiful, traditional copper kettle, that at the same time was a symbol of her oh so comfortable oppression.

Nearly ten years later, its outsize like made an appearance as a piece of art work, tilted at a jaunty angle on an exquisite larger than life sized carved kitchen counter stool, with a cloud of vapour in the shape of a woman escaping from its spout.

This had been Elena's first serious piece of work in her foundation year at Art College.

Rebecca had always loved this symbol of her friend's re-appearance, and what would eventually be her bid for freedom.

Elena had been on the point of leaving Andrew before.

Their daughter was nearly seven and she reckoned they could make it without his financial help.

She and Andrew had been working together to produce a book for the Christmas market whose proofs had been delivered that day. Elena always swore that she had been going to break the news to him that she was going, but they had a drink to celebrate their success. Elena had done all the photography for the book and the layout and editing. They had almost been like comrades once more working on this project, their mutual anger put to one side temporarily. They felt fond of each other and one thing led to another. They had a final fuck to say goodbye and nine months later their son was born.

She stayed. Three years later she started her art degree.

On the celebration evening for Elena's final degree show, Rebecca had been walking round the show with Andrew when they came upon Elena's work.

The centre piece was a carved wooden dining table at Japanese dining size. There were four place settings on the table. The baby's setting was a smooth little plate with baby knife and fork almost without a kink. The bigger child's setting had some groves caused by the raised knife and the tines of the fork were slightly bent and distorted. The woman's place setting, next in size, had even deeper groves in the ceramic surface of the plate. The tines of the fork were bent over each other in a jumble and the knife bent and unusable. Then there was the male setting: supreme and largest of place. The plate was slashed by angry knife marks. The knife and fork curled round each other in an inextricable mess.

It was a shocking, violent, poignant piece of work.

It was called: *For What We Are About to Receive.*

Andrew looked at it dumbfounded, and then said: "She hates me. She really hates me."

Rebecca who could only silently concur, said nothing.

The divorce was long and bitter. It was disputatious in the extreme.

It left Elena and the children in poverty, but thankfully not homeless.

During it she managed to get her Master's degree and somehow bring up two children.

Rebecca helped out as best he could by taking Elena's children together with her own son on holidays.

The year that Rebecca first visited the Alpujarra, she had been on holiday with Elena and her children in a friend's house in a village in Almeria Province.

This was when she had taken her son Daniel and Elena's son Rory with her on the weekend visit Lucinda, who had once worked for Rebecca and had been a friend, and now lived with her partner in a small Andalusian village.

Later, when Rebecca had enough money and bought her house in the Alpujarra, Elena became a regular visitor during the summer holidays. Her husband was a long time ex by then, and her children were grown.

She was teaching sculpture for a living and making fascinating, edgy work.

She and Rebecca were easy together.

Rebecca was semi-retired and making time to do other things and where she could have fun.

They were good travelling companions and once a year for some years had taken to doing long haul trips to places they hankered to see.

The previous year they had gone to Myanmar. It had been a fabulous trip where they had made friends with almost the entire group of people with whom they were travelling.

They were the oldest people on the trip. There were a couple of Australian women in their late forties, and a man of around that age travelling with his daughter and her boyfriend. The others were young; most of them travelling as couples, with a few young women travelling alone. They were all interesting.

Elena and Rebecca had gelled with the Australian women when they shared the most uncomfortable sleeper ever on the most uncomfortable train ever that travelled on the most erratic rail system ever on the overnight journey from Yangon to Bagan.

The evening had started well. They had brought a picnic and some wine, got merry and sang every song they knew.

Rebecca and Elena had hysterics when the Aussies sang

Waltzing Mathilda for reasons they couldn't quite articulate at the time.

It had been fun, but as the journey progressed further into what turned into a polar cold night, the fun petered out.

Their guide had told them that the journey would bring some discomfort and that it might get a bit cool.

They had not been told that it would re-organise their spinal columns and they would freeze all night as they were being thrown violently around and even off the sleeper bunk, as the train pitched and ducked over the track.

Even worse was the bug overrun in the toilet at the back of the carriage, that had iron seats, no flush system and a hole out the bottom of the train and where it proved physically impossible to sit down even if you had dared to try, given the violence of the rocking motion of the train, and impossible to stand, given the same.

By the time morning dawned, going to pee felt like the most dangerous thing anyone had done in a long time.

One of the Australians had a fit bit that told her during the night she had walked over two hundred thousand steps. Their bodies were telling them this might actually be true. But when the morning dawned and it warmed up and with the prospect of breakfast in sight, they all agreed that one day in some far-off distant future, they might be able to laugh about it.

From this point on the holiday was a triumph. They climbed more exceedingly dangerous steps high up on to temples to witness sunrises and sets, saw exotic scenes of children dressed in gauzy multi-coloured splendour riding on baby elephants and jewelled horses down streets, buzzing with massively polluting contemporary traffic jams, enjoying the cacophony of a noisy ancient ceremony emerging from and merging in with modern traffic sound and chaos. They ate exquisite food whilst eschewing the buckets of fried insects they were frequently offered. They shopped and looked at art and had their senses spiced at every turn. They walked through strange countryside where the earth was sculpted into overlapping concentric circles of different coloured rice paddies. They watched the lines of priests queuing with their begging bowls every morning to be fed and marvelled at how all street animals also got fed in a Buddhist culture where every stray pigeon might just have been Uncle Fred returned in a new form.

Their guide, a lovely man who was a Christian christened them 'The Best Group Ever' and it stuck.

At the end of the holiday Elena drew a cartoon of him as a Koala Bear clinging to a tree, and Rebecca scoured Yangon market to find a frame for it, and they collected enough money from the group as a thank you to send his young son to school.

They left exchanging email addresses, became Facebook friends, and Rebecca invited people to visit her in Spain.

The year following this trip Rebecca and Elena were expecting three of the group from Myanmar who lived in Europe to spend a few days with them in the village.

These were young women: two from Belgium and one from Switzerland, who was coming without her partner, Johnnie.

The Belgians – Elisa and Noor – were best friends. They had known each other since school and now shared a flat in Ghent. They were both graduates but not interested in having careers. They wanted to travel, so worked to save the money, in financial services, in insurance companies, where mostly they had phone jobs dealing with consumer enquiries, but thankfully were not called upon to cold call selling insurance. When they had enough, they would plan a trip.

Their next one in the autumn would be back to South East Asia, maybe staying in Thailand on beach to celebrate

Elisa's thirtieth birthday. Sophia, the very beautiful Swiss woman, taught at an Infant school in Aura at the foot of the Jura Mountains.

They spent four very easy days, going with their hosts to the beach and the pool, and by themselves to visit Granada, bringing back lovely thank you presents of a tablecloth and some ceramic bowls.

On the last day they went with Jo to do a recently opened walk around the lower and higher *acequias* near to the village, which had the great advantage of having shade in the late afternoon that made it suitable for a summer walk, when everything else was baking in the glaring sun.

That night they went out for *tapas*. There were six of them around the table, split into separate conversations. At one point in the evening, Noor said to Rebecca: "We really admire you and Elena. Elisa and me we aim to be friends for life as you have been. We met at school too, though we can't match your stories of constant trouble, but like you we travel well together."

"And what will happen if either of you got interested in a relationship with a man?" Rebecca asked. She didn't know or care if they were lesbians, but she thought they probably didn't have a sexual relationship.

"Well," said Noor, "clearly we are both free to go off and have an adventure if we want, but I hope it wouldn't mean we would cease to be friends. I hope we will always find a way of coming back to each other."

"Well we always have," said Rebecca, "despite men making an occasional appearance and children taking up our attention for what seemed like a while – so I'm sure you can do it, too".

Rebecca added, though not much prone to giving relationship advice as she did consider her own sadly failed attempts at personal partnerships as offering any kind of role model for others: "In my experience you just have to hang on in there, particularly if your friend choses a man who turns out to be controlling, and remind yourself that one day she will come to her senses and may need you to help her grow her courage to leave." She paused, then added: "Clearly not all men are controlling, and a good one would not try to close you out – but you may be surprised by the number who seem to need to corral and isolate and then break their women."

Later the lovely Sophia, who had had a fair amount of wine, came to sit next to her.

"You look sad, Sophia. What's troubling you?" and then her story poured out.

Rebecca had her back to the rest of the table so she was shielding Sophia from scrutiny, whilst Sophia's sadness became even more apparent when tears started rolling down her cheeks.

"I have been trying to get pregnant for a long while."

"How long?"

"Two years."

"Are you doing the awful IVF?"

"Yes, and it's not working."

"How many rounds have you done?"

"We've finished the second round before I came away, but I found out today it hasn't worked. I can't think of anything else. I feel as if my life will be completely empty if I cannot have a child of my own."

"How old are you, Sophia?"

"I'm thirty five."

"There is still time. You have at least five years. Look at me, I got pregnant by compete accident when I was thirty eight and looking the other way. There really is still time for you."

Sophia gave her a sad smile: "I hope so."

They hugged and Rebecca wanted to convey in that hug

all the good things that one woman can wish for another across the generations and in the tender understanding of how individual women will feel about and deal with the ever noisier ticking of their own biological time clock and the very personal decisions around the having or the not having of children.

From the other end of the table Jo asked the visitors what they had enjoyed most about their trip.

"For me," said Elisa, "it was the walk today."

The others agreed and they told Elena all about their walk as she had stayed home working on a piece of artwork for an exhibition she was having when she got back. Jo asked them to remind her how they had all met and they told their story and had a lot of fun talking about their wonderful holiday together in Myanmar. They even told Jo about the terrible, epic train journey they had taken from Rangoon to Bagan where from their part of train they had heard the drunken singing of the mad older English and Australian women and all felt envious that they were not in the same carriage sharing the fun.

The evening ended late and their guests were due to leave early the following day to catch their flights home.

The following day they said goodbye and vowed to keep in touch and meet up again in London or Ghent, or maybe Switzerland, though to date they haven't done so – though they keep in touch via Facebook and send each other birthday wishes as the years roll by.

After the initial flurries of thank you emails, Rebecca didn't hear anything else until a Christmas card told her that Sophia was pregnant without the need for a further round of IVF.

Sophie thought it was either an accident or a miracle.

I know how that feels, Rebecca said to herself. *Sometimes in life good things happen to decent people; and doesn't life feel hopeful when they do.*

Some months later Sophia and Johnnie's daughter was born, and two years later she was followed by a son.

THREE NIGHTS OF SEXUAL EXPLORATION
WITH LOUISE

Initially Joanna had not known what to make of Louise. She had made her booking through AirB&B months before her visit, but before making it she had sent a number of emails asking polite and meticulous questions about the region: it's activities; the amenities in the nearby villages; whether it was safe to walk alone in the mountains; what kind of birds and wild flora she might anticipate coming across if she were, for example, to come in May, which was her preferred option. Joanna did her best to answer these questions.

So, in January when there was snow high in the Sierras and the vicious winds of winter were blowing their fullest, as she turned the gas heater up high and sat behind her desk, she tried to imagine herself in the warmer kindness of May. She answered every email diligently and each answer brought forth another batch of seemingly increasingly anxious enquiries. She began to wonder about the age and vulnerability of her potential guest and as subtly as she could she enquired back about Louise's level of fitness and physical robustness, telling her that these mountains were serious and could take their toll on the unprepared and the unfit.

She did make it clear that there was walking to be enjoyed at every level but with heights of up to three thousand five hundred metres (the village was at thirteen hundred metres), walking on the flat was not really any kind of option. What she didn't add was that a family of six had got into trouble climbing the highest peak in August, the previous year and as they were completely unprepared for serious mountain walking. Indeed it was said they had gone up in tee shirts, shorts and trainers, only to experience a white out which reduced summer temperatures to winter in minutes, which also caused them to lose their way. Three of them, including the husband and two of the children, had perished in a tragedy that would excite pity and morbid interest in equal measures for years to come. The others who had been rescued were in a fairly poor state, though they had survived.

Louise's response read firstly as curt and to the point.

"I've just had my sixtieth birthday and I'm a regular walker with a reasonable level of fitness. You do not need to worry about me. I am told I am an artist of self-sufficiency."

The more Joanna read this response, the more she saw a cryptic humour in it. Louise, she thought might be prim and controlled but she might also have enough irony in her soul and humour in her craw to make her interesting.

Eventually Louise made her booking for three nights. She would arrive and hire a car from the airport and drive herself to the village. This in itself perked Joanna's interest. Many women – and indeed men, though they were less prepared to admit it – were scared of the mountain roads.

They were full of hairpin bends in the wrong places and sudden steep drops unprotected by safety barriers. In some travellers the altitude induced minor nausea and symptoms close to labyrinthitus. In others the journey induced fear, but it clearly did not occur to Louise that she should be scared.

Joanna thought about the term Louise had used to describe herself 'an artist of self-sufficiency' and concluded that it might prove to be accurate.

Louise arrived around seven p.m. on the first Wednesday in May and would stay until Saturday. She planned to have days of 'rest n recuperation' as she called it, before driving off to Córdoba and then Seville from whence she would fly back to London. She said she had had a long day and was grateful that Joanna had agreed to provide her with a meal for the evening in addition to daily breakfast as she didn't really fancy having to find a restaurant that evening, and she understood that El Paraje, the only restaurant in the village, was closed on a Wednesday evening.

"Even when they're open," said Joanna, "they don't start serving until nine, and that's considered early in Spanish time. Even though we've been here for six years now we haven't really adjusted entirely to Spanish time, so I plan to feed you at eight after you've had a chance to unpack, get settled in and take a shower if you want one. Is that ok for you?"

"Lovely, that all sounds lovely," said Louise.

Joanna sat with her while she ate. They exchanged some pleasantries. She discovered that Louise was an Employment Law barrister who had a history of political activism and thought her profession might have something to do with her seemingly forensic precision.

First night: Louise Discovers the Pitfalls of Being a Passionate Woman

They were sitting upstairs on the roof terrace in the cooling evening. Supper had been dispensed with and a third glass of wine poured. Louise looked up at Joanna with a shy smile.

"I wasn't always so self-contained," she said. "I feel as if life trapped me in this corner, and in a way this journey is my chance to examine what I can do about it, if anything, while I still have time and before I turn the corner into real old age. Do you mind if I talk about it?"

Intrigued beyond measure Joanna responded: "Actually,

I have to admit to being fascinated and I'd be honoured to listen." Louise smiled a broader, warmer smile than Joanna had supposed possible.

"Well, where to begin?" And, over another bottle, her story began to be told.

"When I was young, I think I was scared of sex. I know I was scared of the consequences of sex – not just the possibility that I might get pregnant: a fate worse than death for a girl in my day of illegal abortion and no contraception. By the time sex became a possibility I was already planning to be the first in my family to go to university. I was on my way out of the working class and each step was into the unknown. I had no idea how to behave in middle clasville – nor did I clearly aspire to being there and, besides, 'there' seemed like such a foreign land across an impassable and impossible chasm.

"I never had what you might call a boyfriend at school. I was wary of the male. Looking back I think what really scared me was the power over me, having sex would, cede to the male. I loved my dad but he was volatile to put it mildly – maybe even a bit mad. So he didn't give me a very useful model of what normal ought to look like.

In those days, the male was the initiator. We knew so little about our bodies. I knew I got pleasure from touching myself, but I didn't even know it was called masturbation. I did have some skirmishes of a sexual kind. They ended abruptly and certainly without taking my virginity. But I was hypersensitive to the way in which the attitude of the boy to me changed as a result of me giving up my power to him. I was not naturally assertive sexually – though I was in many other ways. I didn't know what to ask for and was too embarrassed to put my desires into words.

"I think Erica Yong, years later, in one of her books called what we wanted the 'zipless fuck'. This was some years before feminism came into our lives and we all started examining the clitoris and the cervix and wondering where to find the G spot. We'd been brought up on a diet of romance where the encounter with the hero ended at the bedroom door with you swooning in his arms. We knew there would be a wave of bliss that would somehow be caused by the insertion into the vagina of a penis, but we would somehow be in a floaty parallel universe to these most basic facts of life."

At this Joanna snorted some wine through her nose. No doubt remembering the absurdities of what it was to be a girl before you were a woman, way back then.

"I saw no way out of this dilemma and then a friend introduced me to the pill.

You had to pretend to be engaged and on the point of marriage, telling this story to some seedy bent doctor in the Elephant and Castle, to get six months' supply. He, in any case, was only interested in the money, but you didn't know that at the time. My act was convincing enough as I sat before him twisting the plastic, pretend silver-plated diamante engagement ring I had bought earlier that day for the purpose from Woolworths around my finger.

Equipped with the magic pill, I decided the next move was to lose my virginity. I already had a trip planned to Paris with another friend and on our first day we picked up two guys on the metro and went back to stay with them, emerging some days later.

"It took four consecutive nights of attempts to break my hymen and was unpleasant. I gave him full marks for persistence and effort and nil points for subtlety, but that was probably unfair. Also he turned out to be a really nice young man who wrote to me for years afterwards about the ups and downs of his love life. Still, however unsatisfactorily: mission accomplished.

"This all happened in my final year in the sixth form, when

I was doing 'A' levels and was applying to universities. I had already decided to take a year out before university to travel.

I applied to Camp America, which was just getting established, to be a helper and was accepted. I fetched up in Camp Monroe in New York State and six weeks later I was being inducted into camp life in early June, with camp lasting two months. There were roughly a hundred staff members, split down the middle in gender terms. It was 1969. Rebellion was in the air. Woodstock was billed for later in August and Jefferson Aeroplane and Crosby, Stills and Young were being played everywhere. Also, there was dope and my body had, as a result of my Parisian adventure, moved through the pain of sexual initiation and in our increasing permissiveness as a generation it was the days when it was deemed rude to say 'no'.

"Armed with the pill, I had many sexual adventures. Most were fumbles in the dark and, in the end, totally unsatisfactory. But I was enjoying the adventure and didn't see why I shouldn't do precisely what would have been applauded in the behaviour of the guys.

I became aware that I was getting what was called a reputation, and that what was assumed to be a more liberated time in fact carried all the baggage of Victoriana about its person when it came to the female of the species. I found I had gone from being too good a girl to being too free a girl in the space of a few months.

"I did not at all like the way those young men began to look at me after their fumbled attempts at fucking. No doubt, were I to revisit this short period with a more mature and kindly disposition, I would get to understand the insecurities and pain of their awkward, not yet post teenage selves.

But growing up is brutal, and at the time it feels like there is more pain than gain.

I withdrew from the fray but only because I fell in love

with my boss: the ultimate cliché! Young woman with no power falls under the spell of the most powerful, authoritative man around and seduces him. Not that it took huge effort. In those days I had a body to die for and he was, despite his marital status, up for temptation. Without doubt the sex was better and it really woke me up to desire. It did not entirely satisfy my desire as our meetings were fleeting and often conducted in uncomfortable surroundings: once in an orchard – often outside. Don't ask; and that's probably enough information

"Anyway, I imagined myself in love, and maybe I was. I was grateful that this older man had wanted me – even if it was all slightly tacky. Of course, I never thought about his wife or any of those issues of betrayal in a marriage. To justify myself I had to bury her deep. I am clear of course that sisterhood was not at the top of my agenda – but I was in love and ridiculously believed at some level that he would leave her and come to me. Jokes!

"Anyway, it set up a pattern for the next few years – falling for unobtainable men and having affairs that were meant to be secret.

It made the sex deeply intense and saved me from the tedium of having to work at a real life relationship. I lost myself in the sexual intensity and kept my autonomy intact. To be fair to myself, I never had an affair with the husband or boyfriend of a friend – though believe me I had many offers over the next few years, including said husbands climbing into bed with me when I was staying overnight when I would pretend to be asleep and wait until they were before I got up and left the house.

"I think the real reason I adopted the affairs pattern was that I didn't have the inner strength to keep my identity intact and negotiate a balance of power in a real life relationship.

I think the good little girl inside me would have given up

territory to the needs of the male in my life. In reality I was still not assertive enough – was not sure enough of my own identity to carve out my space and defend it in a partnership of equals – which, of course, we all would have said we wanted and some of us would claim we had friends who had achieved – though later of course many of these marriages ended in tears and loathing, tearing all around them apart. So now at this later stage of my life, I can't decide if my strategies were good survival techniques or simple cowardice in the face of bad luck or bad choice of partners.

Mind you, in so many of the couples I know who have stayed together, rather than achieving equality one partner dominates and the other bends to their will, and in my experience the dominant one is sometimes the woman, but mostly it is the man."

Louise had been talking for hours. It was way past midnight. The second bottle was nearing empty and tomorrow there would likely be headaches. They said goodnight. Louise staggered off to bed and Joanna thought to herself. *Wow! That was quite an evening. Who'd have thought it?*

She made her own way to bed where she found Thomas asleep and partly slumped on her side of the bed. She smiled indulgently and pushed him back on his own side.

The following day Louise turned up to breakfast before nine, already showered and ready for a day's walking. Joanna, who had found getting up to make breakfast more of a struggle than usual, was amazed at the alert togetherness of her guest.

She was still trying to deal with that wine stale feeling that felt like the badger's armpit in her mouth and the regret it inevitably brings. Louise looked positively perky.

"I seem to remember filling up your glass fairly often last night and have no idea how you can look as well as you do this morning."

Louise smiled at her: "Well I didn't tell you but I spent a few years working for a trades union and I learnt a few lessons there about consuming alcohol and recovering from it. If you're interested maybe I'll tell you more this evening."

"I wanted to say how fascinated I was by your tale last night and I'd certainly like to hear more if you're prepared to tell it. But right now just let me clear away and I'll drive you to the start of the walk."

Louise had planned a circular walk in the high Sierra and Joanna had agreed to drive her to the start as it needed a four by four to get up twenty odd kilometres of track in the National Park and over a thousand metres of climb to get there. They said little on the drive up. There was something about the clarity of the air and the bird song audible even over the sound of the diesel engine that kept them silent. Also the intimacies of the previous evening seemed slightly embarrassing between still virtual strangers by light of day.

As they climbed the delicate fresh smell of the spring flowers was just discernible in the still cool of the morning. There were fields of poppies growing through the cultivated crops; their scarlet presence a surprise. The smell of the broom bushes that grow abundantly and from time a time the bold but not unpleasant scent of wild garlic were all borne on the breeze.

There is something about the majestic beauty of these mountains that is balm for the soul to which it brings its easy peace.

They had climbed up through the cultivated fields, up through the olive trees and vines, though almond groves alas beyond the time of blossom, up through the fields being prepared for the later crops of tomatoes and helda beans, up through the black ash trees and the prickly oaks, up through the woods of pines and now beyond the tree line. Still they were climbing. The scenery grew more majestic. There was extensive snow on the peaks – still too far distant to be a problem. There were *cortijos* even this high up where the shepherds would bring the flocks later in the summer.

A few times Louise had heard the sound of bells that announced a herd somewhere in the hills. Joanna told her that mostly they were mixed herds of goats and sheep and that though the herd dogs might sound ferocious if she came across one as long as she made it clear she was not interested in taking any of their charges, they would leave her alone.

From time to time there was a stream, some swollen with the pure run off from the slowly melting snow: others still a trickle but all glinting against their stone beds in the light of a sun rising in the sky.

On the horizon, swooping in circles was a pair of birds of prey. They were too far off to identify, but Joanna said: "I think they're eagles" and the sight was thrilling.

They arrived. There was a path off to the left with a sign to the Sulayr.

"The walk should take you four hours or so. It is way-marked quite well. You've got the map but if you should get lost try phoning me. There are places where you can get a signal. My advice is that you should re-trace your steps back to the last way mark and try reading the map. Sometimes people leave cairns that are mostly helpful in getting you back on track.

Sorry I can't join you. I'd love to as it's such a beautiful day for a walk but it's also market day. We only get two a month and I need to shop. I'll come back to pick you up at the end of the walk in four hours."

"It's fine, Joanna. I'm actually looking forward to some thinking time and a bit of solitude – wonderful though your company would be. Also, I can read a map quite well. I didn't do that six week Rambler's orienteering course for nothing," and with that Louise climbed slightly stiff legged out of the jeep, took up her walking poles, adjusted her backpack and set off.

Joanna turned the jeep around and headed off back down the track and just before she disappeared round a bend they waved.

As she changed up through the gears, Joanna thought: *She's an intriguing character and I'd love to know more of what's on her mind.*

For Louise the walk was all she had hoped it would be.

The eagles seemed to follow her path for a while, hovering over their prey ahead of her. Swooping occasionally and eventually one of the pair rose triumphantly with something – a rabbit – maybe in its talons and they made off.

Later she saw, albeit in the distance some wild mountain goats she had read were shy and reclusive. Otherwise, it was uneventful. She didn't see any of the wild boar people had warned her to avoid, particularly in their breeding season which had to be around now.

At one stage she had a rest and drank some of the water in her drinking bottle and ate the fruit that Joanna had packed for her. She made good time and was pleased to see Joanna's jeep waiting for her as she ended her walk.

Second Night: Louise discovers the perils for powerful women of being sexually available

After her walk Louise indulged in a *siesta*, and then she pottered around the village getting to know it. The church door was open and she wandered in to find the village women cleaning and arranging the flowers.

In Spain there is a saying that unmarried women – spinsters – are good only for dressing martyrs. In every village these women become like unofficial church wardens, lovingly tending the statues of saints and polishing the glass cases of relics and bones of the saints.

She was surprised that the church was a simple but pleasing and peaceful space, with little gold paint and no gaudy artefacts. She had never been a religious woman and would have denied having a faith, but she was tolerant of the faith of others.

She left them to their devotions and found her way back to Joanna's through the narrow winding streets.

Supper was a hearty stew. Tonight she ate with Joanna and Thomas, and after he went off to watch the inevitable football match she found herself climbing the stairs to their roof terrace where Joanna was already opening the bottle. They both swore they would not go on to a second this evening.

"So, what happened to you after Camp America?" Joanna asked her, to get the conversation going. "You said this morning you had worked for a trades union and learnt a thing or two about alcohol?"

"Ah," said Louise, and began.

"Well, I went to university in the North of England, in Newcastle, and got a degree – a good one – so I knew I had a brain.

I'd always been a socialist and at university I became a dedicated second wave feminist. I sat in all male bars until I got served a drink – in most I never got served a drink – but I did sit in the bars until I got very bored and had a sense of humour failure, feeling the hostility and resentment of the men, many of them miners. Some of them I saw at Labour Party meetings and they were very embarrassed to confront me in the bars.

I started the university crèche. I helped to set up a free school. I sat in meetings with other women looking at our cervixes – but only the once. I protested beauty contests and once when the medical student hired strippers for an end of year party I glued the locks so they couldn't get into the room to be told by the irate organiser that no one would want to screw me anyway – which didn't seem remotely relevant, but did have a strange impact on one of the male comrades supporting the action. When I laughingly repeated to him what the medic had said, he put his hand on my arm and consolingly said: 'Oh, I'm sure he didn't mean it,' which temporarily confused me and then made me laugh even harder as some arsehole not wanting to screw you was clearly a cause of pity and consolation. It was clear to me that with many of our male comrades, we had a very long journey yet to undertake on this road to equality.

"I got involved in student politics and after university I drifted into working for a union. What I discovered as I grew into positions of power was that the easiest way to undermine a woman in those positions was through her sexuality. I made it my duty to get other women promoted, too.

I would persuade talented women to put themselves forward for positions. I started women's committees and schools where women could learn how to speak in public and become more confident. I did this right across the political spectrum and even trained and worked with conservative women because if we were going to turn the tide we needed the numbers, and besides sisterhood was pluralistic – it's an all women thing and I'm not by nature sectarian.

I supported campaigns to get women into public life; into parliament, into positions of power in the trades unions, the church, banking and professions and later on to the boards of companies.

At the same time I shamed the male leaders of these organisations who publicly at least espoused greater equality into putting women on their slate for elections.

My younger self was not entirely subtle and as a student I remember telling them that if they didn't support women candidates, I would probably break their legs – but I did get more subtle with age. I remember I had a huge laugh on one occasion before a hustings meeting for local council elections helping a conservative woman write her speech and practically having to put a peg on my nose when she told me what she wanted to say – still mine was not to reason the whys and whats of other people's belief: the bigger picture was all, and the world had to be changed fundamentally if women were ever to be really free and equal.

"So, I was working for a trades union. Hilariously, at my first ever annual meeting of full time officials I inadvertently led a walkout when the newly elected President was making his first address to the officers in a post dinner speech. He cracked a joke about women with their legs open.

What to do? I didn't want to do anything but up with this I could not put. I decided to just leave quietly and that's what I did. Shortly afterwards I was followed by the only other woman full time official in our region. Our male colleagues who claimed – and some genuinely had – a commitment to gender equality, one by one got up and left. This did not go unnoticed and the next day the President asked to see me to ask why I had done it and I explained the jokes about women's uncrossed legs were no longer acceptable. He got to like me – said he appreciated my honesty – and as a result I found myself going on a trade's union delegation to visit our counterpart Union in Poland.

"I hadn't had sex for two years or more. I had had offers and tentative approaches, but I always felt the accompanying power play with a kind of livid embarrassment. I had learnt in America and beyond that a woman could not be a sexual adventurer in a way that would have been applauded in men without falling into the stereotype of the slut in the eyes of those around her. I had learnt that I was clearly sensitive still to the way others would see me and knew that I needed to have my power and authority reflected back to me in the eyes of those around me for it to feel real to me.

I was genuinely growing in experience and skill, but my seeming confidence was still too easily undermined, and it felt like sexuality was the heart of the vulnerability.

I was hypersensitive to the subtle shift in the attitude of men who approached me sexually. Despite their many espoused enlightened views, I did not doubt that getting their leg over would also involve a power take over. Hence, this is the explanation for my lack of sex during this period.

"During our trip we had a minibus, a driver and a guide and interpreter. The guide/interpreter was a very good looking young man and over the period of the week we were travelling together I admit I was drawn to him. He was slightly shy but kind and funny; very blond and blue eyed with a powerful muscular body and really attractive and I was horny.

I was travelling with a few of my union colleagues. One of these was a disgusting, almost obese, chain smoking, nicotine stained, overly hairy, bearded, potbellied and often slightly smelly man with very nasty politics. His name was Barry Savoury and the joke the women in the union made of him was that he should be re-named Barry Un-Savoury.

Despite his myriad physical, philosophical and intellectual challenges he had something of a reputation as a lothario and women, even those who joked about him seemed to make themselves sexually available on a regular basis. He had always left me well alone as he loathed my politics as avidly as I loathed his.

I happened to know from a female colleague on my national women's committee that he had left her with a crop of genital warts that had been hard to shift. He was, nevertheless, the senior member of the delegation and nominally had something of a pastoral role in the care of the rest of us.

"Coming back from a visit to our hotel one night I was sitting next to the lovely young interpreter.

He had been making those special eye connections with me during much of the day. We had a journey of perhaps an hour to go. It was very late and very dark inside the van. He held my hand and I felt that lovely tingling shock of sexual recognition.

One thing led rather to the next and before long I felt his hand creep up my leg inside my skirt and he began to play around the line of my pants. Each stroke was like a gentle, then more powerful electric charge. My legs just opened and his hand found my clitoris and his stroking and probing. His finger found my vagina and the thrill of his entering me was divine and irresistible.

Ostensibly we were sitting side by side looking at the non-existent view given the darkness of the night, but with this furiously engaging sexual encounter going on beneath the surface. I touched his penis through his trousers and it was as hard as my own desire.

"We eventually got back to the hotel. My new friend withdrew his hand and I withdrew mine from him. I whispered: 'Thank you but I can't invite you in and I can't explain why not. I'm sorry'. He looked bitterly disappointed and I felt it, too. I wanted him – but I couldn't have him because I couldn't allow my colleagues to see me as an active sexual being and there was no way to smuggle him into my room unseen."

Joanna was looking at her open mouthed and a little breathless.

Louise continued. "But there is a sequel to this story that is really the point of it.

When we got back to the hotel I went up to my room and the rest of the delegation went to the bar. I had a bath and got ready for bed. In fact I was in bed reading my latest novel when there was a knock at my door. It wasn't locked and I called out to whoever was out there to come in.

Imagine my surprise when in walked my Un-Savoury senior colleague, swaying slightly and clutching a large glass of red wine that he offered to share with me as he sat down in the chair next to my bed. I looked at him in astonishment. He said: 'I've always had a secret soft spot for you,' looking at me with a lasciviousness he had never previously exhibited. Maybe it was the memory of the genital warts' episode, but he made me feel nauseous and every instinct in me felt compelled to get him out of the room. I told him it was never going to happen; that I didn't happen to share what he called this soft spot and asked him if he would please leave, much as I had enjoyed our little talk.

To my surprise he shrugged and got up muttering he thought it had been worth a try. I was fairly sure he had not seen, smelt or otherwise discerned consciously the sexual activity going on behind him in the dark on the minibus – though I couldn't be sure.

Bugger me, I thought, it must be pheromonal this impulse of men to humiliate, undermine and control uppity women of whom they disapprove and with whom they disagree, through sexual conquest.

I was quite shaken up, but I eventually went to sleep thinking about our gentle Polish translator and how delicious it might have been to have him beside me."

At this Joanna started to laugh. "Louise, you are full of surprises: yet another amazing story."

Their conversation drifted on to other things. Joanna told her more about life in these mountains and she shared some of the stories of guests had told her. The next hour went by in draining the bottle they'd brought up with them and their evening ended convivially when Thomas joined them for a beer after his televised football match ended.

"So what have you two found to talk about all evening?" he asked, but neither of them thought it was entirely appropriate to tell him.

The following day was a different walk setting off from the village, walking through a very different terrain but much lower through the Contraviesa where the local vineyards and the almond trees held sway.

Over breakfast and before her walk she asked if she could take Joanna and Thomas out to supper that evening. They didn't usually accept invitations from guests, but Joanna had developed an easy rapport with Louise and didn't feel she could say no when Louise told her it was a sort of celebration for her sixtieth birthday, which had otherwise gone unacknowledged. They agreed nothing fancy – not that that was easy to achieve fancy in any case in the culinary desert that is the mountains – but they would go to the village restaurant for *tapas*. Thomas thanked her for the invitation and said that if they didn't mind he would join them for a drink once that night's match had finished.

Louise had enjoyed her day. She walked, taking a picnic lunch all the way down the hills to the little town of Ugijar where ten years before Joanna and Thomas had stayed while they searched for a place to set up their business and their new lives. There were many more English people in Ugijar than Louise expected, and not just English. She heard German and Dutch and a smattering of French accents and idioms in the cafes where she stopped to have a drink. At four p.m. she caught the bus back to the village as Joanna had instructed her to do. She was looking forward to having some company for her final evening.

Third Evening: Louise faces a sexual and existential crisis.

As they sat on the terrace at El Paraje waiting for their tapas to arrive, they enjoyed the last rays of the descending sun; Louise asked Jo how many foreigners lived in the village.

"Well I think there are about twenty families in this village. The population as a whole is around twelve hundred. Some of the younger ones have children, but most are older people; mostly retired who've come here because they love it but also to eke out English pensions. We're lucky. Thomas works in industrial design and his boss wanted to keep him on – so he works through the internet. I guess he goes back to the UK nearly every quarter to have essential meetings – but mostly he can work from here. This business runs from spring through to November. We don't get that many guests in the winter, but there are some. Winters are short here, thought they can be severe with icy winds and every so often there's snowfall."

Jo wanted to hear the continuation of Louise's story.

"So, did you stop having sexual adventures?" she asked, "Have you ever been married?"

"No to both questions; but I have from time to time lived with men, though the longest I ever lasted was a couple of years. I've had a couple of longer term relationships that endured because we didn't live together, but I am now facing a dilemma. It's really the reason I came, because I wanted to think."

"Can you tell me about it?"

Louise swallowed and then continued. "Ok: here goes...

"Do you know that Joni Mitchell Song *Cactus Tree*? It's from her first album, *Song to the Seagull*, which is still my favourite of all her albums. It came out in my first year at

223

university and over the Easter of that year I had hired a cottage on the coast with my then boyfriend and a mutual friend of ours. This was a guy who ended up going into the music business and he always had the best music first. We played that album on continuous all that weekend.

We were staying in a grey cottage in a grey and bleak little village with April winds whipping grey black clouds through skies full of foreboding and frequent rain showers, but we were inside with wood fires banked, toasting bread for tea and listening to a non-stop diet of Joni and smoking the odd joint.

I remember I cooked the only thing I really knew how to cook then which was spaghetti bolognaise, and we were cosy.

I was drawn to this song and I think it's still my favourite Joni song:

There's a lady in the city
And she thinks she loves them all
There's the one who's thinking of her
There's the one who sometimes calls
There's the one who writes her letters
With his facts and figures scrawl
She has brought them to her senses
They have laughed inside her laughter
Now she rallies her defences
For she fears that one will ask her
For eternity
And she's so busy being free.

"The upshot of the song is that her quest for her freedom makes her heart full and hollow like the cactus tree.

At the time I didn't really know why I liked that song so much, but over the years I recognized that I could only really love if they came to my senses; if they laughed inside my laughter. If I called the shots, I still felt free.

But the sting was the heart that was both full and hollow and boy, I was terrified that one would ask me for eternity and the awful thing is that now one has. Or at least I think he has."

Jo looked at her and seemed on the point of asking a question, but in the end merely said: "And he is?"

"Oh, he is the love of my life. Our lives have been intertwined for the last thirty years.

Many years ago he asked me to marry him; but I wouldn't. In fact, his asking me made me very angry. We were going to spend the weekend together and if he had taken me to a romantic country hotel where we had made rampant love all night it might well have been different – but he didn't.

He wanted the visit to be a surprise and we fetched up in the house of his best – probably his only boyhood friend.

This friend, Andrew, nice enough in his way, was renovating an old country house. He was married to Mary and they had two young children. Mary had given up her career to be a housebound mother. John and I slept on a lumpy old mattress in an attic with bare boards and a lot of dust. The house was cold. We couldn't have sex because every time we attempted it the rafters and joists creaked like the floor was going to fall through – so it was not conducive to intimacy. It rained all weekend. The children were grumpy and Mary so utterly resentful of her lot that she and Andrew bickered and by the end of the weekend weren't even pretending to stop when John and I were around. To top it all, she was a terrible cook and her shepherd's pie was lumpy and grey.

As this awful weekend progressed I grew progressively angrier without being able to articulate why. Well, there was no time just for ourselves as we had to be good polite guests. I was partly relieved when we left but couldn't even talk to John on our drive back as he had one of those boys own sports cars I always hated. You couldn't hear any conversation over the noise of the bloody engine and then – for me the last straw – the canvas hood started leaking water. So I was cold, hungry, wet and very angry.

When we got to London I stopped him at the first tube station we came across and just left.

"I didn't hear from him again for a long time. Then, about two years later, he phoned and asked me if we could meet at a restaurant for dinner that night. I was intrigued and said yes.

Clearly, I wondered why, and it turned out it was to tell me that he was getting married the following day.

I asked him why he wanted to see me: was it to rub my nose in it? Did he want me to rescue him? Did he know why he had wanted this meeting?

Of course he didn't. That was not the end of the story. He turned up again a few years later when the marriage was unhappy by which stage there were children and, inevitably, we became lovers.

Our sexual adventure flourished and I would call what we experienced paradise and the real thing – whatever that is. He was on the point of leaving his wife several times. He never did and at a low point in my life he was guilty of a very painful betrayal of my trust – from which I found it difficult to recover.

"I had not seen him for nearly ten years. Then out of the blue I got a letter from him, delivered by email.

It just happened to arrive on the day I was returning from the funeral of a good friend. This was someone I'd worked with for many years. I had spent the funeral crying with her family and sharing a small part of their grief. I was feeling vulnerable and the moment was poignant.

It was a cold day last December. I got on the train to travel home when the grey clouds parted and late afternoon sun flooded through illuminating the sky in a way that made your heart full and heavy and ping into my email his letter was delivered.

He just said how empty his life was without me in it. That he had been in therapy for the last five years and he now felt he understood and regretted his behaviour.

We've met often since then and we've talked and written endlessly. The sex, when we resumed physical contact, was still divine. Still feels so right. He says he wants to end his marriage: he believes he has changed and he wants to ask me for whatever time we have left. Clearly at our age this will not exactly be eternity...

"I came here to think about what I should do."

"So," said Jo, "Do you know what you want to do?"

"Well," said Louise with a wry smile, "I want to believe him. If what he says is true, maybe there is a chance for us to explore what could be the greatest of human adventures. We are both in our sixties. I'm not going to retire yet but over time I'll work less and travel more, have fun. It would be very nice to have someone to have fun with.

We like similar things: music and theatre and politics. So, one bit of me really wants this to work. The other bit is still fearful of my autonomy; still doesn't know that if I were in a bound relationship I would keep my identity intact or merely collapse into his will.

Yet, another bit is fearful that leopards don't change their spots even when they've been in therapy and those five years, in any case, may not be enough to undo the total screwed up nature of the previous fifty five. I have been so betrayed by him before. So: no.

If this were the agony page of women's magazine I would describe myself as sixty year old confused from Carshalton. I really don't know which way to turn, but maybe I will just go with the flow.

It's not as if there is much drama going on in the rest of my life – but I'm also not sure how much drama I want."

Louise's story was done.

Joanna didn't quite know what to make of it, though she did understand that in anyone's life there is more than one narrative at work and each narrative may have many strands – not all of them are coherent and most are not neat.

"So," said Louise, "tell me something about your marriage. Is it happy?"

"Well," said Jo, but she didn't get any further because at that moment Thomas arrived to claim his post-match drink, and neither of the women felt it was appropriate to talk about such an intimate subject in the circumstances.

"Have you had a pleasant evening?" he asked Louise.

"Yes," she said, "It's been great. Joanna is a wonderful listener and I fear I have done most of the talking and I should probably pay her as a therapist on top of my bill."

"Don't worry," he said with a knowing twinkle in his eye, "Jo tells me it's all part of the service. So, tell us, what route do you plan to take to Cordoba tomorrow?"

"Well, I hoped you might advise me."

"With pleasure," said Thomas, and he began to outline the available routes she might decide to take.

BREXIT HEARTACHE OR DOWN AND OUT IN THE ALPUJARRA AND LONDON

When she thought back on the outpouring of emotion that followed the outcome of the UK's referendum on leaving the European Union, she also thought about the other times in her life she had seen the phlegmatic British give unaccustomed way to possibly equally unaccustomed feelings.

The stereotypes of the British were of moments of cold bloodied calm at times when Johnnie Foreigner was likely to lose his head. The British, with a pole firmly stuck up their bottoms to keep their backbones straight and true, could take command in any crisis as if it were a natural birth right. This trait had underpinned the creation and sustenance of the British Empire.

It was either that image that predominated, or the other equally hard, though infinitely less cultured, image of beer-bodied, much tattooed, lager louts pissing and puking their way through Magaluf, looking for a fight.

The extremes of the toff and the troll: one endlessly polite and formal, the other hopelessly ill-mannered and vulgar, but, both in their own way, ruthless machines.

These were the absurdly male images, remote from and unmoved by the plight of others that summed up the British in the minds of other nationalities. But, from time to time, the outer shell cracked, revealing deep if unarticulated emotion even more powerful and unpredictable for being so well controlled or hidden so much of the time.

The first occasion she had witnessed the cracking of the

shell that she could remember was 22nd November 1963 with the assassination of President Kennedy who, along with super glamorous Jackie, had captured British hearts and minds almost like a faux monarch. It was the first time she had experienced the knowing precisely where you were at the moment when historic events occur, though the emotion it evoked was shock.

The second event was the disaster at Aberfan, and the catastrophic collapse of a colliery spoil tip at just after school starting time on 21 October 1966. The tip had been created on a mountain slope above the Welsh village of Aberfan, near Merthyr Tydfil, and overlaid a natural spring. Previous heavy rains led to a build-up of water within the tip which caused it to suddenly slide downhill as slurry, killing one hundred and sixteen children and twenty eight adults as it so sadly engulfed the local junior school.

A Journalist who witnessed the unfolding tragedy and to illustrate the sorrow the event still evoked in him on its fiftieth anniversary quoted the closing lines to Wordsworth's poem *Ode on Intimations of Immortality from Recollections of Early Childhood*: "*To me the meanest flower that blows can give thoughts that do often lie too deep for tears*".

Queen Elizabeth had delayed visiting the scene for eight days, but when she did go according to onlookers showed a 'poignant grief'. The young Rebecca could remember that each day she had silently urged the Queen to go to be on the side of the people against this terrible crime of corporate neglect and culpability. What she remembered was a genuine and terrible sorrow of a nation in mourning, mixed with class anger but constrained with the dignity a tragedy of these proportions demanded.

The third occasion was the violent untimely death of Princess Diana in August 1997 where it seemed to Rebecca that the previous constraint of dignity had been removed along with the deference of an almost bygone age, but in which class anger had taken a funny turn, vesting its expression in a royal who seemed increasingly more like a rock star. Here the British turned into a nation looking for some kind of existential healing from a royal so cleverly dubbed 'The People's Princess' of a pain that was both public and at one and the same time deeply individualised and personal and which left the nation feeling wrung out and exhausted if united in grief.

In spring 2016 the UK was in the depths of a campaign on the referendum that would define its relationship with its European neighbours for the foreseeable future and the long term. The campaign had been lacklustre and irritable on both sides, but Rebecca had little idea during it just what outpouring of emotion there would be after the vote, or of the level of anger and strife in what had previously seemed like the most consensus seeking and compromise prone of nations. Far from the unifying effect of other tragedies of her experience, this one was to lead to a very uncomfortable civil strife.

Unusually that year Rebecca had booked a flight that would mean she was in her Spanish village in late June 2016. Only afterwards had the date for the UK referendum on European Union membership been set. This didn't really faze Rebecca. Even though it had been a tedious campaign, she felt confident about the result. Also Elena was with her and this was unusual as she normally came in August and her life drawing classes normally continued through June up to the end of July. In most years Rebecca would come out for one of the bank holidays in May or the beginning of June, but this year her family law caseload had been so heavy she hadn't been able to get away.

Her work pattern meant she was busy from September through to New Year and beyond.

It appeared there were two high points in the year for divorces to become inevitable: Christmas and summer holidays.

The theory went that couples at war could hold it together just about in their normal day to day when work distracted but when forced to spend happy family time together the tensions of long held back resentments and loathing exploded. At this stage of her career she was running down her practice but didn't want to stop altogether, just create a bit more time for time to be in the village and for travel to see the world more widely.

Rebecca had been shocked when she had downloaded an app that charted how much of the world you had visited to find she had only seen twenty per cent of it. Previously she had thought she was quite widely travelled until the app had told her how much more of the world she had yet to see. It made her aware that she might be running out of time and that on their death bed no one wished they had spent more time at work during their life time.

Rebecca felt as if since graduation she had had her nose to a professional grindstone and now her son Daniel was almost independent it was time to raise it and smell the humus. Also, although she cared about her clients and did her not inconsiderable best for them, she was jaded by too many forever love stories that flipped into a hatred so profound, the soon to be ex-partner who once could do no wrong was switched into one who now could do no right.

Rebecca's focus was on the children, always.

She found herself wanting to say: "For Christ's sake, grow up and let's get sensible arrangements for them," whilst she watched so many couples probing the fault in the other, locked into the belief of their own paragon perfection.

It wasn't that she had lost her sympathy for women. On the whole, despite all the gains that women in general had made educationally and professionally in her lifetime, in marriage they remained less powerful and certainly mostly a lot less rich than their partner.

This was particularly true when they had children. This was often when those who began the sentence with 'I'm not a feminist' would begin to add the 'but', as the reality of power imbalance between men and women finally dawned, like being hit round the head with a wet kipper.

It was clearly worse if the partner was controlling or violent, when the woman's self-confidence and power to assert herself had been drained by years of calculated or maybe just instinctive undermining on the part of the bully.

She was still sympathetic, but her sympathy had become more theoretical than real to the snivelling victimhood some women could adopt.

When she started to feel the waning of sisterly feeling being replaced by an irresistible urge to suggest a swift kick to his balls might be a better – indeed quicker – solution than dragging a sorry story round the divorce courts, she knew the time was coming when she would just have to stop.

Her best friend Elena unusually had agreed to come with her when she proposed a June trip. Elena had a bad chest from the combination of too many years of smoking and inhaling the cement fondue she handled and breathed in regularly as a sculptor.

Elena, as headstrong as ever had refused to wear the many masks that Rebecca had bought her over the years. She had just got over yet another bout of bronchitis and needed some sun and rest.

Her ever grateful students had agreed to an extension of classes at the end of the year to allow her some time off for this trip.

Besides, both were sick of the paucity of Brexit debates and the campaign and just wanted it to be over. So they escaped.

Before leaving, they had just had time to do a postal vote for Elena, who was in any case a last minute merchant in contrast to Rebecca's by comparison meticulous planner mode. This was the reason that Rebecca organised all their major travels.

In the last few years they had been to Myanmar, China, Vietnam, Cambodia, Thailand and India and were planning next on Mexico.

Elena could reduce Rebecca to tears of hopeless laughter when she tried to grapple with the bizarre visa requirements of different regimes. Though Rebecca might have nagged her, according to Elena and gently reminded her according to Rebecca, Elena would inevitably leave it till the last moment, testing Rebecca's capacity for neurotic irritation to the limit.

It wasn't that Elena couldn't pull it out of the bag when required, after all she had been organising her art classes for years, getting the materials and booking the models. She'd curated exhibitions galore in various galleries. But she was only really good with things that didn't – as she would say – bore the arse off her.

The things that Elena was not inclined to do included the opening of official looking brown envelopes, particularly when they had a tax office or court circuit stamp on them.

Consequently, Elena had missed far more court dates than the average person had ever received. Mainly these were for debts she had forgotten about.

She got quite accomplished at hiding from bailiffs, but indeed had been known to invite them in for a cup of tea and win their sympathy for her poverty to such an extent that they had disappeared with a token, small piece of furniture as a symbol of her good intent.

Rebecca knew that if the Victorian legal system still prevailed she would be reduced to visiting Elena in the Marshalsea or the Clink, for she was always stony broke.

Rebecca thought Elena had a lot to thank the Debtor's Act of 1869 for and always counselled her to pay her council tax, which is the only omission that might still see her sent to nick.

This in itself, however, required her to open the right brown envelope so could not be guaranteed.

Rebecca still remembered Elena's melt down over getting the Indian Visa. Rebecca knew this was a process that had reduced many a grown person to tears or the tearing out of hair. It was the least user friendly Visa process – well except for the Russian one, which was unspeakable – that she had encountered, and it had taken her several goes to get it right.

When Elena phoned her in tears she had taken pity on her and taken her through it step by step, which had taken hours on the phone and several exchanges of digital data and photographs and file conversions to get right. During this it had taken all Rebecca's patience to keep her easily bored pal going to the end.

Elena had shown some gratitude and was relieved and it had left Rebecca with a nice sense of superior smugness – to which, after near fifty odd years of exhaustingly wonderful friendship, she felt she had the right.

Rebecca had real admiration for her friend's ability to duck and roll with the punches of what had been from time to time, a precarious existence. She admired her, but knew she really couldn't have lived like that herself without being driven quickly into nervous exhaustion.

It wasn't that Rebecca was a wimp. Indeed in her career she had taken on and defeated a few very large Goliaths to her much smaller David, but mostly this had been fighting on behalf of others who were too disorganised, too downtrodden or just less agile to tackle the law, the courts or even Parliament in their own defence.

In her private life, however, Rebecca could never have coped with the chaos in which her lovely friend Elena seemed to thrive – well at the least to survive.

Their departure this time had involved something much less perilous than Visa applications. The challenge of their hurried departure was that both had had to fill in and return their voting papers in the referendum for Britain to leave the European Union. Neither Elena nor Rebecca had seen the need for a referendum. They didn't like David Cameron much but knowing that he had caved on the referendum vote not on the basis of what might be in the interests of the country but to deal with a backwoods problem in his own party and the threat to its vote from UKIP was infuriating.

In particular Rebecca loathed Nigel Farage; it was the boorish blokeness of his beer swilling ways she detested. Son of a stockbroker, educated at Dulwich College and admirer of Enoch Powell, he was a representative of the little England that she hated.

She would hazard a bet he had been a member of the Empire Club deploring the removal of Great Britain's pink from off the map as the empire crumbled, decrying the loss of the oh so nobly carried white man's burden.

It was all that nostalgic yearning for a 1950s world of spinsters on bicycles; the sound of leather-on-willow on warm summer afternoon's on English village greens and the swilling of warm beer and all this without dusky complexions on view outside of test match grounds and no Johnny Foreigners in town. Her erstwhile, increasingly right wing, lover had said to her towards the end that he admired Farage and was himself thinking of joining UKIP, after which she had laughed hysterically, showed him and door and said: "Fuck off".

This latter offence is not one she blamed on Farage. She was prepared to admit her own judgement had been at fault – not a concession she often made

She was prepared entirely to concede the critics had a point about the bureaucracy and corruption in the EU. She had seen the gravy train herself briefly when she'd been a member of a European wide consumer body some years before.

She always remembered the sharply stylishly dressed and highly coiffured Italian delegates saying: "You English, you are so serious about the law. Why not just vote the proposition through, then you can ignore it as we shall do?"

Also she remembered, with the hot flush of shame, one particularly arduous debate that went on for a whole afternoon with full simultaneous translation, about regulatory standards for a set of widgets in a boiler. She had been given to a show of much levity about the topic as speaker after speaker droned on, until a union colleague had lent over to her and said: "You do realise, don't you, that this is the Germans trying to kill our central heating industry?"

These two things had made her realise she was utterly out of her depth and entirely inadequate to the task of continuing the fight that had started so long ago on the beaches, now in peacetime finding more docile expression on the floor of a European Council Chamber.

She was an advocate of reform, even big reform, but dissolution, no.

She would also concede this was probably down to her family history of the relatives that had disappeared into Nazi concentration camps who were murdered by gas, or starvation, or disease, or who emerged at war end as broken shadows.

She carried the firm conviction that European Union dreams, then aspiration, then realities, had maintained a peace since 1945, albeit that it was not always an easy peace. It hadn't kept some European nations one could mention from that seemingly inbuilt if mostly buried murderous desire to ethically cleanse their neighbours that had broken out occasionally in intervening years.

Nevertheless, the defence of individual and collective human rights was enshrined in its purpose and mostly upheld in its endeavours, and she thought the world would be an inherently more dangerous and unstable place without it. She was firmly on the side of the Remain camp and had played a small role in some parts of the campaign.

She thought of Victor Hugo who, as president of the Paris Peace Congress in 1849, had outlined an ambitious vision for peace, democracy, and unity in diversity. He called it 'a European Brotherhood'. Advocating a United States of Europe, he said: "A day will come when the only fields of battle will be markets opening up to trade and minds opening up to ideas. A day will come when bullets and bombs will be replaced by votes; by universal suffrage of the peoples; by the venerable arbitration of a great sovereign senate which will be to Europe what Parliament is to England, what this diet is to Germany, what the Legislative Assembly is to France. A day will come when we will display cannon in museums just as we display instruments of torture today, amazed that such things could ever have been possible."

Rebecca had been moved by this in her history class at school. She wasn't sure about the United States bit, but she bought wholesale the economic argument and thought even more fondly of the minds being open to ideas.

For her Europe was a grand idea based on a café society where young people dreamed dreams and fomented revolutions; it was wonderful food and fabulous films; literature rich in challenge and enhancing experience and above all a place where the renaissance had gloriously opened up creativity and curiosity. Her love for it was cultural and ideological and gastronomic, and whilst she recognised that the dream had been tarnished by too many snouts in a trough, where didn't that happen when human greed was linked to power and opportunity?

She had a chuckle to herself when she remembered Michael Gove, the Education Secretary, no less and a leading light of the Leave side at the height of the campaign telling the public that we had all had enough of experts as the long list of professors and intellectuals everywhere had reported how damaging they saw the Leave option for our national life and prosperity. That the Education Secretary had promoted ignorance had seemed to her like a final irony in what had been a distinctly downwards trajectory of the argument to a previously unimagined nadir. She had envisaged the two bête noirs of Dickens those of 'Ignorance' and 'Want' emboldened by this very small man to hold societal sway. Even above her contempt for the intellectual poverty on display, what she really didn't want was to be pushed back into the narrow, xenophobic blokey bloke world of Farage and the awful Dominic Cummings that she felt she had been fighting since first she drew political breath. Hence, she was looking forward to them being put in their place.

The vote took place on the 23rd June with results coming in overnight. Rebecca and Elena had eaten supper at home. They'd made an arrangement to meet other friends in the village the following night to either celebrate or commiserate the outcome.

At 10 p.m. a YouGov opinion poll released at the closure of the polls predicted Remain were on course for victory with 52% and Leave on 48% and at 10.15 p.m. Nigel Farage conceded the Brexit campaign might be beaten and said Remain 'will edge it' – but promised that "UKIP and I are going nowhere." At 11.25 p.m. Gibraltar was the first area to declare, with a predictable landslide for Remain at 96% of the vote. It was 12.25 a.m. Spanish time and the pound had just surged against the dollar. Rebecca, relieved but tired, decided to call it a day. So, she missed the turning point in the voting record of Sunderland and the subsequent down-hill drama.

At 12.04 a.m. the first big result was declared, with a narrow win in Newcastle for Remain with 50.7% against the Leave result of 49.3%. At 12.20 a.m. Sunderland voted to Leave by a significant margin, with 61% in the Tyne and Wear town in favour of Brexit compared with 39% backing Remain. This was to prove the turning point.

At 12.30 a.m. Sterling tumbled against the US dollar as jitters over a possible swing to Leave wiped earlier gains off the pound, with a near 4.7% drop – greater than that of the Black Wednesday crash in 1992. At 1.55 a.m. the City of London count was announced as vote to Remain in the EU.

Then at 2 a.m. bookmakers changed their odds in favour of Leave winning the referendum, with Ladbrokes putting odds of 1/2 on a Brexit result. Having had an 86% chance of Remain winning at the close of polls, the odds shrank to 6/4, or 38%. At 2.01 a.m. Swansea voted Leave, with 61,936 backing a Brexit against 58,307 voting to remain. At 2.17 a.m. Nigel Farage, who earlier said he sensed Remain would take victory, tweeted that he was 'so happy with the results in North East England'. At 2.35 a.m. Former Bradford West MP George Galloway, another odious bloke, appeared to claim victory for Leave, tweeting: "First they ignored us. Then they laughed at us. Then they attacked us. Then we won #Lexit #Brexit."

At 3.27 a.m. Sheffield came out for Leave, backing an exit from the EU by little over 5,000 votes. Nigel Farage appeared again at 4.05 a.m. this time to claim victory in the EU referendum, saying: "Let June 23 go down in our history as our Independence Day." He called the votes for the Leave campaign 'a victory for real people, for ordinary people, for decent people', and when asked if David Cameron should resign if the UK votes for Brexit, he replied: "Immediately." The implication being that there were no decent people in the Remain camp – but to be fair it's pretty much what the tribal fold on the Remain side felt about those who voted Leave.

Then in rapid succession at 4.13 a.m. people in the rest of Wales voted to leave the European Union, despite a Remain win in Cardiff. At 4.15 a.m. turnout data from all 382 counts came in and indicated the estimated winning post would be 16,768,027 votes. Then at 4.39 a.m. both the BBC and ITV called a Leave victory based on analysis of the votes. At 4.53 a.m. Jenny Watson, who acted as National Chief Counting Officer, estimated the turnout for the referendum at 72.2% of the UK population eligible to vote. There had been 33,568,184 ballot papers from an electorate of 46,501,000. Many were to claim it was the highest turnout ever, which in a slightly nerdy way Rebecca knew to be false as the turnout in the election in 1992 had been higher at 78% of voters registered.

Finally, at 6.02 a.m. the Leave campaign officially passed the estimated winning post 16,763,272.

Forty-three minutes later the Foreign Secretary Philip Hammond said voters had 'spoken clearly' and the Government's job now was to 'get on with that decision, protecting the economy and doing all we can to get the best outcome for Britain'. Nineteen minutes after that the final count of the EU referendum showed Leave won 51.9% of the total vote to Remains' 48.1%.

Rebecca had woken up at around 7.30 a.m., still an hour ahead of the UK and at around 7.45 she had turned the radio on to BBC Radio 4 rather than Radio Nacional de España whilst she had put the kettle on to make a cup of tea, at precisely the point that Hammond was making his comments on the outcome. She remembered standing there in her kitchen with the steaming kettle in her hand in a state of total shock. She had felt so confident that her side would be successful. She had wanted the vote to be reasonably narrow to strengthen the government's hand in the negotiation she felt must surely come for reform. In the real world, while she slumbered the narrow margins had reversed and she couldn't quite take it in.

She managed to make a cup of tea and take it in the wake Elena up with the news.

"No," said Elena. "I don't believe it. What the fuck happened?"

But Rebecca had no explanation, though she did recognise something dark and deep had arisen in Albion; something that she had not recognised previously was even stalking the land.

She did not understand her own emotional response to the news. She felt gutted like a fish cut open on the fishmonger's block. At first, she put this down to her chagrin at the jubilation of the political forces of darkness she so disliked. But this mixture of pain and shock was not like anything she had experienced before as the result of any previous political outcome and in her life, she had known both the joy of victory and the sting of defeat – but this felt different.

This response was visceral. It was a sharp pain in the solar plexus. It was a tightening in the diaphragm that made it difficult to breathe. It was a tumult in the gut that made breakfast a bad idea and it was pain between the eyes and a vague sense that the world as she knew it had crumbled.

As she probed these feelings, she realised it was a bit like bereavement: something rather than someone she loved had died; just maybe it was not only a dream about internationalism, but also her image of the country in which she lived and which she had always loved for its slow tolerance and liberalism.

It felt as if the unenlightened fringe had taken over the

mainstream or the lunatics the asylum. However, this turned out, it shook her baby boomer confidence in a shared destiny of continual social progress across plural political forces. It made her feel that the dialogue across the political spectrum that had long been her practice and that she took for granted had just suddenly died.

Later the recognition that she could not see a way for the nation to heal its divisions would take over, but at this moment the major feeling was pain and shock that went way beyond an acknowledged dislike of being on the losing side.

What Rebecca heard when she became conscious was the announcement of David Cameron's resignation as Prime Minister. He said he would go by September because the people had spoken and 'the will of the British people is an instruction that must be delivered'.

She felt rage that the idiot who had unnecessarily called this referendum in the first place and who had only ever argued about the economic damage that would be done if it were lost was off to make his fortune on the after dinner speaker circuit, leaving the mess to be sorted out by someone else.

Rebecca and Elena decided to go to the beach for the day. They moved slowly like invalids who needed to take care of themselves and cosset the bruises that went further than skin deep. Mostly they spent the day in stunned silence punctuated by the outpourings of the first ideas that came into their heads that might possibly explain what had gone on and so badly wrong back home.

Elena, who was more of an extremist than her pal, put the result down to the pure evil in the Leave camp. It was the consequence of xenophobic, racist, anti-immigrant ranters mired in nostalgia for a post World War Two glory golden age Britain, when it ruled the waves and was a benign and enlightened ruler of a magnificent empire that kept foreigners of all colours and creeds firmly in their place and out of ours.

Rebecca accepted that most, maybe all these elements were at play.

"But Lena, there must be more to it than that. Not all those who voted Leave are racists. Many of them will have Black partners and mixed-race children. Lots of them are poor from areas of the country that only ever benefitted from EU money, but probably don't know it. What's clear is that many of them feel like the forgotten; like they are reclaiming something. The question is: what?

I just don't want to rule out 52% of the country. How could we go on living there if that were true?"

But this was not a set of questions that could be answered immediately by either of them.

They had as mellow a day as possible in the circumstances – as David Cameron might have said 'chillaxing' on the beach. Rebecca had certainly felt chilled when she got her courage to the sticking place and took a swim in the still too cool waters of the Med.

On the drive home they still felt oddly displaced mentally, but it helped Rebecca that she had to concentrate on the road ahead. It did not do when climbing back into the mountains from sea level to lose concentration on some of those hairpin bends.

At 8 p.m. that evening they met up with other English people who lived in the village. Joanna and Thomas, Elizabeth and Toby, Karen and James, and Mike and June a lovely couple of paramedics who lived in an isolated farmhouse on the hill directly opposite that could be clearly seen from Rebecca's sun terrace. They were all gloomy apart from James, who sometime later it turned out had voted Leave, but was not going to advertise it among this group. At the time no one much had noticed how quiet James had remained during their evening, though Karen had said to Rebecca a few days before the referendum that she would not like to predict how James had voted on their postal ballots. Rebeca had deliberately not asked him, not wanting to be responsible for the lynching that might have been the outcome.

As a group they shared the sense of shock, though Jo reminded them that Leeds had voted by a narrow majority to Remain and Mike and June who had lived in Brighton, where 68.55% had voted Remain, felt like they had passed some sort of exam summa cum laude.

Rebecca consoled herself with the thought the just under 60% of Londoners voted Remain and Elena did the same with the 57% who had done the same in Bath.

That night they realised two things. The first was that they lived or had lived, in the case of those them now living permanently in the village, in bubbles in the UK, clearly cut off from in what in this vote had been the majority of the country – however narrow the margin.

"Maybe that's why we all like each other," said Rebecca and Mike, taking up the theme said he'd drink to that and proposed a toast, which was the first of many.

The second thing they realised was that theirs was a completely divided nation where the feelings would run just as deep as they did in a family visited by divorce. In the nation a knife edge fine majority on the hugest turn out in years had decided to get a divorce from Europe but would drag the unwilling other half of the partnership of nation – the part that wanted to stay hitched with them however unwillingly through it.

"Well," said Rebecca, who we know knew a thing or two about the pains of divorce, "I think it's going to feel like a disintegrating marriage where both parties are condemned to live in the same house with a partner they regard as evil incarnate or psychopathic forever more and no one knows what the hell will happen to the children."

"On that happy note, Rebecca, maybe it's time you moved here for good. I'd drink to that," said Mike chivalrously, and so they did.

Then Rebecca stopped them all in their tracks when she said: "But what if the Spanish won't want you to stay? Well, given the mad xenophobes in our government the Spanish may retaliate."

As the evening degenerated somewhat into silly, slightly drunken jokes someone mentioned the likelihood of England and Spain going to war over Gibraltar on the basis that it had happened before and it caused endless mirth.

"Battle of Trafalgar?" Asked Karen.

"Spanish War of Succession and the Treaty of Utrecht 1713 and then there were the fourteen sieges over five hundred years but nothing much has happened since the end of the Second World War," said Thomas, who was the historian amongst them.

Then it turned out that Spain had already put in a bid for British rule of the rock to end and it didn't seem quite such a funny joke anymore. The evening ended with many more than slightly drunken embraces for solidarity.

Rebecca and Elena left a few days later and returned to a more turbulent world. Things moved fast and politicians tumbled.

On her return, as was her wont, she went to visit Aunty Betsy, her dead mother's now very elderly sister. It turned out Betsy had voted Leave and Rebecca was surprised at her instantaneous response of wanting to punch her. She didn't, of course, but the Neanderthal urge was in her.

So maybe in her soul she was more lager lout troll in Magaluf than pole up backside straight spine toff, thought Rebecca with some embarrassment for what previously she had been proud to think of as a higher level attainment of civilised thought and behaviour.

Betsy explained that she had been against going into the EU in the first place and had never changed her mind.

"And Betsy," said Rebecca, "did you not care when they lied to you about the £350million a day that would be put into the NHS when we leave Europe?"

"No one took that seriously," said Betsy, proving that tribalism is stronger than logic or truth, which was why Rebecca was so very suspicious of it. As the time, however, a bit of her, maybe the same primitive bit of her of which she had been previously unaware that had produced her uncivilised urge to give Betsy a slapping, longed for a tribal embrace.

So, Elena joined the first of many demonstrations by the Remain side. She hadn't been on a demonstration since the politics of protest when she was a student and in the years beyond that where sometimes they hadn't even known what the demonstration was about or which 'Two' or 'Three' they were marching to 'Free' this week.

She went to ascertain the mood and the feel of the thing. Also, she was feeling the need for some continuing solidarity with people whose views and values she largely shared. She knew from long experience that she might not feel right at home with the entire crowd. At the wackier fringes of politics where Earth departed company from Mars, she knew she would have no connection. Nor would she have much with sections like the Morris Dancers for Europe who would merely make her giggle, but she was keen to see them in action.

There was no chance of meeting anyone in this crowd, which was huge, but she had come with a couple of friends who stayed with her. They got behind the gay boys, who had the best music, and boogied their way through central London.

There were many posters declaring undying love for the EU and the Brussels bureaucrats which stopped her in her tracks somewhat, as love for the gnomes of Europe was not what she felt, but nevertheless in war you pick a side, so she went with the flow.

What she hadn't been prepared for but what made perfect sense when she remembered her own visceral response to the outcome of the vote was the depth of the raw emotion in the crowd. People were jubilant to be with their own, yes, and there was a party atmosphere but there were also tears and the genuine outflowing of deep regret and sadness. After all, they had just lost the vote.

The jubilation came in spending time with their tribe in a world they assumed they had known, but that had shattered and could no longer be understood. It was a tribe that instinctively understood the emotion and that validated its expression. Everyone felt the soreness of wounds so very far from being healed.

Later when she got home foot sore but still a bit elated, Rebecca was struggling to remember if she had ever seen such emotion pouring out on the London Streets. Then, in the bath with bubbles both in it and in the glass of cold prosecco she'd taken with her, it came to her.

She ran through the death of Kennedy and the Aberfan disaster as moments of national pain, but the last time she had experienced this level of passion on the streets of London was after the death of Princess Diana and her funeral on 6th September, after which there had been a spontaneous and spectacular week of mourning outside Buckingham and Kensington Palaces. The many thousands who came built altars and memorials of flowers and in the warm September air the smell of progressively rotting flowers became overpowering as the human numbers swelled daily of those holding silent vigil or sobbing quietly locked into their own deep sense of pity at the loss of the People's Princess.

Rebecca had witnessed this mourning closely. It was a mystery to her.

She had met Diana a few years previously whilst she was still nominally inside the royal marriage. It had been at a charity event held to benefit the charity Rebecca ran, which had teamed up with a more respectable, larger charity which had had the royal contact and got Diana as the guest of honour.

The event was a performance of *The Marriage of Figaro* with Bryn Terfel in the lead role. She and the director of the other charity had had to line up at the entrance to the Coliseum with other worthies to greet the princess and then afterwards she had spent some time with her in the Green Room before they had taken their seats for the performance.

What struck her immediately was just how physically lovely she was in real life; even better looking than in her photos, of which god knows there had been a daily diet for years that would have satiated the appetite of the most voracious royal watcher.

They had been left alone for five minutes. It was just after Diana had got into trouble for having smacked Prince William on the bottom when he ran away from her at his school sport's day. This event had caused huge outrage in the press with furious arguments for and against from her detractor's and supporters. Rebecca had thought about and rejected this as a topic of conversation as she doubted that even in the interest of the hundred thousand pounds this event would raise she could be enough of a toady to express any support as she herself then had a five year old, Daniel, whom in a million years she would never have hit.

She also wickedly wanted to tell Diana that on the occasion of her marriage to Charles, Rebecca had worn a 'Don't do it Di!' badge, but like the newly fledged grown up she was trying to be, she resisted that urge, too.

Instead, rather more prosaically, she asked Diana how she'd like the Opera. She was probably thinking about the princess's well-known liking for Wham and George Michael. Diana gave her a warm smile and said she was not to worry because she also liked Opera and was really looking forward to the immensely talented Bryn's performance. They had sat together throughout the whole evening and Rebecca found it impossible not to take the occasional peak sideways at her companion who did seem to be genuinely enjoying herself, while Rebecca was feeling somewhat overawed in the presence of such starry stardom and downright loveliness.

Clearly, she couldn't claim in any way to know Diana and always wondered just how much of an airhead she really was – after all, Dodi Fayed?

"Really, Diana, what were you thinking?" she had wanted to ask her before the terrible accident in Paris claimed their lives.

Almost the whole world had seen that photo of her alone outside the Taj Mahal on what has since been known as the Diana Bench. Well, Rebecca knew it was not quite the whole world as when she had visited India with Elena, they had both had pictures taken on the Diana Bench and Rebecca had sent hers to the erstwhile lover who had a 'pash' on Nigel Farage and it had drawn a complete blank.

Rebecca had to walk through St James's park to work each day. She saw the crowds of mourners' ebb and flow. To Rebecca, it was like an exercise in grief in contemporary Western societies.

Two thousand people had attended the funeral ceremony in Westminster Abbey, while the British television audience peaked at over thirty two million, one of the United Kingdom's highest viewing figures ever with estimated two and a half billion people watching the event internationally, making it one of the biggest worldwide televised events in history.

Somehow Diana had become a symbol of sacrifice representing people's deepest personal pain.

In mourning her they seemed to be mourning the selves that they had brought to her to be healed. She had become a saint moderating both the pain of loss, and the need to rebuild life and adapt to a changed world.

So, there amongst the overwhelming perfume of the funereal lilies and other slightly nauseous intense perfume of over-abundant, slowly dying flowers, they paid homage to their saintly goddess who in her role as People's Princess had somehow become a commoner: like them.

Rebecca had been shocked and bemused by the depth of the emotion, which was clearly genuine if more than a little hysterical for though she felt sadness for this tragic life played out entirely in the public domain and ended too soon, she could not elevate it the level of the cult that had these mourners enthralled.

Rebecca knew of people who had joined the throng. They had all had deep psychological trouble and mental health issues but they had felt comforted in the bosom of their tribe and the embrace of the princess who suffered even the little children to come unto her, and who had been both deeply loved and then sacrificed to the perfidy of others.

It seemed to Rebecca that the demonstrations for the Remainers had something of a similar quality of mourning.

Clearly there was not a mythical figure for it to cohere around and it had more to do with the death of a culture than a person, but people similarly felt the need of some healing for their loss.

These memories were swirling round in Rebecca's head four years later when she was staying in London, unable to get to her Spanish village in the Covid 19 lockdown for the foreseeable future.

She, like everyone else she knew, had taken part in the weekly applause for front line workers in the National Health

Service and essential workers elsewhere. This was a time of further chaos and uncertainty but perhaps the wounds that had come with the Brexit vote were beginning to knit together, though the nation could hardly be called healed when so many were dying from a potentially deadly virus.

Yet, there was a feeling of solidarity through support for the last bastion of social solidarity in the National Health Service.

For weeks she had watched the incompetent Prime Minister blustering Boris and his hugely unimpressive government of also rans and yes men, whose dithering had been responsible for the deaths of so many people and particularly of those around her more advanced age.

He had been the victor ultimately through his sudden anti-European conversion when he judged it was in his longer-term political interest to emerge as the leader of the Vote Leave block in the Tory Party.

For years she had watched as Boris snatched every opportunity for his push up when climbing the greasy pole of political power; disliking him more at every turn as it became clearer, he did nothing unless there was advantage in it for him.

That evening she had watched him defend the flouting of lockdown restrictions with a supposedly pee and beverage free two hundred mile car journey to Durham, by the odious Dominic Cummings who had been their architect as well as being the genius behind the Leave Campaign – or 'Coming and Goings' as he was now being called in social media.

All she could think when she looked at the level of contempt shown to those obeying the rule, had been unable to see loved ones before they died was: *with this shower of shit in control and no Covid vaccine, and on our way out of Europe with a trade deal growing ever more unlikely, what the hell happens now to us as a nation?*

Index

Finito di stampare nel mese di novembre 2020
presso Rotomail Italia S.p.A. - Vignate (MI)